D0287012

# TREACHEROUS

# TREACHEROUS

BOOK SIX IN THE ON THE RUN BOOK
INTERNATIONAL MYSTERIES

SARA ROSETT

McGuffin Ink

*Treacherous*

Book Six in the *On the Run International Mysteries* series

Published by McGuffin Ink

Copyright © 2017 by Sara Rosett

First Paperback Edition: November 2017

ISBN: 978-0-9988431-4-8

All rights are reserved. Without limiting the rights under copyright reserved above, no part of this work may be used, stored, transmitted, or reproduced in any manner or form whatsoever without express written permission from the author and publisher.

This is a work of fiction and names, characters, incidents, and places are products of the author's imagination or used fictitiously. Any resemblance to persons, living or dead, incidents, and places is coincidental.

❀ Created with Vellum

*To Alicia, reader extraordinaire*

# PROLOGUE

Robert Novall didn't need to wait until his last colleague left the room for lunch. No one suspected anything, but it wouldn't do to make a mistake at this point.

The printer whirred to life, and Rob picked up the five pages from its tray. It was laughable really, the amount of time and money the company put into monitoring their activities while completely overlooking one thing—paper.

Footsteps sounded in the hall, someone coming back. The new guy darted in, grabbed his jacket, and asked if Rob was coming with them. Rob tossed the stack of pages on his desk to deal with later. The first four pages were various memos and reports that he needed, but the page on the bottom was different. He left it with the others at the side of his desk and went to lunch.

On his way out, he passed through the metal detector as well as the full body scanner, then retrieved his personal phone from his locker, and dropped off his lanyard. The whole process had to be repeated in reverse when he returned. No personal phones, cameras, or any other sort of digital equipment were allowed inside the office. Computer activity was highly monitored—files accessed, search queries, downloads—it was all tracked, but they were so focused on plugging any digital holes that they didn't even think about someone going analog.

No one monitored or cared what was printed, and his current work project gave him legitimate access to the files, so what he was doing didn't raise any red flags. In fact, it *couldn't* raise any flags. No flags were in place to be raised. No one had set any warnings connected to what came off the printers. Who would bother to print anything sensitive—especially at their company?

Rob made sure he was back from lunch before everyone else.

He settled at his desk and removed the bottom page from the stack. He folded the paper into fourths lengthwise, then leaned over, lifted his pant leg, and slipped it inside his sock. It stayed there for the rest of the day, tucked against his calf. He logged off his computer at the end of his shift and headed to the elevator. He rode the elevator down, then walked through the metal detector and the body scanner. The single sheet of paper didn't create a wrinkle or bulge that could be picked up on the screens. The security guard waved him through with a bored nod.

Rob kept up his easy pace as he walked to the Metro, then stopped for a calamari sandwich on his way home. When he arrived at his apartment, he closed all the curtains before removing the paper. He smoothed the creases, took a tube of lip balm from the drawer of his desk and removed the cap, revealing the port of a flash drive. He plugged it into his laptop, and quickly transcribed the single page of text. He hit *save*, then added the printed page to the growing stack on the corner of his desk under the Rubik's cube.

Rob disconnected the flash drive, replaced the cap on the lip balm, and dropped it in the desk drawer. He stretched his arms over his head then logged into the forum. "Tuck05" was online, discussing the latest article from a tech blogger. Rob jumped into the discussion, hitting a couple of threads, then he transitioned to a secure, private connection and sent a message. *Rbn: I'm close. Another week or two and I'll have it all.*

A few seconds later a reply popped up. *Tuck05: Glad to hear it. No problems?*

*Rbn: None. Easy.*

*Tuck05: Watch yourself.*

*Rbn: No worries. No one has any idea what I'm doing.*

# 1

———

**Monday**

Zoe could feel him gaining on her, his steps pounding on the asphalt, seconds behind her. She forced her legs to pump faster. In one last burst of speed, she flew by the mailbox at the curb in front of the house. She thrust her arms into the air as if she were breaking the tape at the end of a marathon instead of finishing her afternoon jog. Jack came alongside her, his hand raised for a high-five. "You beat me today, but I'll get you tomorrow."

She slapped his raised palm. "You're sure confident for someone who just lost."

Hands linked, they slowed to a walk. Jack tilted his head in the direction of the brown delivery truck that had pulled away from the curb in front of their house a few moments earlier. "It was the incentive of a package that gave you that final kick of speed. If you hadn't seen a package being dropped off on our porch, I would have beaten you. I know how much you love opening boxes."

They turned and headed back to their house. "So you're saying I have no impulse control, that I have some sort of Pavlovian response to a sealed box?"

Jack raised his arm and used the sleeve around his bicep to wipe the sweat away from his forehead. "Boxes, gift bags, letters, junk mail. You're not a girl who likes to wait around and savor the anticipation of opening something later."

"Why would you want to wait?" Zoe asked as they walked into the shade under the cottonwood tree in their front yard. "That's no fun."

"So what's in the box today?" Jack opened the mailbox and removed several flyers and a catalog then handed them all to Zoe. "Office supplies? Clothes? A gallon of milk?"

"I know I order a lot online, but I do draw the line at dairy products—at least for now. If we get one of those services that delivers in an hour, then all bets are off."

"I'd expect nothing less."

They walked up the sidewalk to the porch, and Zoe picked up the box as Jack opened the door. "It's those hanging file folders I ordered the other day," Zoe said. "And to show you I do have self-control, I'm not opening it right now. I'll wait—until we get in the kitchen, at least."

Jack grinned and stepped back so she could go inside first. "I'll stay out of your way then."

She swatted him on the arm with the catalog and transferred the box to a better position in her arms. "This seems awfully heavy for twenty hanging file folders." She tilted the box so she could read the label as she walked into the kitchen. "Did you order something from Spar Eon? Is this yours?"

"No, I don't have anything being shipped here."

Zoe put the box down on the island and reached for a pair of scissors to cut the tape. Her phone, which she'd left on the island, buzzed with a call. It was Harrington Throckmorton, owner of Throckmorton Enquiries.

Zoe put down the scissors. "I better get this. He may have an update on the Milam file." Since Harrington was based in London, they usually spoke in the morning, Zoe's time. It was late afternoon now, but if he had news he'd call immediately.

The Milam home—or a more accurate description would be

mansion—in Highland Park, one of Dallas's most expensive neighborhoods, had been broken into last week. A Miró had been stolen along with some rare coins. The Milams had hired Harrington's firm, which specialized in discreet recoveries of art and other valuables. Zoe worked for Harrington as a consultant and was handling their search for the missing art and coins. Zoe had been in touch with every contact she and Harrington had in the art world. So far, she hadn't uncovered so much as a whisper about any of the stolen items.

"I have that late meeting," Jack said. They exchanged a quick sweaty kiss before Jack trotted up the stairs to shower. Zoe sat down on a barstool at the island, which was her work area, and answered the call.

Harrington's crisp British accent came over the line. "Hello, Zoe. Do you have a moment?"

"Of course." As ever, Harrington was infallibly polite. Zoe hitched the barstool closer to the island. With the phone tucked between her ear and her shoulder, she pushed the cardboard box aside and pulled her laptop closer. A few clicks brought up the Milam file.

"So how is everything in Dallas?" Harrington asked.

Zoe thought he meant how is everything going with the Milam case, and she was about to launch into a list of who she'd talked to recently, but then Harrington went on, "Jack is well?"

"Yes. He's fine. If you want to speak to him, I can have him call you back." Zoe glanced at the clock. As fast as Jack showered, he might actually be back in the kitchen before she hung up. "He's planning security for a new skyscraper that's going in downtown, so if you had something for him he might not be able to take it on right now." A few times in the past, Harrington had asked Jack to step in as a consultant when clients were interested in making their valuables more secure.

"Oh, no. Nothing like that on my agenda at the moment. How is Dallas? Are you enjoying some cooler weather, now that it is September?"

A thread of unease twisted through Zoe. It wasn't like Harrington to beat around the bush. He always was polite and asked how she was doing, but then he moved on to business. "Yes, it's so nice that Jack and I just got back from an afternoon run." During the summer the humidity was so intense that the only time they could run was in the late evening—or in an air conditioned gym.

"Excellent. Right." Harrington cleared his throat. "I spoke to Mr. Milam this afternoon..."

Zoe sagged. She could tell from his tone what he was struggling to say. "They want you to work their case, not me."

"Er—well, that is a stark way to phrase it...but, yes, they do." Harrington sighed. "I'm sorry. I tried to convince them that my plate is full, but Russell insisted."

Russell. Of course Russell Milam and Harrington communicated on a first-name basis. Zoe would never be able to call a man forty years older than her "Russell." She just couldn't do it. It would feel disrespectful. But Harrington could do it, and do it genuinely. Russell Milam and Harrington Throckmorton had known each other socially before the Miró was stolen. The flat in London was just one of several properties that the Milam family owned around the world, not to mention their yacht in the Mediterranean. Russell Milam and Harrington had dinner together when the Milams were in London.

Zoe rubbed her forehead then straightened and forced an upbeat tone into her voice. "It's okay." She closed the computer file with the data on the Milam robbery. "I know you did everything you could to convince them to stay with me as the lead in the case."

"Oh, I did. I'd much rather have you working this than me, but well..."

"Yes, I know. And I understand, too." Who wouldn't rather have the famous art recovery expert Harrington Throckmorton work their case instead of the unknown consultant, Zoe Andrews? Well, actually that wasn't true. She was known. Unfortunately, when anyone searched her name online, her history of being a participant on a reality show popped up first. The fact that it was when she was a kid and her stage mom had engineered the whole thing wasn't highlighted. If someone scrolled down, then they'd find out she'd been linked to a multi-million dollar fraud case that had been under FBI investigation. It had all worked out. She'd been an innocent person caught up in an international incident, but the articles that reported the happy resolution that cleared her name ranked much lower in the search results than the ones from early in the investigation that shouted about her possible guilt.

"I'll send you everything I have."

"That would be helpful. I'll get in touch if I have any questions. I may have some admin tasks for you next week."

"Sure. I'm happy to help." It would be what she'd been doing for months for Harrington, mostly administrative tasks with a little research and background work thrown in. She was happy to do it, but what she really wanted was to lead the search for the missing valuables. So far, she'd been in charge of one successful recovery. She wanted to get more cases under her belt. Besides the fact that Harrington wanted to transfer some of his workload to her, she wanted to establish herself in the field. A thought whispered through her mind. *And prove that her one and only successful recovery hadn't been a fluke.* Zoe shook off that thought and reached for a pen. "Is there anything I can do for you right now?"

"As a matter of fact, there is." Harrington sounded relieved. Zoe was sure he was glad he'd gotten through breaking the bad news about the Milam case. "It's about that Jenson case," he said briskly. "One small detail..."

Zoe grabbed one of the flyers from the mail, flipped it over, and made some notes on the white space around the address.

While she was writing, Jack walked into the kitchen, his dark hair still damp from the shower. He was in his business casual attire, an open-collared blue dress shirt and dark pants. He took one look at her and raised his eyebrows. "Everything okay?"

With the phone still pressed to her ear, she raised a shoulder and made a face that she thought expressed her feelings: not great, but nothing tragic. Zoe mouthed the word, *Later*. Having a client who preferred to work with your well-known boss wasn't anything that should hold up Jack. She waved a hand, motioning him to the back door.

Jack pressed a kiss to her forehead then picked up his keys and computer bag. Zoe went back to making notes. After Harrington ran through several small tasks that Zoe could do for him, he said, "That's it for now. I'll be in touch again after I read your notes."

"I'm sending them to you right now. I'll start on these other things. I'll probably have them done in a few hours."

"Yes. I know," Harrington said. "They are rather pedestrian." He paused. "I am sorry about the situation with the Milam family."

"It's not your fault," Zoe said. After a beat, she added, "This is the third time, though."

"A run of bad luck, is all—well, or..." he lowered his voice, "... bad people, rather. Samantha Bascom is an old woman who likes to make as much trouble as possible. She insisted on working exclusively with me simply because she knew it would inconvenience me. She quite likes to make life difficult for everyone around her, even her art recovery specialist. And the Robbie case, you and I both know that was a power play on the husband's part. His wife wanted to work with you, so he insisted on working with me to annoy her. I wasn't at all surprised to hear they filed for divorce."

"I wasn't either." That case had been a nightmare and, truthfully, Zoe had been glad to step down. Recovering valuables is difficult enough without adding relationship issues to the mix. "But you can't deny it's a pattern."

"A string of bad luck." His tone was firm. "You're not to let it bother you." He sighed. "Sometimes dealing with people is more difficult than finding a stolen painting. You're a valuable asset to Throckmorton Enquiries, and I know that in time others will recognize that as well."

"Thanks for the pep talk. You're good at it. You could give motivational speeches at business conferences."

"I'd rather deal with the Samantha Bascoms of the world." Zoe heard the shudder in his voice. Harrington didn't like to be in the spotlight. When his recoveries drew press attention, he made his way through the interviews in a workmanlike way, answering reporter questions, but never allowing his photo to be taken. "Let them run a photo of the art, not me," he always said. He knew that the publicity was good for business, but he was most comfortable recovering lost items discreetly.

Zoe hung up, and after a quick shower to clean up after the run, she focused on work, knocking out the tasks Harrington had given her. She was done in a few hours with the admin tasks of sorting and collating data into spreadsheets, and a few emails that needed a standard reply. Zoe sent off the last email then stood and rotated her shoulders. It was nearly six-thirty. She made a circuit around the island a few times. She always thought better on her feet. Being dropped from the Milam case stung, no matter how nice Harrington had been about it.

The fact remained that a client didn't want to work with her. Zoe was an unknown while Harrington was the established expert. She paused to do a few stretches that she should have done after the run. As she stretched her quads, her gaze roved over the ceiling, which looked uniformly smooth and even with its new coat of white paint. You'd never know that part of the ceiling drywall had been torn away after a pipe leaked. She couldn't afford the repair and it stayed like that for months. That had been when she and Jack were on the outs. For quite a while, she'd had a view of the two-by-fours and pipes in one corner of the kitchen ceiling, but now it was all patched over. Kind of like her and Jack.

She grinned as she switched to stretch her other leg. She and Jack were together, and with Jack's business and her work for Harrington, they had a comfortable life. Nothing excessive. They weren't moving into the Milams' neighborhood, that was for sure. But they had enough to pay their bills, keep up the house, and even indulge themselves sometimes with a night out or even a trip.

Zoe had once liked skipping from one freelance gig to another. She'd loved the freedom it gave her. But while she occasionally took

on a few freelance jobs—she still got an occasional copy-editing job
—she had to admit that she enjoyed the work she did with Harrington. She wanted to do more of it, and not just the support stuff.

She eased out of the stretch, her fingers drumming out a quick
beat on the island. There really wasn't anything more to think
about, she decided. She loved the art recovery work, but if she was
going to do it, she needed to establish her own reputation. It was
obvious to her now that she couldn't ride Harrington's coattails any
longer. She needed to prove herself. In short, she needed to build
up her own portfolio of successful recoveries so that clients would
see her as an expert, not just Harrington's helper.

Harrington said she'd had a run of bad luck with clients. Well,
she wasn't going to wait around and hope things changed. She'd
make her own luck.

And she might as well start close to home. She went to the
refrigerator. Poetry magnets held up pizza coupons, the schedule of
the martial arts class at the gym, and Jack's doodles. Tucked away,
behind a postcard reminder about a dental cleaning, was a newspaper article. She plucked it out and skimmed it as she made her
way back to the island.

*Old Master Stolen From Dallas Museum*, ran the headline. Two
months ago, a curator doing inventory at the Westoll Museum, a
small private museum, discovered a Canaletto was missing from
their storage area. A thorough search revealed another missing
painting, a Picasso.

Zoe picked up her phone and scrolled through her contact list until she found the name she was looking for.

"Ruby Wu."

"Hi, Ruby. It's Zoe. Are you busy?"

"Not if you can give me a second."

"Sure."

Classical music came on the line, then Zoe listened to a voice-over recite the museum's hours. Ruby's voice cut into a description of one of the Westoll's current exhibits about Caravaggio. Zoe hadn't realized that her call would make Ruby think that she'd made a discovery about the lost art. Zoe had met Ruby a few months ago when Zoe was doing research for Harrington. His name opened lots of doors, and Ruby had taken Zoe on a private tour of their galleries. Since then, they'd met for lunch a few times.

Over the last few months, Zoe had made an effort to meet as many people in the local art community as she could. Her contact list was now filled with gallery owners, curators, and artists. She was making her way through the pawnshops and flea markets, too.

Ruby came back on the line. "Okay, I'm back. Do you have news?"

"No. I'm sorry. I should have told you that right away. How are you doing?" Zoe asked.

"Well, I still have my job, so that's good."

"But you're not in charge of security."

"Someone has to be blamed, and I *am* in charge of the artwork. The fact that two pieces of art have disappeared doesn't reflect well on me." She sighed, then her tone became brisk. "But enough about that. What can I help you with?" Zoe could picture Ruby tucking her long black hair behind her ears and straightening her glasses as she got down to business.

"Actually, I was calling about the theft. I know the Westoll isn't interested in hiring us—"

"Which is absurd, but you know my thoughts on that."

"Right. Maybe they'll come around soon."

"But by then, where will our lovely Canaletto be? And the Picasso? I'm afraid they're already out of the country by now, don't you think?"

"I hate to say it, but that would be the smart play for the thief," Zoe said. Getting art away from the place it was stolen, and in particular, into another country was the ideal way to avoid getting caught. It was one of the things that made finding art so difficult. The police and investigators worked within jurisdictions and one of the simplest ways to confuse things was to cross into another jurisdiction. "But that's not to say that the local area shouldn't be checked. Maybe the thief couldn't leave the country for some reason, or maybe they aren't that savvy."

"We can only hope. As long as they don't do something stupid like...destroy them. Or damage them. I'm sure climate controlled storage is the last thing on their mind."

"They know those are valuable pieces. It's in their best interest to take care of them." It was true, but Zoe avoided mentioning the cases she'd read about when art had been transported wrapped in dirty blankets or left in damp basements. "Look, I know you're busy, and I don't want to keep you, but I'm going to do everything I can to find the Canaletto and the Picasso."

"But you know the board won't hear of calling in anyone. They swear our security is able to handle it. They don't even want to work with the police, if you can believe that."

"I'm not surprised," Zoe said. As strange as it sounded, many art institutions didn't want to call the police when something went missing. They feared bad publicity might spook future donors who might pull back their bequest or loan if they thought it wouldn't be safe. "This is completely on my own. I'll work on it in my spare time. I know you can't tell me anything specific about the robbery, but I wanted you to know—"

"Got you. Thanks, Zoe. If you can find them it would be...well, it would be wonderful."

They talked for a few more minutes, making plans to go to lunch again soon. Zoe hung up then worked her way through the contacts that she thought would be most helpful. Most people didn't have any information and hadn't heard anything about the paintings, except for Evelyn at Salt Grass Gallery. Elegant and efficient were two words that came to mind when Zoe thought of Evelyn.

Zoe had met her at an art show in December. A slim woman in her forties, she had crossed the open space of the gallery, making a beeline for Zoe. She had been dressed in a designer suit and had her auburn hair swept up into a chignon. Evelyn held out her hand and said, "I've been looking for you. Harrington said you'd be here. Can I show you around?"

Evelyn was single, a co-owner of the gallery, and an accomplished photographer, who specialized in portraits. Zoe had later met her after one of her photography shoots when her hair was pulled back in a ponytail, and she was in casual jeans and an oxford shirt, but she still looked impeccable and had the air of someone who knew exactly what was next on her to-do list—and she'd get it done, whatever it was. When Zoe asked if Evelyn had heard anything about the two paintings stolen from the Westoll, she said, "No, I'm afraid—um, actually...there was one thing..."

Uncertainty wasn't Evelyn's usual style. Zoe picked up a pen and turned the flyer that she'd made notes on earlier to a new angle where she had more room to write. Since Evelyn was speaking slowly, Zoe knew she was weighing each word before she spoke, which was not like her usual brisk style of speech.

"A man came in last week and asked several questions. Now that I think about it, he might have been hinting. Subtly trying to see if we were open to something shady. He mentioned Canaletto."

"Really?" Zoe asked. If the person was hinting around at art galleries, hoping to unload artwork by major artists, he wasn't a very smart thief.

"I know," Evelyn said, the cadence of her voice picking up. "But that's definitely what happened."

"Did you get a name?"

"No, we didn't get to a point in the conversation where I could ask."

"What did he look like?"

"A young Giacometti."

Of course Evelyn categorized people in terms of famous artists. "Um, not all of us have your art education," Zoe said. "I'm learning as fast as I can, but I don't know what Giacometti looked like."

"Puffy dark hair standing out all around his head, prominent nose, thick brows. Oh, I'm not good with words. Let me look at the surveillance recordings. Maybe we still have the footage from the day when he came in. Too bad I'm a photographer, not a painter or sketch artist."

"Do you think you could draw his face? Even something rough would be helpful?"

"Only if you want a drawing of a stick figure," Evelyn said. "There's a reason I'm a photographer. I'll check the recordings."

Evelyn had been her last call, so Zoe opened a new file on her laptop and made a few notes, then shut it down and hopped off the barstool. She ordered Chinese takeout and sent a text to Jack to let him know about dinner.

He texted back. *Great. I'm finished here. I can pick up the food on my way home. See you soon.*

As Zoe cleared her work-related things off the island, she felt a rush of rejuvenation and excitement to see what she could find out about the Westoll art. She might not find anything, but she would chase down every possibility.

She turned to the cardboard box that she'd shoved out of the way earlier when Harrington called. She checked the return address.

Zoe had never heard of Spar Eon. So it definitely wasn't the file folders, but she did order quite a bit online now. It must be another order she'd placed. Maybe Spar Eon was a subsidiary of another company or it handled the shipping for another business.

Using a knife from the butcher block, she slit the tape. Layers of shredded paper sprang out, showering across the island like confetti as she folded back the flaps. She pawed through the fragments of paper until she came to a heavy bundle in bubble wrap.

The object was long and narrow, but she couldn't see through the distortions of the plastic wrapping. It was something dark, black or brown. That was all she could make out. As she unwound the layers of plastic, Zoe mentally scrolled through everything she'd recently ordered online, but couldn't think of anything of this size, shape, or weight.

She flicked the last layer away and was able to see a base of some sort, thin and nearly circular. With a flick of her wrist she untwisted the remaining wrapping and nearly dropped it. It was a sculpture of a ballet dancer—a Degas ballet dancer.

## 3

"A Degas?" Jack asked. "I thought Degas was a painter."

"He was, but he also sculpted." Their Chinese takeout dinner sat forgotten on the kitchen counter. Jack had arrived home to find Zoe scrolling through websites, searching for information on the sculpture.

Jack circled around the figure and studied it from all sides. About twenty inches tall, the sculpture portrayed a dancer balanced on one foot as she looked at the sole of her other foot. It conveyed a feeling of graceful motion. The surface was dark brown with some lighter golden highlights and wasn't completely smooth. Several cracks traced along the rough exterior.

After the surprise of seeing it, Zoe had immediately set it down on the island.

"At first I thought some neighbor's box had been delivered to the wrong address, but then I saw the stamp and the foundry mark."

Jack leaned against the island. "I take it that's important?"

"Yes."

Zoe had known a little bit about Degas from her reading and gallery visits, but in the last half hour, she'd given herself a crash course in his bronzes. "Degas originally worked mostly with wax for his sculptures. After he died, his family commissioned a foundry to create copies of the sculptures in bronze, but only a limited number were made." Zoe pointed to the sculpture. "This one is marked with a number and letter, a reference to the original sculpture in Degas's series that this sculpture belonged to. That reference number along with the foundry mark...well," Zoe pushed both hands through her hair, drawing it off her face, "that means this *could* be one of the original bronzes cast in the nineteen twenties."

Jack raised an eyebrow, picking up on her doubt. "You think it's a forgery?"

"I don't know. Maybe. I've been concentrating on paintings lately. I know nothing about bronze sculpture."

"I'd say you know a little more than nothing. You recognized the artist and are bringing yourself up to speed on the artwork."

Zoe waved a dismissive hand. "But that's not the biggest problem." Zoe swiveled the computer toward Jack. "This piece—if it's real—is stolen."

Jack gave her a long look. She nodded. "Once I realized it might be a real Degas, I switched to searching for who owned it. It came up on the first stolen art directory site I checked."

Jack had been leaning over the computer, scrolling down the page while Zoe talked. He stood up. "What a headache."

"You're telling me." Zoe realized her voice sounded shrill even to herself. She took a breath and brought it down a notch. "The site doesn't list who owns it. It only describes the piece, so I don't know if it was taken from a museum or a gallery or an individual. I'd contact the company that shipped it to us, but I can't find anything about it online, and there wasn't anything else in the box." Zoe picked up a handful of the paper shreds that she'd dumped on the island. "No packing slip, no identifying tag or sticker on the sculpture. Nothing."

Jack sifted through the paper. "And all the paper used to make the packing materials is blank as well."

"Right. So no hint of where it came from, at all. Even the shipping label doesn't help. It's just a P.O. Box. I suppose I could pack it up and return it to the sender, but I don't think that's a good idea."

"No, having a possibly stolen sculpture is bad enough. Let's not compound things by sending it through the mail—I think that would be a Federal offense."

Zoe groaned. "This is *so* not what I need. I want to work on the Westoll's missing paintings, not spend my time sorting out this..." she gestured to the box "...mess."

Jack dropped the shredded paper and faced her. "So the Westoll came around and hired you guys?"

"Not exactly." Zoe pulled out a barstool and dropped onto it. "Let me tell you about Harrington's phone call. The Milam family will only work with him."

Jack sat down beside her. "That stinks."

"Yeah. It does. And what's worse is that it's not the first time it's happened. So I decided I need to establish myself. I need my own reputation. I'm looking into the Westoll theft on my own."

Jack said, "I think that's a great idea."

"You do?" Zoe turned her head and looked at him out of the corner of her eye.

"Yes."

"I thought I'd have to convince you that I should do it."

"I know better than to attempt to sidetrack you when you lift your chin and get that determined look on your face." He leaned forward and gave her a quick kiss. "Besides, I think you're right. If you want people to trust you, then you have to show them you can do the job by yourself. Part of business is about who you know, but another part of it is about what people think of you. If people consider you Harrington's assistant—and even though he hired you as a consultant, that's how they see you—then you'll have to keep fighting the battle again and again to have them trust you."

"Glad you agree," she said. "I might have even found a possible lead." She told Jack about Evelyn and the security footage. "It's not much to go on, but it's a place to start." Zoe's gaze slid to the sculpture and the open box on the counter. "I'd done all I could for today, and it was getting late, so I opened the mail." She tilted her head toward the ballet dancer. "I can't believe I was working away while it was sitting on the island right beside me. If we hadn't returned from our run as the delivery truck left, anyone walking by could have swiped it off the porch."

"It's a pretty quiet neighborhood," Jack said. "Most people would never think of taking a package off someone's porch."

Zoe rubbed her forehead. "I almost wish someone *had* taken it. Then it wouldn't be our problem. That's terrible to say, I know...but this isn't good."

"No." Jack swiveled to the box. "You said you checked the return address?" He read the first line of the label. "Spar Eon. Never heard of it."

"Me either. And I can't find anything on the web about them. No website, no mentions anywhere. And look at the address."

Zoe pointed to the return address that listed Denver, Colorado as the city and state. "This Zip code doesn't exist. I think the whole return address is made up, just a placeholder to fill the space."

Jack was staring at the label with intense concentration. "What is it?" Zoe asked.

He picked up a pen. "Got a spare sheet of paper?"

She handed him the flyer that she'd made notes on earlier. "Not much room on here," he said.

"I know. I need to invest in something more professional like an actual notepad."

"I'm sure the budget will stretch to that," Jack said, throwing her a grin before he began jotting down letter combinations. He wrote for a few moments, then said, "I think it's an anagram. 'A person' sent this to you."

"What?"

Jack handed her the flyer. "If you rearrange the letters, you get this." He tapped the last line of his various letter combinations.

Zoe's hand dropped to her side. "Is this a practical joke?"

"Odd sort of joke."

"I know. It's not even funny. Only strange." They both studied the ballet dancer for a few seconds.

Zoe shook her head. "Harrington wouldn't send me something with a misleading label, even as a joke. Not his style."

"Definitely not." A smile flickered over Jack's face. "He's far too formal to be interested in practical jokes."

Zoe tossed the flyer on the island. "I've met a lot of people recently in the art world, but I can't think of a single one who'd mail me a sculpture of a Degas ballet dancer." She leaned her elbows on the island, and examined the dancer, her face a few inches from it. "I wish I knew if it was real or a fake." She straightened and sighed. "Either way, I don't see how I can get around calling someone official to look at it."

"The FBI?" Jack asked.

Zoe wrinkled her nose. "I suppose. I'd rather not talk to Sato, but I don't see any other option."

"He's the best choice, I think. He's not a bad guy."

"That's generous of you, considering he wanted to arrest you for murder and who knows what else. Oh, and he wanted to arrest me, too, don't forget."

"But that's all in the past. He was helpful, there at the end."

"Right. Once it was all wrapped up, and we'd done all the work for him. I'll admit, I'm still a bit touchy about all that, but it will be better to talk to him than someone at the police station. At least he can probably get in touch with the Art Crime Team quickly." Zoe reached for her phone.

She'd known in the back of her mind from the minute she saw the dancer that she'd have to make the call, but she'd been putting it off, hoping something would come to light that would make it unnecessary. But she had to admit that whether the ballet dancer was real or a fake, a threat or a joke, it was listed on a directory of stolen art.

She didn't have the expertise to make the call about the sculpture's authenticity, and while she might be able to recruit someone out of her new list of contacts who could tell her, she wasn't going to hold onto something that seemed to be hot art. She found the number for Special Agent Greg Sato and dialed.

# 4

Zoe would have rather talked to Sato's former partner, but Mort Vazarri was retired, and probably puttering around his garden, doing whatever gardeners do in the fall. She had mentally prepared a quick summary to leave on Sato's voicemail, but he came on the line.

"Oh. Hi. This is Zoe Andrews. You'll remember me as Zoe Hunter."

"I remember. Congratulations on your wedding."

"Thanks. I should say congratulations to you, too. Jenny sent me a note after the wedding with some pictures." Jenny was a freelance journalist who ran a popular blog called *The Informationalist.*

"Thanks," Sato said. "How can I help you?"

Sato had never been one for chitchat. Zoe cleared her throat and launched into the short explanation about the ballet dancer. She'd barely mentioned the sculpture, before Sato cut in. "Let me stop you right there. You still live in Dallas, correct?"

"Yes," Zoe said. But what did that matter?

"I've transferred to Denver."

"Oh, I didn't realize," Zoe said. "I haven't heard from Jenny in a while, so I didn't know."

"Just happened about a month ago. Work transfer for me. We're still unpacking. Jenny has been a good sport about it. Says she can do her work from anywhere."

"That's great."

"So you should call Dirk."

"Dirk?"

"Dirk Sorkensov," Sato said in a tone that meant Zoe should recognize the name.

"Um…I don't think I know him."

"That's right. He was my partner after Mort retired, but Dirk was out when that whole thing around the fraud case went down. His wife had a baby, and he took some time off, so you wouldn't have met him. Good guy. Here, I'll give you his number." Zoe scribbled the number down as Sato continued, "He looks like he went to work for the FBI about fifteen minutes ago, but he knows his stuff. I'm sure he'll be happy to hear from you."

Was there a shade of sarcasm in those last words? Zoe suspected there was, but only said, "Okay. Thanks. I'll give him a call."

"Good. I'll tell Jenny you called."

Zoe hung up and saw Jack's raised eyebrows. "Sato and Jenny have moved. He gave me his old partner's phone number, a guy name Dirk…um…something. I didn't quite get the last name."

Zoe dialed the number and left her succinct message on Dirk's voicemail. She slipped the phone into her pocket and crossed her arms, her gaze fixed on the ballet dancer. "And now, we wait."

---

**Tuesday**

"Jack, the FBI is here," Zoe called, then paused to give her head a shake on her way to open the front door. "Now, there's a sentence I'd hoped to never say again."

As Jack trotted down the stairs, he slipped on his suit jacket. He smoothed his tie and gave her a firm kiss. "It'll be fine."

"I know," Zoe said with a confidence she didn't feel. "Thanks for being here." Jack had a meeting downtown at the future site of One Heritage Plaza, which would be the eventual name of the skyscraper that he was providing security input for, and he needed to be there in an hour. He'd normally have already left to make sure he had plenty of time to get there, but today he'd said he would stay with her until the FBI left. "I can always reschedule," he'd said.

Zoe opened the door to a young man with dark hair and an open, cheerful face. He wore a plain suit jacket over a white shirt and dark pants. "Special Agent Sorkensov." He showed his badge. "Zoe Andrews?"

"Yes, that's me," Zoe said. "And this is my husband, Jack. Come through to the kitchen, Agent Sorkensov," Zoe said, stumbling over his name as she led the way through the hallway to the back of the house.

"Call me Dirk," he said with a quick smile. "It's much easier."

Zoe immediately liked him with his easy manner and relaxed attitude, which was so different from Sato's aloof personality, but Zoe caught herself. "Dirk" might be putting forward a non-threatening attitude, but he was still an FBI agent, and she'd had enough brushes with them to remember not to let down her guard. A glance at Jack's face confirmed that he felt the same way.

Zoe waved a hand at the ballet dancer, which still stood on the island, the packing materials and box surrounding it. "It's quite a mess," Zoe said. "But once we realized it was stolen, we decided to leave it as it is until you got here." That wasn't to say that Zoe hadn't asked her new art world contacts if they'd heard any mention of the statue, but no one had. She'd also tried to find out more about the fake address the box had been shipped from, but hadn't had success there either. Possible fingerprints on the box were the only other thing she could think of that might give a clue about who had sent the statue, but since she didn't have access to vast databases with fingerprint records, she'd have to leave that one to the FBI.

Dirk circled the island, looking over everything without touching it. In the bright light of the kitchen, Zoe could see that despite his young-looking face, he had bags under his eyes. He completed the circuit and reached into the outer pocket of his suit jacket. "When did it—" As he pulled a notebook out of his pocket, a plastic toy bottle clattered to the floor and rolled over to Jack's foot. Jack handed it back.

"Sorry," Dirk said. "My daughter is two. She likes to hide things, thinks it's a great game."

"No problem," Jack said.

Dirk shoved the baby bottle back in his pocket and cleared his throat. Zoe answered all his questions, running through the details from the moment they found the box on the porch to her decision to call Sato.

Dirk used a pen to push the flap of the box down so he could read the address. "We'll look into this address," he said. "And check everything for fingerprints, but..."

"We've probably ruined anything that was there," Jack finished for him. "Sorry about that."

"I didn't realize when I opened it," Zoe said.

Dirk pulled on a pair of gloves and proceeded to bag everything from the sculpture down to the last shred of packing paper. As he worked he looked at Zoe. "You work for Harrington Throckmorton?"

"Yes, as a consultant," Zoe said. "I called him last night and told him about it. He didn't send it, and he doesn't have any idea about who might have."

"I'll need his contact information."

"Of course." Zoe gave him Harrington's business card.

"Anyone you can think of who'd send this to you?"

"No. I've worked with Harrington for a while, but the cases I've helped him with have involved paintings. Harrington checked his files and said he hasn't been involved in any cases of a theft of a Degas sculpture."

Dirk nodded, his gaze fixed on the piles of evidence bags now spaced across the island. "I'll contact the Art Crime Team, of course. I'm sure they'll be in touch."

As he bundled everything into his arms, Zoe asked, "You haven't heard anything about that theft at the Westoll, have you? A Picasso and the Canaletto..."

"Not a thing."

"Oh. I'd thought since it was local..."

"No, not a murmur," he said as he walked to the front door where he paused. "Great meeting you both," he said with a wide smile. "I always thought you were innocent in that other case."

"I bet Sato didn't agree," Zoe said before she could stop herself.

"I'd say we had divergent theories of the case, but he came around in the end. The evidence always plays out." He gave a nod and went to his nondescript four-door sedan that was parked at the curb.

"That was weird," Zoe said. "It was almost like...I don't know... we were some long-lost friends."

Jack closed the door. "He knew about us from the fraud case, and I think he was excited to meet us."

Zoe walked back to the kitchen. "Strange. That had to be the least stressful interview ever."

"Let's hope he stays our new best friend and puts in a good word for us with the Art Crime Team."

"Yeah, they probably aren't predisposed to be in our corner."

---

*Rbn: Wrapping up here.*

*Tuck05: Still no glitches?*

*Rbn: None. The boss told me how much he appreciates the long hours I'm putting in.*

*Tuck05: Irony. What's your timing?*

*Rbn: A week to 10 days.*

*Tuck05: Ok. Looking forward to it. Can't wait to see it hit the news.*

## 5

**Thursday**

Zoe hadn't expected to hear back from Dirk right away. She spent the next few days working on more admin and research tasks for Harrington and finishing off copy edits for a short nonfiction book, a freelance project that she'd picked up. But she felt antsy, waiting for a call from the FBI Art Crime Team. She hadn't heard back from Evelyn either, and when she checked in with her, Evelyn said, "I'm sorry. I've been overrun with work. Haven't had a chance to get to the video footage, but I will. I promise!"

When the phone finally rang on Thursday, Zoe was not surprised to see an unknown number.

She answered and heard a male voice ask, "Zoe Andrews?"

"Yes, speaking."

"Hold for Mr. Thacker please."

Mr. Thacker? While techno music played in her ear, Zoe skimmed through her mental contact list of friends, family, and work associates, but came up blank. The name Mr. Thacker did sound familiar, though. He couldn't mean Fredrick Thacker...could he? No, surely not.

Zoe tucked the phone between her ear and shoulder and went

on with her packing while the hold music played. Jack was attending a conference in Denver on Friday and Saturday. Since her workload was so light, Zoe was going with him. She planned to sleep in at the hotel, then lounge around the pool while Jack worked. On Sunday, they would go to the mountains for a day of hiking before they returned to Dallas on Monday. She placed a folded shirt into the open suitcase on the bed then crossed the bedroom to the desk where Jack's laptop was. Once the browser came up, Zoe typed in the name Fredrick Thacker.

A deep masculine voice came on the line, replacing the hold music at the same moment the search results loaded and an image of Fredrick Thacker with his narrow face, aquiline nose, and thin lips open in a half-smile filled the top of the screen.

"Zoe Andrews, it is a...*pleasure* to talk to you," he said. "Fred Thacker here."

"Um, it's nice to talk to you, too," Zoe said. Could she really be speaking to *the* Fredrick Thacker, the tech entrepreneur and owner of Eon Industries, turned avant-garde philanthropist?

"I had to call...to thank you." He spoke again with the same cadence. The pause in the middle of the sentence added significance to the final words.

Zoe cleared her throat. "Um...thank me for what?"

"You mean they...*didn't* tell you?"

A frisson of nervousness jolted through her. This was a wealthy and influential guy. He obviously thought she knew something that she didn't. She considered trying to bluff her way through the strange conversation, but decided that could make her look even worse than admitting she was confused. "I'm afraid I'm lost," she said. "Tell me what?"

"Typical government inefficiency," Thacker muttered, then went on in his regular tone of voice. "Let me be the first to thank you," he paused again with what Zoe realized must be his typical conversational style, then said, "for the recovery of my ballet dancer. I'm thrilled to have it back."

"That's wonderful," Zoe said. "I had no idea. It arrived here in the mail, and I called the FBI. I didn't have much to do with getting it back to you."

"Nonsense." His voice was firm. "You did the right thing. A less scrupulous person might have been...*tempted* to keep it for themselves." His deep voice and whispery emphasis gave the word extra impact.

"I couldn't do that," Zoe said. "Besides the fact that I would never be able to enjoy something that I hadn't purchased fair and square, there's also my job. I work in art recovery."

"Yes, I know. With Harrington Throckmorton."

"Oh, you know him?" Did everyone in the world know Harrington? He had been in the business for years, but the thought of how long it would take to get to the half-way point of his knowledge and contacts was daunting.

"Only by reputation...and his reputation is *excellent*." His voice shifted from conversational to brisk. "But back to the reason I called. I appreciate the part you played in getting my little dancer back to me." He waited a beat, and Zoe realized his speak-pause-speak pattern resulted in a cliffhanger aspect that had her listening extra intently to see how he would end his sentences. "I understand you'll be in Denver with your husband for a short trip next week," he continued.

How did he know that? With anyone else she would have asked outright where he'd learned about the trip, but with Thacker...well, he was a powerful man and she didn't want to get on his bad side.

"You're wondering how I know this?"

"Well, yes."

"Your husband is attending a cybersecurity conference in Denver. His name is listed on the website as one of the attendees. I made an educated guess that you'd accompany him because...who wouldn't want to visit Denver in the fall?"

"You guessed correctly. I am a bit of a travel junkie. I love to visit new places."

"Then while your husband is attending his lectures, come visit me in Vail for a day. I would love to meet you...in person."

"You won't be at the conference yourself?" The meeting focused on cybersecurity, an area that Jack was moving into with his business. Until last year, he'd focused mainly on advising clients about physical security issues like how to make sure buildings were secure or how to make sure your fine art stayed in your home instead of ending up on the black market. But lately Jack had decided to branch out and add cybersecurity to his list of consulting services.

He'd taken several night classes to get up to speed on the topic. Attending the conference was part of his learning curve and would also be a networking opportunity. Zoe didn't know a lot about the tech world in general or the cybersecurity world in particular, but even she knew Fredrick Thacker had made his money in a startup that brought high-tech home security options to homeowners by cutting out the middlemen of established home alarm companies. Thacker had been the company's spokesperson and several of his funny ads had gone viral, making him a household name.

Thacker laughed. "Me? No, I'm retired now...well, semi-retired. Mostly, I leave things like that to the kids, like your husband. What do you say? You can drive up Saturday and stay the weekend in a small apartment we own. Your husband can join you on Saturday after the conference. A weekend in Vail...is a *wonderful* thing. I wouldn't pass it up, if I were you. You can meet my wife, Mary, and I'll tell you all the details about the sculpture. I think you'll find the story quite...*entertaining*."

She wouldn't get as much relaxing time at the hotel while Jack was at his conference, but this opportunity was too good to pass up. "I'd love to."

## 6

Saturday

Z oe saw the sign for Vail and put on her blinker. She had
departed Denver early that morning, leaving Jack to attend
his last conference sessions. He had grumbled in a good-natured
sort of way, "Go ahead. Go to the mountains without me. Have
lunch with a multimillionaire. I don't mind. I'll just stay here
and work."

Zoe knew he was joking. "It's only a few hours."

As soon as the conference ended tonight, Jack was scheduled to
catch a Denver-to-Vail shuttle, which would drop him off at the Vail
town center. Zoe and Jack would have the evening and the whole
day tomorrow to explore the village and the mountain.

Zoe parked in the multilevel parking garage, which seemed sort
of an odd thing to have nestled next to a ski village, but she
supposed it was needed during the winter season when the area
would be packed. For now, there were only a few cars, and she
easily found a parking space, which she assumed meant the village
wasn't quite as busy during the fall as it would be in a few months.

She stepped out of the car and took a deep breath of the crisp
evergreen-scented air as she zipped up her jacket. She'd known the

mountains would be cooler than Dallas, but the air had a sharp edge that made it feel like winter was only days away.

She followed the directions in the email she received from someone named Kaz Volk and made her way through the village to Fredrick Thacker's cabin. If she hadn't known she was in Colorado, she might have thought she was in a Bavarian village. The towering mountains in the background, the steep roof lines, the overflowing flower baskets, and the fretwork on the wooden balconies, combined to give the village a definite Alpine air.

It was odd to think that this morning she started her day on the flat plains to the east side of the Rocky Mountains in Denver, and in only a couple of hours she had driven a road that had taken her through small mining towns into the heart of the mountains. She had enjoyed the drive as it traced along the course of a sparkling river and through a tunnel that burrowed through one of the mountains where she crossed the Continental Divide.

As she walked past designer boutiques, high-end art galleries, and restaurants with umbrella-shaded tables outside, her phone buzzed with the text from Harrington. Zoe had texted him after speaking to Fredrick Thacker, but because Harrington was out of the office and on a trip to Japan, she hadn't expected to hear back. Her steps slowed as she read the message.

*Interesting that the ballet dancer belonged to Thacker. Good idea to meet with him. Be careful, though. I've heard some interesting rumors about him that hint at unsavory things.*

Zoe resumed walking. Interesting that Harrington wanted to give her a little warning about Thacker. She strolled by fancy boutiques and a couple of ski rental shops, then managed to resist going inside a gourmet chocolate shop. She found Thacker's cabin on the far side of the village. Tucked up at the base of the mountains, it was a perfect location. Walk out the door, and you'd be on the slopes.

It was more extreme luxury home than cabin. The multi-story building with fieldstone and wood accents had a ground floor with two double garages and three stories of living space above. Zoe climbed the wooden staircase to the deck that looked as if it encircled the whole building then crossed to the huge wooden front door.

She was surprised when Thacker opened the door. She'd expected someone like a housekeeper or maid to greet her. Zoe recognized him immediately, even though it had been several years since his online ads had gone viral. His narrow face was a little bit more padded, and his longish straight brown hair was now tinted with gray around his temples, but otherwise he looked the same. He held a glass of white wine in one hand. "Welcome, Mrs. Andrews. Come in, come in."

"Call me Zoe, please."

As she stepped inside, Thacker said, "And you must call me...Fred."

Zoe hadn't been quite sure what he was going to say and had braced herself for anything from Chairman of the Board to Supreme Overlord.

"Of course...Fred," Zoe said with a pause of her own. She didn't think she'd be able to toss his name off easily, but she'd try. He had presence even dressed down in a worn sweatshirt with the word *Vail* printed across it in capital letters, a pair of faded jeans, and red cowboy boots. It was not at all the look she expected a multimillionaire to have, even on a Saturday afternoon at home.

He waved the wine glass. "Come this way," he said, indicating a large living area dominated by a flagstone fireplace that filled one wall running up to the rafters. Wood beams traced across the openness of the two-story ceiling. The room was furnished with a mixture of casual furniture in leather with a rustic edge to the design. The living area connected to an open kitchen and beyond it, a glass wall gave a view of the mountains. A plump blonde woman in a bright multicolored floral top with black leggings was moving back and forth across the kitchen from the glass-fronted cabinets to the professional gas range.

"Mary," Thacker said, "Zoe Andrews is here." He motioned to the living area and said to me, "You can leave your stuff in here."

The painting over the fireplace drew Zoe's attention. She thought it might be a Salvador Dalí and wondered if it was an original, but she didn't have time to look closely. She dropped her messenger bag on the couch and draped her jacket over it, then followed Thacker to the kitchen.

Zoe guessed Mary was near Thacker's age, which was listed on his Wikipedia bio as fifty-eight. With her bouffant blond hair, chunky gold jewelry, and perfect makeup that included hot pink lipstick that matched her pink fingernails, Mary resembled many of the society wives that Zoe had met on her recent tour of art gallery openings.

"Nice to meet you." Mary shook Zoe's extended hand, then said, "I'm a hugger," and gave Zoe a quick embrace as a cloud of flowery perfume enveloped her. Mary stepped back and tugged at the frayed neckline of Thacker's sweatshirt. "I can't believe you're wearing this ratty old thing."

"It's my Vail sweatshirt," he said. "I wear it every time I'm here."

"I *know*," Mary said to Zoe in a what-can-you-do tone of voice. "Men and their clothes."

She patted Thacker on the shoulder. "Go change into that nice cashmere sweater I bought you the other day. Lunch is almost ready."

Thacker said to Zoe, "You can see who runs things here, right?" He set his glass of wine on the granite countertop. "I shall return... shortly," he said before climbing an open-tread staircase.

Mary waved Zoe into the kitchen. "Can I get you something to drink?"

Zoe felt as if she was technically at work, so she said, "Water or a ginger ale, if you have it."

A woman with dark hair pulled up in a bun, wearing a plain T-shirt and jeans, glided through the kitchen as silently as a ghost, carrying a laundry basket full of clothes in her arms. Mary checked the stainless steel refrigerator then said to the woman, "Bring in the extra ginger ale from the other refrigerator." The woman nodded and slipped out, then returned a few minutes later with a ginger ale.

She added several cans of it to the refrigerator then poured a glass for Zoe. Zoe took it with a smile. The woman's expression didn't change. She told Mary she was going to pick up the dry cleaning and left.

Mary opened the oven door, and the aroma of roasted chicken wafted through the air. She looked critically at the roasting pan, then grabbed a couple of dishtowels, and used them like potholders to lift the pan out of the oven.

"It smells delicious," Zoe said.

"We'll sit down to lunch in a few minutes. I'm so glad you could come."

"It was nice of you and Mr. Thacker to invite me."

Mary took out a chef's knife, efficiently carved the chicken, and placed it on a platter. "Freddie does like to have his entertainments." Mary's tone had a critical undercurrent, which drew Zoe's attention, but Mary's face was blank as she focused on cutting the meat. Zoe didn't like the idea of being anyone's entertainment, but she kept her thoughts to herself.

Mary walked to a dark hallway that branched off the kitchen and called, "Kaz, lunch," then she retrieved the platter of chicken and put it on the table.

"Can I help?" Zoe asked as Mary crossed in front of her to the large refrigerator and took out a deep wooden bowl filled with salad.

"There's not much to do. You could put the bread in this basket." Mary gestured to rows of bread cooling on a rack.

Thacker thumped down the stairs in a rush. He retrieved his wineglass and peered over Mary's shoulder as he gave her waist a quick squeeze. A look that could have been irritation traced over Mary's face as Thacker said, "Looks good." He said to Zoe, "There's a reason I asked you to lunch. Mary's culinary skills deserve a wider audience than just me and Kaz."

Zoe picked up the basket of rolls and turned to place it on the long glass-top table beside the expansive windows. She nearly dropped the basket. "Is that the—?"

She took a step closer and realized it was exactly what she thought it was. The sculpture of the ballet dancer examining her foot sat in the middle of the table surrounded by four place settings. Zoe wouldn't have been surprised to see an arrangement of flowers or a bowl of fruit in the center of the table. Seeing valuable art so casually displayed caught her off-guard.

"Indeed, it is." Thacker released Mary and topped off his wine. He lifted the bottle and raised his eyebrow at Zoe. She shook her head, and indicated she already had a drink.

Mary brought the salad to the table and waved Zoe into the seat on the side of the table opposite the window. "You sit over there where you have a view." Mary walked around the other side and drew out a chair. "I get to see the mountains all the time." As Thacker set his glass down, Mary said to him, "You know, we really should think about getting a round table instead of this long rectangular thing."

Thacker nodded, but clearly he wasn't interested in chatting about decorating. Mary let out a small huff, presumably because Thacker didn't respond to her. Zoe wasn't sure if he intentionally ignored Mary, or if he just wasn't aware she was annoyed. He waited until Zoe was seated, then motioned to the sculpture. "Our ballet dancer has been returned home, just where she should be." He picked up the platter. "Chicken?"

Zoe transferred a couple of pieces of chicken to her plate then carefully reached around the sculpture to hand the platter to Mary. "Sorry that I'm staring. It's so unusual to see it sitting here on your table, just like it was sitting on the island in my kitchen. I didn't think you'd have it back yet or that it would be out..." she waved her hand, "...in the open."

"You think I should have it tucked away behind glass with special lights and alarms?" Thacker passed Zoe the salad.

"Something like that." She placed a serving of salad on her plate and passed the bowl to Mary.

"I don't understand all that rigmarole." Thacker waved his fork. "It's a whole lot of stress and worry...and *expense*," he said.

"No offense taken, I hope, considering the work your husband does."

"No," Zoe said. "It's your artwork. You can do whatever you want with it. How did you get it back so quickly? And who stole it? Did the FBI figure it out?"

"And therein...," Thacker said with his characteristic pause, "... lies the tale that you've travelled so far to hear."

Quick footsteps sounded behind Zoe. A skinny man in his late twenties circled around the table. He pushed up a pair of square glasses with earpieces so thick that they almost looked like blinders as he sat down beside Mary. "Sorry," he said as he placed his cell phone beside his plate. He wore a red T-shirt under a tan zip-necked fleece with a pair of jeans, and hiking boots. Springy curls of black hair covered the top of his head, but the sides of his hair were cut short around his ears.

"How's the rubber ducking going?" Mary asked.

"Slowly," he said. This must be Kaz, Zoe decided as the man focused on filling his plate.

Mary turned to Zoe. "If you're around these guys long enough, you'll pick up some of the jargon," she said. "Kaz is debugging code. Kaz, this is Zoe. She helped Freddie get his little ballerina back."

He nodded at her.

"Nice to meet you," Zoe said. "I think I had an email from you."

Kaz bobbed his head again and applied himself to cutting his chicken. As Zoe buttered her roll, she couldn't help but compare the two men at the table. While Thacker was relaxed and affable, Kaz sat hunched over, his gaze often straying to the screen of his phone, which flickered with incoming notifications. Zoe assumed from the email comment from Mary and the fact that Kaz was eating with them that he was on a slightly higher level in the household than the woman with the laundry basket since she was retrieving the dry-cleaning instead of eating chicken with them.

Thacker sipped his wine then leaned back in his chair. He'd already eaten half of his chicken, while Mary only nibbled at her mound of lettuce.

Thacker admired the sculpture for a moment. Zoe thought that if it were possible to caress something with your gaze, that's what Thacker was doing. He leaned forward and wrapped his hand around the sculpture's torso and picked it up.

He held out the sculpture to Zoe. "Here."

"Oh, no. I don't think I could—"

Thacker continued to hold out the ballet dancer. "I insist. It's part of the story."

Zoe set down her fork. She held the ballet dancer with one hand under the base and the other wrapped around the torso. Her palms suddenly felt sweaty.

"Take a look at the base," Thacker said. "No, the underside." Thacker waved his hand in a circular motion, meaning turning over.

Zoe didn't want to be handling such a valuable piece of artwork, but she tilted the sculpture so that she could see the underside of the base.

Thacker leaned forward, his gaze intent. "Do you see anything interesting—any *marks*—on the base?"

It was relatively smooth except for a few shallow scratches on the surface.

"Keep looking," Thacker said.

"Some of these grooves..." Zoe said. "They look a little like a letter. Maybe the letter *C*."

"Yes," said Thacker. "That's it exactly, which stands for copy."

Z oe looked from the sculpture to him and back at the
sculpture. "You mean not the original sculpture? It's a copy?"

"Yes," said Thacker. "Amazing to think that this ballet dancer,
which is exactly like the original bronzes, is not worth nearly as
much as ones made in the nineteen twenties."

"So that's why you got it back so quickly," Zoe said. "The FBI
didn't hang onto it longer. It wasn't one of the original Degas
sculptures."

"Correct." Thacker served himself another piece of his chicken.
"I have copies of all my artwork made."

"You mean you have the original as well?" Zoe asked.

With the bite of chicken poised on his fork, he gestured with his
knife, making a circular motion that included the whole house. "It
would be a bit careless to have the originals out. But I do want to
enjoy the things I purchase." He pointed the knife at the artwork on
the far wall of the dining room, a painting of a blue butterfly.
"What's the use of having beautiful art if you can't look at it?"

"You mean you have the original of *this dancer* as well," Zoe
asked again because she wanted to make sure she had the details
completely clear.

"Of course. I always have the original, before I have a copy made." He leaned toward her and lowered his voice as if he were telling her a secret. "I'm trusting you with this information. It's not...*general knowledge*. But I know that you can keep a secret, especially in the line of work you and your husband are in."

Zoe carefully set the sculpture down in the center of the table. She didn't feel quite so nervous handling it now that she knew it was a copy. Actually, it was a copy of a copy. The bronzes from the nineteen twenties were made from molds from Degas' original sculptures. "Displaying copies is actually a good system to keep the originals safe," she said.

Zoe peered at the butterfly painting at the end of the dining room. She wasn't good enough to know if it was an original or a copy, but she assumed from Thacker's words that everything in the cabin was a copy. She looked from the butterfly painting to Thacker, eyebrows raised.

He nodded. "You got it. It's a copy."

Zoe resumed eating, but her gaze kept straying to the ballet dancer. "I think there's more to this story."

"Much more," Thacker said. "How you got the copy—that's what you want to know, isn't it?"

"Yes, I'd love to hear the whole story." Zoe glanced around the table and saw that Kaz, who had been eating with machinelike precision, cutting his meat and shoveling his food in, had already finished his first helping, and was reaching for another. Mary's salad had a little dent in it, but most of her plate remained covered with food.

"A computer glitch was at the base of it," Thacker said. "Kaz can explain all the technical jargon."

Kaz, who was focused on his phone, glanced at Thacker but didn't say anything. Zoe noticed that Mary was pushing lettuce around her plate as she tilted her head so that she could read the screen of Kaz's phone over his shoulder.

Thacker went on, "Of course, all those details are...boring." He touched his napkin to the corner of his mouth then said. "We were trying out a new program at Eon."

Zoe realized he was talking about his company, Eon Industries.

"It didn't work," he continued. "One of the biggest goofs we've had in a long time. Thankfully, Kaz caught it after only one package went out—yours."

"Faulty mail merge."

Zoe glanced across the table, surprised that Kaz jumped into the middle of Thacker's story. "But the package came from a company called Spar Eon," she said.

"That's an old company of mine," Thacker said. "I closed it down a few years ago, but the details were still in our database. Eon Industries is a much better name."

"And the zip code that didn't exist?" Zoe asked.

"Placeholders," Kaz said.

Thacker said, "Those numbers were supposed to be replaced with the correct zip code before labels were printed, but an overzealous employee—not Kaz, here, who checks and double checks everything—took...*initiative*." Sarcasm laced his tone. "She had those labels printed, and the first package mailed before anyone noticed what was wrong."

Thacker twisted and reached behind him to a sideboard made of rough wood. He picked up a padlock. "Your husband was on a list of names to receive this." He handed it to her. "A new digital lock. The idea was to send this lock as a promotional item to security specialists around the country to generate interest in a new promotion we're running."

"Freddie doesn't know what it means to be retired." Mary speared a tomato. "He can't leave it alone. He's always doing something new."

"*Semi*-retired. But I do hand things off, eventually."

"Not soon enough," Mary said.

Thacker laughed. "Any time spent on business is too much for Mary," he said to Zoe.

Since work was a touchy subject between the two of them, Zoe said, "So we should have gotten a padlock, not a sculpture."

"Yes," Thacker said. "The little ballerina had been packed for transport to our home in Florida on Star Island."

"It will look perfect on the coffee table down there," Mary said.

"I left instructions for the first set of promotional items to be sent out..." Thacker exchanged a look with Kaz, "...but only after the addresses had been checked. That didn't happen. The box with the Degas copy was sitting with the promotional items. Someone placed a label on the first box, which was the sculpture—not a lock —and sent it out."

"So it was a series of glitches and coincidences—that's how I received the copy of the ballet dancer." It was hard to believe...a little too hard to believe? Zoe wasn't sure. It *could* have happened. But there was something a little *too* extraordinary about it for Zoe.

But who argues with a multimillionaire who invites you to visit his mountain cabin and serves you homemade roasted chicken? "That's quite a story," Zoe said.

"As bizarre as it is, that's what happened."

## 8

"Everyone ready for dessert?" Mary stood and collected plates. "Chocolate mousse."

Kaz said, "I have to finish coding that program," and left the room, disappearing down the short hallway off the kitchen.

Thacker said to Zoe, "Come take a closer look at my butterfly painting while Mary gets dessert."

Mary asked as she opened the refrigerator, "Who wants whipped cream?"

"I'll always take whipped cream." Zoe followed Thacker to the other end of the table.

Instead of focusing on the painting, he rested his hand on the piece of furniture below it. It had shallow drawers and reminded Zoe of a map cabinet at a library. "This is my cabinet of curiosities." He reached for a drawer.

Zoe wasn't sure she wanted to see what Thacker considered a curiosity, but when he opened it Zoe saw that he meant curiosities in the Victorian sense of the word.

The drawer contained a framed collection of various sizes of butterflies, all of them yellow, each labeled with a scientific name. Thacker closed that drawer and opened another one. Another framed collection of butterflies rested inside it. This time the butterflies were white with black accents. Another drawer held a collection of beetles. He closed the drawer and waved a hand up and down. "All vintage," he said. He tilted his head toward the butterfly painting. "This seemed the appropriate place for this painting—or rather, this...*copy*."

"It's lovely," Zoe said. Besides capturing the stunning iridescent blue of the butterfly's wings, the painting also showed the smallest details, down to the faint lines that ran through the shimmering wings.

In the painting, a shadow fell over half of the butterfly, throwing one side of its wings into darkness, but even in the shadow, the painter had picked out the faint contour and muted coloring of the wing. A brown and taupe background focused all the viewer's attention on the butterfly.

"It's a blue morpho," Thacker said. "Not hard to come by now." He opened the top drawer of the cabinet and took out a framed box with several different blue butterflies. "At the time this was painted, many Europeans hadn't seen a blue morpho, especially not a live one. Martin Johnson Heade went to Brazil to study plants and animals in their native habitat and then paint them. You might not have heard of him. He wasn't well known during his lifetime. Critics thought he was all right, but nothing special. Lately, he's been recognized for his groundbreaking compositions and beautiful paintings." Thacker took a few steps away to a bookshelf in the living area and returned with a large art book.

He found a page with a painting of a hummingbird and an orchid. He handed the book to Zoe, who had noticed that his pattern of speaking with pauses and emphasis had disappeared when art was the topic. He was clearly passionate about art and butterflies, and his showmanship with his speech had slipped away. "Look at that unique composition. See how the orchid dominates the frame, and yet the hummingbird is full of movement and life. And in the distance, the mountain and the rain—brilliant."

Zoe said, "They're so detailed. They look like botanical illustrations."

"Yes, they do. Worthy of being included in any Victorian field guide or wildlife guide. But besides the exacting detail, you also have to consider the arrangement of the elements, the presentation." He turned to another page. "Notice the vegetation. See this passion fruit flower? And look here." He flipped to another section. "Here's a banana plant and a coffee plant. The accents and backgrounds are spectacular in their own right." He set the book down on the table, open to a page that featured the orchid and hummingbird in the foreground and a rainy tropical vista in the background. He stepped back and looked at it, resting his chin in his hand. "Do you feel it? That the background isn't just filler or a placeholder?"

Zoe tilted her head as she studied the steamy rainforest background. "It does give the painting... atmosphere. A mood."

"Yes," Thacker said, his voice quickening with enthusiasm. "I *knew* you were the right person to talk to about this."

Zoe was flattered, but she wasn't quite sure how to respond. Fortunately, Thacker went on. "There is another blue morpho butterfly painting by Heade." An excited light came into his eyes. "I should say, it's *thought* that there is another one."

"The documentation on Heade's work is incomplete?"

Thacker let out a bark of laughter. "I'll say. Heade was prolific. He made his living through painting. He sold enough to maintain his lifestyle—and that's a lot of paintings."

In the background, the clinks of dishes sounded, then the distinctive swish of the whipped cream nozzle. Thacker seemed oblivious to anything except talking about the art. He went on, "Heade was productive, and he traveled widely. The trip to Brazil was just one of his tours. The upshot is that no one is quite sure exactly how many paintings he produced."

Thacker raised his eyebrows as he tilted his head toward his butterfly painting. "Even this one has some questions around it. Officially, it's part of a series that he painted while he was in South America. The series features mostly hummingbirds. The blue morpho is an outlier. After Heade visited Brazil, he went to England where he produced many paintings similar to the ones he painted in Brazil, cranking them out for an appreciative fan base there. There is some debate about how many hummingbird paintings he painted in Brazil versus what he painted later in England." Thacker waved his hand, brushing that topic away. "But I'm going off on a tangent. What's important is that if there's another painting with a blue morpho butterfly in a different composition, I want it."

This was the first time Zoe had come face-to-face with a collector's passion. She wouldn't describe the light in his eyes as feverish, but his gaze had an intensity, a determination, that hadn't been there during the meal. He would have his painting, if it was at all possible. His fervor was on a completely different level than Zoe's desire for a new pair of shoes or that cute handbag she saw last time she browsed online.

Thacker propped an arm on his cabinet of curiosities. "And I think you're exactly the right person to help me find it."

"If it even exists?" Zoe asked.

"That would be the first step," he acknowledged with a laugh.

"Dessert is ready," Mary called.

Thacker closed the art book and handed it to Zoe. "You'll need this."

"But I haven't said that Harrington and I will find your painting, if it even exists." The job sounded tempting but she bristled at his attitude that her participation was a foregone conclusion.

"Oh, I think you'll take this on," Thacker said. "I can see you're interested. Think about it for a few days and get back to me," he said in a tone that indicated he knew that thinking about it was only a formality. "And I don't want to hire Harrington. I want you to do it. He's a great guy, but it won't be long before he retires. You know I'm right. I can always spot the up-and-coming people. You're one of them."

The words were flattering and gave Zoe's battered self-esteem as an art recovery specialist a boost, but she didn't want to get sidetracked from the main topic, the art. "Why do you think there's another blue butterfly painting?" The book weighed heavily in her arms.

"See, I knew it—you're hooked." Thacker replaced the framed collection of blue butterflies in the cabinet. "There's a rumor that a painting similar to my blue morpho surfaced in Florida a week ago."

Zoe opened her mouth to ask a question, but Thacker raised his hand. "I know you're wondering how I would have heard about this, but let's just say that it's well-known that I collect Heade's paintings, and that I've been looking for the other blue morpho painting for a long time. People tell me things."

He pushed the cabinet drawer closed. "Several new paintings belonging to Heade have been discovered over the last couple of years as he's become more well-known. It's not unthinkable that someone could have purchased one of his paintings, not known its value, and sold it for a few dollars at a yard sale. Or it might have been inherited, and the person who received it knows nothing about Heade."

"What does this rumored blue butterfly painting look like?"

"It's similar to mine, but besides the butterfly, it also incorporates either a hummingbird or multiple hummingbirds. It would be more similar in composition to the orchid paintings with the hummingbirds."

"You seem to know an awful lot of details, for a painting that's never been confirmed to exist."

He lifted his shoulder. "It's all rumor and speculation. The second blue butterfly painting is mentioned in Heade's correspondence, which is where the possibility of a second painting originated."

Mary called again, and Thacker gestured to the table, indicating Zoe could lead the way back. He continued speaking as they walked. "There's also a mention of a another blue butterfly painting in a newspaper from 1866, which fits with the time my blue butterfly was produced."

Zoe sat down at the table as Mary placed dishes of chocolate mousse at each place. Zoe picked up a spoon. "And you think this second blue butterfly painting has been undiscovered since the mid-1860s, tucked away in someone's garage or on someone's wall with them not realizing it?"

"It's happened many times. One family was using one of Heade's still lifes to cover a hole in their wall. It sold for over one million dollars. Another painting of his was stored away in an attic for years."

Mary took a seat and drew her tiny serving of chocolate mousse close to her. "Is he bothering you about that other blue butterfly painting?"

Before Zoe could answer, Thacker jumped in. "I'm not bothering her about it. I'm hiring her to find it."

"I haven't actually taken on this job," Zoe reminded him.

"Yet," Thacker said. "You'll agree. I know you will. I can see that you're interested. You're curious about this painting. Once that happens..." he shrugged. "You won't be able to *not* look for it."

Mary waved her spoonful of chocolate mousse at Zoe. "You might as well go ahead and take the job. Freddie usually gets what he wants. I should know, I was one of his first hires." She winked at him.

## 9

**Sunday**

"So how did you leave it?" Harrington asked.

Zoe switched her phone from one ear to the other and caught Jack's attention. He was across the store examining the spiky crystals inside a geode. Zoe tilted her head toward the door and mouthed the word *Harrington*. Jack nodded and went back to examining the purple crystals inside the rock cavity as she headed outside. "I told Thacker that I would consider it," Zoe said. "I didn't want him to think it was a done deal, but he acted like he didn't even hear me."

"That's quite common," Harrington said. "These high-powered businessmen don't like hearing their plans may not be executed exactly as they would like."

"And he said he wanted to work directly with me, not Throck-morton Enquiries," Zoe said, figuring it was best to get that detail on the table.

"Did he?" Harrington said. "That's excellent."

"Not many people would say that in your place." Zoe was relieved that Harrington had responded the way she thought he would. He'd never been jealous or stingy and she hadn't expected him to start behaving that way now, but she couldn't help being a bit worried about what his reaction would be to the news that Thacker didn't want to hire Throckmorton Enquiries.

Harrington chuckled. "That may be true, but I have more work than I can handle. I'd be delighted for you to intercept a few cases that would normally come my way. The Milam case is taking much more time than I thought."

"How is that going?" Zoe asked as she paced back and forth in front of the window of the store with its display of fossils and geodes. She walked as far as the life-size model of a raptor dinosaur, an eye-catching attraction that the store had placed out front, then reversed course.

"Unfortunately, it appears that I have run into a dead end here in Japan. I'm on the next return flight to London."

"I'm sorry to hear that."

"I've heard of another possibility and will track it down next. It may involve another trip, so I'll most likely be out-of-pocket again. The timing for you to take on the Thacker case couldn't be better."

"But then there's the issue of working with him," Zoe said. "You said you heard some rumors..."

Harrington cleared his throat. "Nothing that I've been able to confirm. I've heard some—indications—let's call them, that a few of his art purchases may not have been completely aboveboard. However, he is an important collector and rumors are just that— rumors. Nothing has been proved. It's not a good idea to turn away someone of his stature."

"So you would advise to proceed with caution," Zoe said with a smile, thinking that that was usually Harrington's advice.

"Don't I always advise that?"

"Without fail. And I'm sure that's why you've been in this business so long."

"Possibly." Harrington's voice shifted. "How is Vail?"

"Gorgeous. Mountain scenery is one of the most beautiful landscapes in the world, at least in my book. Jack and I are actually in Breckenridge today. The chairlift in Vail is closed for repairs. We wanted to go to the top of the mountains so we came over here."

"You're at the peak of the mountain? You're able to get mobile reception there? The connection is wonderful."

"No, we haven't even made it through the town to the chairlift yet."

"Well, I'll let you get to it then."

Zoe ended the call and was about to return to the store, but Jack met her on the sidewalk. He handed her a small bag. "For you."

Zoe opened the bag and found a pair of gold earrings shaped like aspen leaves. "They're beautiful Jack. I love them."

"I saw you looking at them before you got your call." As Zoe removed the earrings that she was wearing and switched to the new ones, Jack said, "They're real aspen leaves coated in gold."

Zoe gestured at his empty hands. "But no geode?"

"I decided I don't need to spend a couple hundred dollars on a rock, no matter how cool it looks."

"Practical as ever," Zoe said, with a teasing tone in her voice. But she was secretly glad he hadn't bought it because something like that would make a perfect birthday or Christmas gift. "In that case, I think we should head for the chairlift."

"Good idea."

They strolled through the rest of the town on their way to the chairlift. While Vail had a glitzy almost European feel to it, Breckinridge's atmosphere was closer to a frontier mining town. A few buildings in rough wood siding at one end of the town showed Breckenridge's authentic roots in the early mining days. Of course the little town was now a ski resort and had its share of T-shirt stores and kitschy shops selling refrigerator magnets and baseball caps.

They stopped at a grocery store and bought sandwiches, a couple of apples, and some water bottles before climbing onto the enclosed chairlift that took them halfway up the mountain. They switched to a second chairlift, this one an open-air lift, which would take them all the way to the top.

With the bar settled in place across their hips, the second chair-lift moved away from the base station, rocking gently. A light breeze flicked Zoe's hair into her face. She caught the long strands as she looked over her shoulder. The chairlift station receded behind them, and the ground dropped away. They floated across a meadow dotted with wildflowers and a small stream that disappeared into a stand of pine trees. The air felt even crisper and sharper than it had in Vail. Everything—the trees marching up the slopes, the dots of wildflowers, the wires on the chairlift—seemed to almost sparkle with a new sort of clarity in the thin air at the high altitude.

"So how was Harrington?" Jack asked.

Zoe brought Jack up to date on what she and Harrington had discussed then said, "So it looks like I'm free to take the Thacker case. Harrington wasn't offended at all that Thacker wanted to work only with me."

"Do you want to take it on?"

"It's intriguing." Zoe studied the mountain peaks above them as they rose steadily upward to the more barren section near the tree line. The chairlift rocked over one of the support posts with a clatter.

"Phantom art," Jack said.

"Right, so I might be setting myself up for failure. And there are still the other paintings, the Picasso and the Canaletto, that went missing in Dallas. I haven't heard back from Evelyn. If she can find anything on her surveillance video, I might have a lead there."

"You can't do both?"

"I suppose I could. I do find it a bit odd that Thacker wants to work only with me. Makes me a bit suspicious since everyone else hasn't wanted to do that."

"He's known as forward-thinking. Didn't he tell you he realizes Harrington will probably retire soon?"

"Yes."

"So he's smart enough to realize he should shift his business to the promising newcomer. That's you."

"No one else seems to think so."

"I do." Zoe gave Jack a look, and he said, "You think I'm humoring you, but I'm not. In a few years you'll be the go-to person in art recovery. Thacker is smart enough to see it now."

"I'd like to think that's it." Zoe shifted slightly on the seat, causing the chairlift to rock. "So what about you? I haven't heard much about the conference. I've been doing all the talking."

When Jack arrived in Vail on the shuttle from Denver, they had gone straight to the condo that Thacker had let them borrow. It turned out to be just as nice as Thacker's cabin. It was furnished with the same streamlined Western-style theme but the whole place was much smaller, only a living room, a kitchenette, and a bedroom. The deck off the bedroom was nearly as large as the whole condo and had a gorgeous view of the slopes as well as a good-sized hot tub. Jack and Zoe had a meal at a nice restaurant, strolled around Vail, and then soaked in the hot tub. Zoe had spent most of yesterday evening telling Jack about the interesting lunch, and the rather strange journey the ballet dancer sculpture had made to Texas and back to Vail. They'd never gotten around to talking about the conference.

"It was a typical conference," Jack said. "Met some new people. Reconnected with a couple of old friends, picked up a couple of good ideas."

"Okay, thank you for the summary version." Zoe gave him a playful punch on the shoulder and the lift quaked again. "Now let's hear the details."

Jack told her about the different sessions he attended, then said, "And there was a hacking contest."

"Now *that* sounds interesting." The roof of an open-air building that housed the end of the chairlift came into view.

"A business sponsored a contest to see if anyone could hack into their software. If anyone succeeded and turned over the hack to the company, they got a cash prize."

"Did anyone do it?"

"Yes. Two teams did." Jack reached for the bar. "Here we are. Ready?"

They hopped off and scooted out of the way as the chair swept by them. "That looks like the trailhead over there." He slung his backpack with their lunch onto his shoulders and reached for Zoe's hand.

They found the trail that they were looking for and set off to see the mountain. It was an easy hike, and Zoe was thankful for that. The altitude made even the easiest trail challenging. The narrow path wound through a treed area where the scent of pine was heavy in the air. They emerged into a wide meadow. Zoe said, "It makes me want to throw my arms out and spin around like Julie Andrews in *The Sound of Music*."

Jack pulled his backpack off his shoulder. "I think this is a great place for lunch."

They settled down to eat. Zoe devoured her ham and cheese sandwich, then ate her apple down to the core. It was only when they were cleaning up that she noticed her phone, which had been in the backpack, had a new message. "This must have come in when we were down the mountain, and I didn't hear it. "It's from Evelyn." She clicked the message open.

*No go on the surveillance tapes. Everything has been erased. Sorry. I'll keep an eye out though, maybe he'll come back.*

Zoe tapped out a quick reply then said to Jack, "Looks like I'm going after that phantom painting after all." A buzz of excitement raced through her at the thought of a new case, and one that was all her own, too. But she felt a trace of worry. Working with Thacker could be a huge boost for her career—as long as she was successful.

## 10

**Monday**

*Tuck05: You've been dark for a while. Everything still good?*

...

...

*Tuck05: Status update? You ok?*

*Rbn: Not sure. I think someone followed me back from work today.*

*Tuck05: You better watch your back. Do you have enough to go with it now?*

*Rbn: No. Incomplete. Only a few more days.*

*Tuck05: Let me know.*

**Thursday**

Zoe lowered the car window, and the humid air flowed over her. It would have been the perfect temperature and moisture consistency for a sauna. Unfortunately, Zoe wasn't in a sauna. She was in Tampa, Florida, trying to track down the original sighting of the possible second blue butterfly painting. Once she'd worked out an agreement with Thacker, she contacted the art dealers she knew and told them she was looking for a Martin Johnson Heade painting with a blue butterfly. No one had anything like that for sale, and no one had heard rumors or hints that a painting like that might be available. She told everyone to keep an eye out and let her know if they heard anything.

Since she didn't have any luck with the dealers, Zoe decided her next move should be to verify whether or not the blue butterfly painting actually existed, which meant going to Florida. The information Thacker had given her said the painting had been part of the estate of a woman who was recently deceased. If there had been an estate sale, Zoe was sure at least a couple of the neighbors would have checked it out. Hopefully, someone in the neighborhood would remember the blue butterfly painting and could describe it for her.

A young man wearing the uniform of a security company stepped out of the gatehouse as Zoe slowed the car. He leaned down to her window, pen poised over his clipboard. "Address?"

Zoe was relieved to see it was a different guard from the one who had been on duty last night. He'd turned her away from the rather ritzy neighborhood when she couldn't give him an address as her destination. Today she was ready. "I'm going to 17254 Blue Heron Way."

The guy noted the address then frowned. "That residence is empty. I can't call and confirm your entry."

Unlike last night, Zoe was ready today not only with a destination, but she had also figured out how to get around the requirement of the security guard calling the homeowner. "It's empty because it's on the market. I'm going to look at it this morning."

He still seemed reluctant to let her inside the neighborhood, so she added, "The agent is Alma Murray."

He scribbled the name on the clipboard then asked for Zoe's ID. Zoe handed over her driver's license with a glance at the rearview mirror. The line of cars behind her waiting to enter Palmetto Palm Estates was getting longer by the moment, curving back around the large pond with its spray fountain.

The security guard handed Zoe her ID, punched a button inside the gatehouse, and the arm barring her way went up. She closed her window, cranked up the AC another notch, then accelerated, but only to twenty miles an hour, the maximum speed limit inside the neighborhood. Helpful signs informed Zoe the speed limit was strictly enforced.

She followed the directions on her GPS, creeping along residential roads. The houses had a Mediterranean flair with red tile roofs and stucco exteriors in pale pastels of ivory, taupe, and pink. Lush plants surrounded the homes. Zoe cruised along the street lined with tall palm trees, their skinny trunks rising to a round burst of palm fronds that resembled giant dandelions.

Palmetto Palm Estates actually had several smaller neighborhoods within the main gates. Zoe cruised by entrances to three separate neighborhoods before she came to the entrance to Blue Haven Preserve. A gate also barred the neighborhood, something Zoe hadn't counted on. She'd figured once she got past the main gate she could canvas the neighborhood easily. At least there wasn't another security guard stationed here.

She pulled over to the side of the road a few yards back from the keypad entry box and took out her phone, settling in to wait.

Zoe unfolded the printout of the newspaper obituary that Thacker had sent her. Nancy "Birdie" Martindale's husband had died five years earlier, and she was survived by a sister and a great niece. The obituary stated that she'd gotten the nickname of Birdie because she loved bird watching. After retiring from a local community college where she had taught English Lit, she spent most of her time adding to her Life List, the comprehensive list of birds she'd seen.

A car approached the gate, and Zoe put away the obit. The driver punched in the code, and the gate labored open in a slow arc. Zoe waited until the car was halfway through the entrance before she put her car in gear and followed. She easily made it into Blue Haven Preserve before the gate closed.

She took a left and followed the curving street, passing houses that looked nearly identical except for their exterior colors until she found the house she was looking for with a For Sale sign planted in the yard. Zoe parked a few houses away. She didn't have an appointment with the realtor, but she was *looking* at the house.

Zoe scanned the neighborhood, considering where to start. A woman directly across the street from Birdie's house came out her front door with a Jack Russell terrier on a leash. Under the woman's short iron gray hair, her tanned face was lined and dotted with age spots. The Jack Russell terrier sped down the walk, straining at the leash. The woman was lean and looked as if she played tennis and golf—maybe both in the same day. She settled a pink sun visor on her forehead that matched her white tennis outfit that was trimmed in pink piping. As she came down the driveway, she gave Zoe a long look. Zoe waved then quickly picked up her phone. The woman didn't look like she would welcome questions and certainly didn't look like the chatty soul that Zoe hoped to find.

As the woman in the pink sun visor moved away, a minivan barreled down the street. It veered into the middle of the street to give the woman in the pink sun visor a wide berth, then swung to the other side to avoid Zoe's parked car. A final swoop brought it into the driveway of the house that was for sale as the garage door scrolled up.

A heavy-set woman in booty shorts and a flowing tank top hopped out and slammed her car door.

Zoe took a deep breath. After a quick check of the obituary, she stepped out of the car. Zoe didn't think this was the realtor. If she was the realtor, she was the most casually dressed realtor Zoe had ever seen. No, the woman was probably one of Birdie's relatives, which was a great opportunity for Zoe, one she hadn't expected.

Zoe approached the garage, which was still open. The woman had moved her reflective aviator sunglasses to her head, nestling them in her spiky brownish-blond hair. Hands on her hips, she surveyed the mix of furniture and household items crammed in the garage. She blew out a breath and checked her watch.

Spotting several frames propped against one of the garage walls, Zoe picked up her pace. "Rochelle?"

The woman turned. "Where's your truck?" she asked, her gaze taking in the only car parked at the curb, the compact rental that Zoe had picked up at the airport yesterday.

"Umm, I'm afraid I don't understand." Zoe had thought up quite a few different approaches to the people she intended to talk to today, but she hadn't expected that question.

"Aren't you here for the charity pick up?"

"Oh, no. Sorry."

Rochelle's dark brown eyes narrowed. "So you must read the obits—that's how you know my name, isn't it? You're a vulture, are you? Come to pick over the leftovers? The estate sale was last weekend. You missed it, but you can take whatever you want." She tossed a suntanned arm at the household goods and furniture filling the double garage, her bracelets jingling around her wrist. "All of it's going to charity today anyway. Have at it."

Zoe decided not to waste time correcting Rochelle's assumptions. Zoe went straight to the paintings, which were turned toward the wall. It only took her a few seconds to flip through them. Most were prints, which was disappointing, but all the artwork depicted birds and wildlife. She leaned the frames against the wall. "Whoever lived here must have liked birds."

Rochelle rolled her eyes. "That's practically all Aunt Birdie could talk about." Zoe moved to the back of the garage. It was packed with furniture of good quality, but it was worn and dated and would have been in style about twenty years ago.

Zoe moved to the other bay of the garage to make sure she hadn't missed anything. "Do you remember seeing a painting with a butterfly?" She spotted stacks of cooking utensils, pots and pans, piles of clothes still on their hangers, and a precarious tower of paint cans.

"No, but that doesn't mean that Aunt Birdie didn't have one. She had all sorts of crap related to birds."

Zoe stepped on something lumpy and reached down to pick it

up. She brushed her footprint off the leather cover of a small book about four inches tall and three inches wide. The name Birdie Martindale was written in elegant script on the inside front cover. Flipping through a few of the pages, Zoe recognized scientific names along with locations and dates.

She walked outside the garage. Rochelle had returned to her minivan. She had the engine running and was sitting in the driver's seat, scrolling down the screen on her phone. Zoe went to the open driver's door where blasts of icy air were fanning Rochelle's face. The overflow felt great to Zoe. The day was getting hotter as the sun climbed higher.

"Can you believe it? They're running late," Rochelle said. "They didn't even call or text. So *rude*. And it's not like I have *time* to run out here and sit around and wait for charity trucks. I live an *hour* away."

"I don't see anything I can't resist," Zoe said. "I found this on the floor. I thought you might want it."

With her attention still fixed on her phone, Rochelle reached out for the little notebook. She dragged her gaze away from the phone as she used one hand to angle the soft leather of the cover into a curved shape so that a few of the pages splayed open. "Perfect. More birding stuff. Just what I need."

The rumble of a heavy engine filled the air. A truck lumbered down the street, the branches of the water oaks along the sidewalk brushing along the top of it.

"Finally." Rochelle jumped out of the van. Zoe stepped out of her way. Rochelle went to a rolling trash can positioned at the side of the garage, tossed in the notebook, then walked to the foot of the driveway. Rochelle's voice carried to her as Zoe walked to the trash can and lifted the lid. "I don't appreciate you keeping me waiting. You'd think that since people are *giving* you things, you could at least be *on time*. You're getting it for free, after all."

The leather book rested on top of crumpled packing paper. Zoe plucked the notebook from the trash. She tucked it in the back pocket of her jeans, making sure the hem of her white cotton shirt covered it. It just didn't seem right to throw something like that away.

While Rochelle directed the truck to park so that her van wouldn't be blocked in, Zoe went to the houses on either side of Birdie's house. No one answered at the first house. At the second, a woman told Zoe that she had moved in three weeks ago and hadn't met her neighbors yet.

As Zoe walked down the street to the next house, the woman with the pink sun visor rounded the corner at the end of the block and headed in her direction. The terrier still looked just as perky. Zoe decided that despite the formidable look on the woman's face, she might as well give her a try.

Feeling that nothing less than the truth would do, Zoe approached her and said, "Hello, my name is Zoe Andrews." She took out one of her business cards. "I'm an art recovery specialist. I would love to talk to you about your neighbor Birdie Martindale. Did you know her?" The terrier danced around her feet. Zoe leaned down, let him sniff her fingers, and then rubbed his ears.

The woman flexed the business card in her fingers. "I knew her a lot better than that one." She lifted her chin, indicating Rochelle. Zoe glanced back at Birdie's house where the men from the charity were carrying a couch up a ramp to the truck. "And Pepper seems to like you."

At the mention of his name, the dog looked at the woman, tilting his head inquiringly. They exchanged a look, then she said, "Come on. We can talk at my house."

## 11

A wall of fumes hit Zoe as she followed the woman through the front door. She removed her pink sun visor and dropped it on a chest, then unhooked the leash from the dog's collar. "There you go, Pepper."

The dog darted off, his nails clicking against the white ceramic tile. The woman turned back to Zoe. "Sorry about the smell. I didn't realize he would start painting so early."

She raised her voice and called out, "Artie, we have a guest." She led the way across an open-plan living room that was furnished in dark rattan with cushions covered in a pastel tropical print. "I'm Pat, by the way." She clicked on the overhead fan then opened the sliding glass door where Pepper waited, his short tail quivering.

A burly man entered from a hallway, carrying a square of cardboard with a mass of metal on top of it. He had a thatch of glossy white hair and a paunch that pressed against his oversized red polo shirt. A pair of denim shorts, tube socks, and tennis shoes completed his look. He balanced the piece of cardboard with one hand underneath it, like a waiter carrying a tray. He held out a beefy hand. "Hi there."

"I'm Zoe."

Pat handed him Zoe's card. "Zoe Andrews. She's an art recovery specialist. She wants to talk to us about Birdie."

"Then come out here away from the fumes." He pushed the sliding glass door open wider and maneuvered the flat piece of cardboard outside ahead of him to a screened-in covered patio. Zoe could now see that a dismantled vintage typewriter covered the cardboard.

"I can't believe you're painting in the house again," Pat said to Artie, but looked at Zoe and shook her head.

"Just dibs and dabs," he said. "Only a few touchups."

An arrangement of the furniture sat in the middle of the screened-in patio. Artie hit a switch, and a ceiling fan as well as two fans mounted in the corners of the covered patio whirred. Pepper had been patrolling the borders of the yard but as soon as Artie stepped onto the patio, the dog raced for the doggie door placed in the screen door that separated the screened patio from the backyard.

With the dog pirouetting around the man's gigantic feet, Artie deposited the square of cardboard with its dissected typewriter on a workbench on one side of the patio then reached down to pet the dog. Another vintage typewriter rested on the workbench, but this one looked like it had just been removed from the box. Zoe said, "That's quite a contrast."

He gave the dog's ears a final rub and stood. "It's just a matter of taking it all apart, a little oil, and a little elbow grease, a little paint, and then putting it all back together."

"Easier said than done, I'm sure. This one looks brand-new. It's in fantastic shape." The paint on the typewriter glowed a glossy black and each circular key had the correct letter inside its glass-topped metal encasement.

"I just finished refurbishing that one. It's one of the first portable Remington typewriters. Circa1920. I'm waiting for the paint to dry before I mail it back to its owner."

Pat joined them, carrying three water bottles. "Don't let Artie bore you, if you're not into vintage typewriters. He can go on all day."

"I'm not bored. I think the workmanship on these is amazing."

"Have a seat over here by the fan." Pat motioned to the wicker sofa. "It's a pleasant breeze." She offered Zoe a water bottle, and Zoe opened it as she took a seat. The cool air from the fan coursed over her. Pepper hopped up on the cushion beside Zoe and angled his face toward the fan, catching the breeze as if he were riding with his head out a car window.

"Pepper, down. Shoo."

"It's okay. I don't mind." Zoe ran her hand down Pepper's lithe form. His lungs were working overtime, and he briefly favored her with a doggie grin as he panted, then returned his adoring gaze to the fan.

Pat transferred a tennis racket case and a package of tennis balls from a wicker chair to the ground, then sat down. "So why are you interested in Birdie? She wasn't into art—only birds."

Zoe set her water bottle down on a nearby table. "I'm looking for some artwork that she might have owned."

"The neighborhood won't be the same without Birdie." Artie dropped onto a metal glider that creaked ominously under his weight. He wiped his palm across his forehead then drank his whole water bottle in two gulps.

"That niece has a charity truck over there now, clearing out the last bits and pieces from the garage," Pat said to Artie.

"The niece, Rochelle, has gotten rid of almost everything that was in the house within a week," Artie said to Zoe.

Zoe raised her eyebrows. "That's quick work for a house that size."

"She's a fast worker, that one." Pat sniffed. Pat and Artie exchanged another look of what Zoe thought was mutual disapproval. "She hardly showed up when Birdie was alive. But now that Birdie's gone, she can't turn that house over quick enough. It's all about the money, of course. First thing she did was sell Birdie's car then she had dealers in looking over the furniture the next day."

"Well, it sounds as if she might have missed something important, if that makes you feel any better," Zoe said. "I don't know anything for sure, though. That's what I'm here trying to confirm. Do you know if Birdie had a piece of artwork with a hummingbird and a butterfly?"

"You mean her blue butterfly painting?" Pat tapped her hand against the arm of her chair. "I knew that painting was special."

Zoe's heart kicked a bit at Pat's casual description of the color of the butterfly, which Zoe had intentionally not mentioned. She didn't want to prompt any responses, and she felt the best way to go about this would be to let Pat and Artie fill in the blanks. "That might be what I'm looking for."

"It was one of her favorites. She had it right behind her chair in the living room, where she could see it every day," Pat said. "She inherited it from a relative, she said."

Artie cut a glance toward Pat. "But she had lots of artwork of hummingbirds." He shifted his gaze to Zoe, his tone dampening. "Pretty much everything in that house had a bird or butterfly on it, including the wallpaper."

"That's true, which might impact the time it spends on the market," Pat said with what Zoe thought was satisfaction. "But Birdie only had one painting of a blue butterfly."

"You're sure it was a painting, not a print?"

"Oh, yes. It was an oil," Pat said.

"Could you draw a sketch of it for me?"

"I can do better than that." Artie hitched himself up off the glider and slipped his phone out of one of his shorts pockets. After sliding his fingers across the phone a few times, he handed it to Zoe. "How about a photo?"

Zoe couldn't keep the excitement out of her voice. "This is wonderful." It was an informal snapshot of two women. Pat was one of the women, and the other one must have been Birdie. She favored her nickname with her small build and delicate features. Birdie sat in a chair, and Pat leaned over the arm so that their faces were on the same level as they smiled. A painting of a blue butterfly and hummingbird hung on the wall behind them.

"I think that's one of the last pictures we took of her," Artie said.

Pat had moved around to look over Zoe's shoulder. "Yes. It wasn't long after Artie took this photo that she had to go into long-term care. Birdie liked to sit in that chair and watch for the birds. With the retention pond behind her house, she got a lot more wildlife over there than we do here."

Zoe reached into her back pocket and pulled out the small leather notebook she found in the garage. "Would you like this? I found it in the garage at Birdie's house, but her niece wasn't interested in it." Pat took the notebook, but she didn't have to open it to know what it was. "Her Life List." She cleared her throat. "Yes, I'll take care of it. Thank you."

Zoe looked away to give Pat a moment to compose herself. Zoe asked Artie, "Can you send me that photograph?"

"Of course." He tapped on his phone, and after they had exchanged phone numbers, the image popped up on Zoe's phone.

"I'd have bought that painting myself, but I wasn't quick enough," Pat said, returning to her wicker chair. She balanced Birdie's notebook on her knee.

Artie looked at Pat. "You would have? I thought you didn't want to give any money to *her*."

"I didn't. But for something like the butterfly painting, I might've made an exception. That nice Indian lady from the antique store beat me to it. I told Rochelle I wanted that painting, but she said it was already sold. But the Indian lady didn't get it either."

"I don't understand."

"The Indian saleslady was one of the dealers Rochelle called in. I know she was with the store because her car had one of those advertising panels on the door with the store's logo, World Décor Bazaar, and she's the one who helped me when I bought a lamp there. But back to the point, Rochelle said the woman from the store bought the hutch in the dining room, one of the bedroom suits, and a couple of the paintings, including the one with the butterfly."

"But something happened?" Zoe asked

Pat said, "It disappeared."

## 12

The metal glider creaked as Artie dropped back onto it. "It was stolen, is what Pat means."

"What?" Zoe inched forward in her seat. Her hopes, which had begun to swing upward, plummeted.

Pat nodded. "That's what we think happened. The woman from World Décor Bazaar send a truck the next day to pick up the items she wanted, but when they got here the painting was gone. I was walking Pepper, and saw the whole thing play out. Rochelle came over and asked if I'd seen anything suspicious, but I hadn't noticed anyone creeping around. The crew sent to load the truck checked the whole house. The sliding glass door at the back of the house had been forced open, and the painting was gone. It was the only thing that was missing."

"What did the police say?" Zoe asked, her spirits plummeting even more. She knew the odds of recovering the painting would be low.

"Rochelle didn't care enough to call the police," Pat said, exasperation in her tone. "Can you believe it? Shortsighted, that's what she is. All she can think about is how much money she'll be able to get once she sells the house."

"But if the woman from the store had purchased it, then she could call... " Zoe trailed off because Pat was shaking her head.

"She hadn't actually paid for it yet. She'd only told Rochelle which pieces she wanted. Once Rochelle realized it was just the single painting that was gone, she waved away the idea of calling the police. Said she didn't want to get involved in an investigation."

---

"You actually found a picture of the painting? That's great," Jack said.

Zoe moved the phone to her other ear and looked out the coffee shop's window, keeping an eye on the store that was located across the shopping center parking lot. "Not really. I have a picture, that's all." Zoe explained that the painting was missing. "So all I have is a photograph, and it's not clear when I zoom in. The painting wasn't the focus of the photograph, the two women were, so I can't see the fine details of the painting."

"But even a blurry picture is progress."

Zoe sighed. "I suppose so. And I did get some details on the history of the painting." Zoe had asked Pat if Birdie had ever talked about where she got the painting. Birdie had said she inherited it from a relative whose father bought the painting from an artist in London around the time of the American Civil War. "I won't go into the details, but the dates are right for a Martin Johnson Heade painting. So that's something, except I'm at a dead end on what to do next." If Rochelle had filed a police report, there would at least be a record that the painting was stolen, and Zoe could have gone in that direction.

"Won't the fact that it's stolen, even if the owner didn't report it, complicate matters? When you eventually find it—because I know you will—couldn't the niece claim it was hers?" Jack asked.

"I asked Kaz about that, and he said to keep looking. He said Thacker's legal team will sort out any disputes, if any come up. I'm sure Thacker has more than enough money to make little details like that go away. Kaz said my job is to find the painting and not to worry about anything else." She had been told to call Kaz with her updates, and he'd pass the news on to Thacker. She'd just gotten off the phone with him.

"Where are you now?"

"I'm sitting in a Starbucks, waiting for World Décor Bazaar to open." She looked at her watch. "Only about ten minutes to go. I figured I better check it out. It's all I can think to do now besides to wait for a call from the art dealers. They know I'm looking for a blue butterfly painting and will call if they hear about one. It looks like the store is opening a little early," Zoe said as she watched a short muscular man with a shaved head inside the store walk to the front doors and unlock them. "I'll call you later."

She tossed her cup in the trash and left the coffee shop, walking into the wall of heat and humidity. When she approached World Décor Bazaar the double doors swished open, and a rush of frigid air flowed over her.

She took a few brisk steps into the store and then slowed as she took in the merchandise. Much of it was oversized. Zoe stepped around a massive king-size bed with posters the size of small tree trunks, feeling like she'd reached the top of the beanstalk. An antique gilt framed mirror that was twice her height and in such an ornate style it would have looked right at home at Versailles reflected her image. A chandelier made of intertwined antlers hung overhead. She threaded through the furnishings toward a granite-topped counter at one side that seemed to be the checkout counter.

An Indian woman was rearranging a display of amber beside the counter. The guy with the shaved head must have gone into a back room. Zoe didn't see him anywhere.

"Excuse me," Zoe said to the woman. "I'm looking for a painting of a blue butterfly. I spoke to a resident in the Blue Haven Preserve neighborhood, and they said that a woman from this store tried to buy the painting of the blue butterfly from the estate of one of their neighbors. Was that you?"

The woman held three boxes, which she slotted into position on the shelf. "Yes, I tried to buy it." She was in her thirties and had a manner of quiet efficiency as she continued to arrange the boxes. Her glossy black hair was pulled back into a ponytail, which slid across her shoulders as she shook her head. "But it didn't happen."

Zoe took out her phone and zoomed in on the picture of the painting that Artie had sent her. "Is this the painting that you wanted?"

The woman paused. "Yes, that's it. It was so lovely. But we have other paintings," she said. "They're nice as well." A phone on the counter rang. The man with the shaved head emerged from an open door behind the counter and answered it.

"No, the blue butterfly painting is the one that I was after," Zoe said. "I heard what happened—that it was stolen." Zoe felt the man's gaze on her. He spoke into the phone but was watching her. She pulled her attention back to the woman. "Have you heard anything about it? About where it might be?"

"Of course not." Her chest swelled as she drew in a breath. "We don't have contacts with those sorts of people or deal in that kind of merchandise." Her tone indicated that kind of merchandise was slimy and that she'd never touch it.

The man put his hand over the phone. "Irene, it's for you. You want me to take a message?"

"No, I'll take it," she said to him, then turned back to Zoe. "I'm sorry I can't help you with that painting. Have a look around. We have some wonderful art. Or if you like, give your contact information to Barry. We'll let you know if we find anything similar."

Irene went behind the desk and took the phone from Barry. Zoe turned and headed for the doors, thinking about how she'd phrase her update when she spoke to Kaz.

She was about halfway across the store when Barry caught up with her. "Hey, you said something about a blue butterfly painting?"

"Yes, that's right, but your coworker says it never made it to the store."

"That's true," Barry said slowly, his tone implying the exact opposite of what his words said.

Zoe tilted her head. "You know where the painting is?"

"No, nothing for sure," he said quickly, "but certain...information...might be available. If you're curious. I might be able to make a call or two and, uh, point you in the right direction. If it's worth my time, you know, for me to hunt around for it," he said casually, but his gaze was sharp and speculating.

Zoe stared at him for a moment. He apparently didn't have the same scruples as the woman he worked with and did have some contacts of the shady sort. Zoe didn't like to do things this way, but if she had a chance—even a slim one—to get back on the trail of the painting, she would take it. "I'm interested."

Barry stood straighter.

"Okay, then. His gaze raked over the antler chandelier then came back to Zoe. "Two hundred dollars," he said in a firm voice, but only after another quick glance at Irene, who was still on the phone.

"Done."

His eyebrows flared. "Oh, in that case—"

"And not a penny more. That's all I'll pay," Zoe said swiftly to cut off any attempt from him to renegotiate the deal. "When will you have it for me?"

"When will you have the money?"

"I can give it to you now, if you can get the info."

The man ran his hand over his shaved scalp. "Give me about ten minutes. Meet me in the Starbucks across the parking lot."

Zoe left the store and popped the trunk of her car. A lot of the transactions that Throckmorton Enquiries dealt with involved people who insisted on cash payments, so Harrington made it a policy that if he or Zoe were meeting with anyone about purchasing artwork, then they had access to a fairly significant amount of cash.

Zoe had thought it was a good idea to continue the practice. She had left the money locked in the trunk of her car. She slipped the cash into her purse, then went inside and ordered a chai tea.

Before she finished her drink, Barry came in. Without making eye contact, he ordered a coffee. When his drink was ready, he picked it up and walked by Zoe's table. When he came even with her, he dropped a piece of paper. He stooped. "Is this yours?"

"Yes, thanks."

Zoe slid a folded napkin closer to the edge of the table.

He pocketed it with an almost imperceptible nod and left. Zoe had placed two crisp hundred-dollar bills inside the napkin. She watched Barry's steps slow as he exited the building and glanced at the napkin. He tucked the bills into his pocket and walked jauntily back to World Décor Bazaar.

Zoe unfolded the paper. A string of numbers was written on it in black marker. Under the numbers, was a line of text. "Here you go. Tell LeBlanc that Barry sent you."

Zoe went to her car, cranked the AC, and dialed the phone number.

"LeBlanc here."

He spoke with a slight accent, but she couldn't place it. "Hello. My name is Zoe Andrews. Barry from World Décor Bazaar said I should give you a call. I'm looking for a blue butterfly painting."

"What was that? You're breaking up. A blue what?"

"Sorry, the connection isn't good." Zoe spoke louder and tried to enunciate clearly. "I'm looking for a painting of a blue butterfly by Martin Johnson Heade. Barry at World Décor Bazaar said you were the person I should talk to."

"Oh, *Barry* told you to call." A pause filled the line, then the man's voice came through. "Pretty difficult...come by, something like that."

"So you're familiar with it?"

"Familiar with it? Darlin', I got it right here with me." His voice came through clearly for a few seconds with the feel of a ringmaster announcing a spectacular performance on the high wire.

Zoe decided she would overlook the "darling" comment. *Just get the painting, don't get sidetracked,* she reminded herself. "I'd like to come see it. I have a buyer who might be interested. Do you have a photograph?" Zoe asked.

"Sure. Let me send you one. I'll even include something with today's date so you'll know I'm not a scammer." He laughed and ended the call, saying he'd text a photo to her in a moment.

Her phone pinged, and she opened the image. It showed the painting that she'd seen in Artie's photograph. She zoomed in and checked the details, swooping across the image. It looked the same, and he'd propped it up against a computer monitor with a web browser open to a news article with today's date.

Zoe called him back. "I'm interested in seeing it in person."

"Well, come on. I'm out at my camp. I don't have a physical store. I do all my business on-line, but if you want to see the actual painting you're welcome to come out."

Zoe turned the scrap of paper over and grabbed a pen from her leather messenger bag. She jotted down the street address he gave her.

"Is that Florida's Highway One? I'm in Tampa."

"Barry didn't tell you? That's Highway One in Grand Isle, Louisiana."

---

*Rbn: I was right. Tailed to and from work today.*

*Tuck05: That's bad.*

*Rbn: They won't see anything. I'm a model employee. A couple of days of this and they'll be bored out of their minds.*

## 13

Friday

Another day, another rental car, Zoe thought as she drove through the flat green countryside on a road that traced the same path as the placid water of a bayou. Zoe had booked a flight from Tampa to New Orleans as soon as she could. She had spent most of the afternoon on the flight, then she'd picked up the rental car, and navigated through one of the most interesting cities in the world. She wanted to stop and see the French Quarter, tour Jackson Square, and eat beignets dusted with powdered sugar at Café du Monde, but she was on a schedule. She would have to come back later when she had time to explore the city.

Once she navigated through the congestion of New Orleans, she had the road mostly to herself, except for a black BMW that flitted in and out of her rearview mirror. It had a special vanity plate on its front bumper that caught her eye, a logo of the New Orleans Saints football team, a fleur-de-lis.

The phone, propped on the console, rang, and she put it on speaker. She expected it to be Jack, but the voice on the other end of the line had a touch of an accent. "LeBlanc here. Is this Zoe?"

"Yes, it is."

"Good. Good. Are you still coming out to the camp today?"

"Yes. I tried to get in touch with you, but couldn't leave a message." The recorded message had told Zoe that the subscriber she was trying to reach wasn't in the service area. She'd wanted to coordinate with LeBlanc about authenticating the painting. She would have rather brought somebody with her today, but since she couldn't speak to LeBlanc and the authenticator Thacker wanted to use was in Seattle, she'd have to check the painting first, then coordinate authentication.

Thacker hadn't seemed that worried about authenticating the painting. "Just find it first," he'd said when he hired her. "Then Kaz will help you set up an authenticator. I have several people I use. It won't be a problem."

LeBlanc asked, "What time do you think you'll get in?"

"Let's see..." Zoe glanced at the navigation app on her phone, which was in a holder on the dashboard. "I should be there in about an hour."

"Excellent. I'm sending Phil to meet you. It's a little tricky getting in here. You can follow him." LeBlanc gave her the name of a gas station at the corner of two intersections where Phil would meet her. "He'll be inside, and he'll be eating something, I guarantee." He pronounced the word "guarantee" as gar-RON-tee. "Phil's a skinny little thing," LeBlanc continued, "about as big as a sapling. Has more hair than sense."

"I'm sure we can find each other. I tend to stand out. I have red hair." She could have added that she was wearing a cap-sleeved green top and khaki pants, but she figured the hair color would be enough for Phil to find her.

Zoe hung up, pulled over and reset the GPS for the truck plaza, then merged back into traffic. It was only about twenty minutes away. The low-slung truck plaza was surrounded with families climbing out of vans and cars for a break as well as 18-wheelers, pulling in to refuel at the far side of the complex. As she pulled into a parking space, she noticed that the black BMW with a fleur-de-lis license plate that she had seen so often during the last hundred miles or so had also stopped.

Zoe locked the car and went inside the building that contained a fast food sandwich shop, a convenience store, and 24-hour private showers for truckers. Zoe detoured to the restrooms then headed for the sandwich shop. Several families were gathered around a couple of tables, but there was only one guy eating alone. He looked like he was about eighteen or nineteen. Arms as skinny as rails stuck out of the flappy sleeves of a black T-shirt. He'd pulled back his wiry black hair into a ponytail that reached past the nape of his neck. Hunched over the plastic table, he was scarfing down a meatball sub.

Zoe walked over to him. "You must be Phil."

He swallowed, and stood, extending his hand. "That's right. Zoe?"His speech had the same cadence that LeBlanc's did.

"That's me."

"Glad to meet you. Can I get you anything? LeBlanc is cooking up some lunch but it won't be ready for an hour or two." His tone implied that an hour or two was an eternity to wait for food.

"No, I'm fine."

"Do you mind if I finish this?" He motioned to the last half of his sandwich and a large dark chocolate cookie with white chocolate chips.

"No, go ahead. That would be a little messy to eat in the car."

"Great. It won't take me a moment."

"I'll get a drink."

Phil wasn't kidding about being a fast eater. By the time Zoe had bought a ginger ale from the convenience store and made her way back, Phil was devouring the last bites of his sub.

She sat down and popped the top on the can. "Don't hurry on my account."

"No worries." Phil crumpled the sub wrapping paper into a ball and took a long slurp from his drink. He broke the cookie in half and offered part of it to Zoe.

"Thanks, but no. You go ahead," she said.

"So how did you hear about LeBlanc?" Phil asked after he'd consumed half of the cookie in one bite.

"From a guy in Florida named Barry at World Décor Bazaar."

Phil's dark eyebrows crunched together. "Okay. That's a new one." He looked toward the parking lot where Zoe's blue rental car was visible through the windows. "Bring anyone with you?"

"No, I'm on my own today."

"And you just flew in this morning?"

"Yes, that's right."

"From where?"

"Tampa." Zoe glanced around the restaurant, feeling slightly uncomfortable with the questions. Phil certainly didn't look like a threatening guy with his rather pasty skin and stick-like build. She didn't have any doubt that if she needed to she could either outrun him or deliver a few swift kicks that would give her an advantage over him. She and Jack had been going to a martial arts class at the gym, which had helped her brush up on her self-defense. But the string of questions seemed odd. "Anything else you want to know?"

"Hey, it's not me. It's LeBlanc. He always wants to know who's coming to visit him, and if anyone's coming with them. It's just his way."

"And which city they've traveled from?"

His mouth full of the last bite of cookie, Phil nodded then swallowed. "That too, yeah."

"Do you escort a lot of LeBlanc's visitors to him?"

"Some."

Zoe's phone rang. "I need to take this. It's my husband." It couldn't hurt to let the rather mild-looking Phil know that other people knew where she was and what she was doing.

Jack's voice came online. "Hey, where are you now?"

Zoe angled slightly in her chair so that she was facing away from Phil. "I'm in southern Louisiana on my way to see LeBlanc."

"Everything good?"

"Everything's good...so far."

After a pause, Jack said, "You don't sound one hundred percent sure."

"I'm not." Phil mimed that he was going to get a drink refill and ambled away from the table. Zoe waited until he was out of earshot. "LeBlanc has sent someone to meet me, a skinny guy named Phil. He's asking a lot of questions that seem sort of odd."

"It seems weird that LeBlanc would send somebody to meet you."

"I know, but apparently these roads can be confusing down here. But don't worry, I'm following Phil in my own car, and I have my GPS. If he takes me anywhere else besides Grand Isle, I won't go there."

"Do you feel comfortable about this? You know if you don't, you can walk away."

"I know that. Alarm bells aren't going off, or anything like that. It's just...a little strange. But then it *is* southern Louisiana. Which is kind of a law unto itself, isn't it?"

"I've never been there, but that's what I've heard."

"I haven't been here before either. I wanted to explore New Orleans but didn't have time today. We definitely need to make a trip there."

"Sounds good. I'm in."

"How's the planning going at One Heritage Plaza?"

"Oh, you know, another meeting. Hopefully, this is the last one this week."

"Well it's Friday so that might actually happen."

"Then it's off to London for me," Jack said.

"That's right. I'd forgotten about that meeting. When do you leave again?" One of Jack's friends had recommended him to a company in England that wanted him to assess their security set-up.

"Saturday, but I don't arrive until Sunday. I'll have the meeting Monday morning, then turn around and come back home that afternoon."

Phil was returning to the table, his soda in one hand and a set of car keys in the other.

"Time to get back on the road. I'll call you later," Zoe said.

In the parking lot, Phil motioned to a white Honda Accord with custom wheels and black tinted windows. "That's mine," he said as he sauntered toward the car. "Just keep me in sight, and I'll take you all the way to LeBlanc's. We're only about thirty miles out. Shouldn't take that long."

As Zoe settled in her rental car and turned on the GPS app, she noticed that the black BMW with the Saints license plate had already left. She wondered if she would see it again. Was the driver going all the way to Grand Isle? Plenty of small towns lined the highway, and one of those could be its destination, but Zoe thought that most of the traffic on the road was probably passing through on the way to or from Grand Isle.

About twenty minutes later, the road swooped in a massive curve, and Zoe knew they were getting close. The land had flattened even more and the bayou had given away to long stretches of water and sea grass. She'd even seen several brown pelicans flying low, their massive wings spread wide as they skimmed over the water.

A car approached on Zoe's left in the passing lane, and she checked her rearview mirror. It was the black BMW with the Saints license plate. It accelerated, blowing by her so quickly that she only had an impression of a driver wearing a baseball cap. In front of her, Phil continued at his steady pace of four miles over the speed limit.

They crossed over a strait of water, then the road swooped again in another curve as they reached land. They passed a marina, and the map on her phone showed that they were on the straight line of Highway One, which ran the length of the narrow barrier island from west to east.

She cut back on her speed and took in the surroundings. The Gulf of Mexico was to her right, and houses on wooden pylons stretched along the beachfront property, but she couldn't see the water. A high berm blocked it from view. The houses on pylons ranged from small bungalows and trailers to sprawling homes with observation decks. Each property had a name, and Zoe smiled at some of them: Paradise Found, Land's End, Maggie's Place, and Bordeaux Getaway.

Grand Isle felt different from some of the other coastal vacation spots that Zoe had visited, which were glitzy and upscale with high-rise hotels, beach cabanas, and designer boutiques lining the main drag. Grand Isle, with its houses of vinyl siding and quirky names, felt down-home and casual.

After they had gone a few miles, Phil turned on his right-hand blinker and pulled into the driveway leading to a good-sized house that faced the Gulf. The nameplate on the wooden balcony that encircled the whole building read, "The Coast is Clear."

A couple of cars were parked on the concrete foundation under the raised house. Phil pulled in between two of the pylons. Zoe maneuvered the car into the next slot and parked between Phil's Honda and a black BMW with a Saints license plate.

---

*Rbn: I think I've got a problem.*

*Tuck05: ??*

*Rbn: Tail still on me and someone's been in my apartment.*

*Tuck05: Searched? Did they find it?*

*Rbn: Yes, they looked, but didn't find it. It's somewhere they'd never think of.*

*Tuck05: You sure you're good? What about the original stuff?*

*Rbn: It was cool enough last night that I had a nice little fire.*

*Tuck05: Good idea. You should call the police, report a break-in! That might throw them.*

*Rbn: I refuse to use an emoji, but LOL. Seriously, I don't want them to know I'm aware.*

*Tuck05: What are you going to do?*

*Rbn: Release it tomorrow.*

*Tuck05: Make sure you're good to go off-grid after.*

*Rbn: You know it. I'm about to become a ghost.*

## 14

P hil waved his arm in a follow-me gesture. At the far end of the foundation, several men were gathered around a picnic table. Zoe locked her car and slipped her keys into her pocket along with her cell phone, then moved through the shadows between the thick wooden support beams. Waves of heat were coming off the surface of a stainless steel grill beside the picnic table. An enormous stockpot sat on an exterior gas burner connected to the grill.

A hefty man in a Panama hat and tropical shirt printed with a repeating pattern of swordfish, held a lid in one hand as he stirred a spoon around the stockpot. The movements pulled at the colorful shirt he wore, and Zoe saw the butt of a gun sticking out of one of the pockets on the leg of his cargo shorts. He replaced the lid and the fabric fell back into place, covering the gun. He saw Phil, who tilted his head toward Zoe. "We're here."

"Zoe Andrews." He shuffled over to her, his hand extended. "Glad you could make it out. I'm LeBlanc." Under his Panama hat, his face was flushed pink.

"Thanks for having me. This isn't quite what I expected when you said you had a camp." And LeBlanc wasn't the sort of high-end dealer she'd been meeting at art galleries and shows in Dallas, but she refrained from adding, _and you're not what I expected either._

He laughed. "That's what we call these places down here. You'd probably call it a beach house, but to us it's a camp. How about some food before we do business? I was about to throw some chicken on the grill. If you're vegetarian, we have beans and rice."

"Sounds delicious. I'd love some chicken. And beans and rice, too. I haven't eaten since I had a package of pretzels on the plane."

"You know if you come to Louisiana, we have to feed you. It's a shame it's not crawfish season. We do it up right. Have you ever had crawfish?"

"No. I'm sorry I missed it."

A movement in the shadows under the house caught Zoe's eye. A man leaned against one of the pylons. In the dimness, she couldn't make out many details about him except that he wore a baseball cap and had a droopy mustache.

"Phil, get Zoe something to drink," LeBlanc said then moved to talk to the mustached guy. Phil hurried over to the ice chest at a completely different speed than the loping stride he'd had when he and Zoe left the truck plaza. He offered Zoe water, soda, or beer. She took a bottle of water as she kept an eye on LeBlanc.

He exchanged a few words with the man in the shadows, then the man with a mustache left. Zoe shifted slightly so that she could see the row of cars parked under the far side of the house. The man got in the black BMW and drove away.

LeBlanc rejoined her. "Would you like to see the beach? We've got a few minutes."

"Yes, I'd love to."

LeBlanc said to Phil, "Put the chicken on the grill. We won't be long."

"On it, boss," Phil said, heading for the grill with a quick stride.

LeBlanc took a beer from the ice chest, opened it, and motioned toward a path that led up over the berm that shielded the house from the Gulf. When they reached the top, the wind, which had been rattling the fronds of the palm trees around the house, hit Zoe full force, whipping her hair away from her face and making her shirt pulse around her. Except for a couple of people strolling hand-in-hand and a few groups of sunbathers, the beach was empty. The water was choppy, flowing in and breaking into a fringe of white on the dark brown sand.

"Would you like to stroll?" Leblanc asked.

"Sure." They made their way down through the seagrass and vines until they were on the sand. It was so hard packed that it was almost like walking on a sidewalk. Zoe walked easily in her sandals, and LeBlanc ambled along beside her, his flip flops kicking up hardly any sand. Zoe couldn't help but notice that the pocket with the gun beat heavily against his leg as they walked.

Zoe asked, "So do you always have your guests followed?"

He looked at her out of the corner of his eye. "Now why would you say that?"

"The black BMW. I don't think that it was a coincidence that it took the same route I did and also ended up here at the same house on Grand Isle."

Jack had taught her a few things about following and being followed. She'd noticed the black car not too long after she left the airport. It wouldn't have been hard for someone to watch for her arrival at the rental car center at the airport. When she first spoke to LeBlanc she'd told him that she would arrive today from Tampa. There weren't that many flights coming in from Tampa, and a quick internet search would turn up her photo. It would just be a matter of keeping an eye out for a red-headed woman at the right time of day.

"I like to know who's coming to visit, and if they're bringing unexpected guests."

Zoe watched the seagulls swoop back and forth overhead. If she had a lineup of all the art dealers that she had met in her recent tour of the art galleries in Dallas, Leblanc wouldn't have blended in at all. Most of the dealers she'd met were slick, highly groomed, and consummate salespeople.

She'd been feeling slightly uneasy since Phil's questions, and now that uneasiness intensified into wariness, but this was where the trail for the blue butterfly painting had brought her. All she needed to do was check the painting then coordinate for an authenticator to look at it later. She had her car keys in her pocket. If anything went wrong, she'd leave.

"I always check up on anyone I don't know." LeBlanc half turned to her as they continued walking and gave her a quick smile. "Barry is a good guy. Even though he sent you my way, I always do my due diligence."

"And what did you find out about me? What's the verdict?" She wondered what portion of her history Leblanc had found.

"You have had an interesting and varied life."

Zoe laughed. "That's one way to put it."

"And from what I can tell, it seems that you were once hunted, but now you're on the side of the hunters."

"That's true." Zoe unscrewed the lid of the water bottle that she was carrying. "I got mixed up in something that was much bigger than me. It took me a long time to figure out what was going on. But that's all behind me now."

"And now you hunt for paintings of blue butterflies?"

"Exactly. So you have the blue butterfly painting?"

"I brought it with me to the camp when I came out earlier this week." A jogger coming toward them gave a wave as he passed. Zoe waved, and LeBlanc lifted his chin in acknowledgment.

"From a reputable source?" Zoe asked.

"One of the oldest dealers in the state."

Since the painting had been missing for several days, Zoe knew that it had probably already changed hands several times before it came to LeBlanc.

In fact, she suspected Barry was the first person in that chain. If Irene had described the painting or perhaps showed him a photo of it, Zoe had no trouble imagining Barry snatching the painting before it went into the store's inventory. He would have passed it along to a fence. The fence would sell it on to a dealer who didn't mind accepting stolen goods. The dealer would sell it on to someone else, someone like LeBlanc, who could legitimately claim to have no knowledge that the painting was stolen since he'd

bought it from a "reputable" dealer. The speed at which the transactions took place made it difficult to catch criminals who stole art.
If her guess about Barry being the start of the chain was right, she
was sure that Barry expected a kickback from LeBlanc if he sold the
painting to her.

"Your client, this person is a serious collector?" LeBlanc asked.
"Not just someone who dabbles? Because there's no bargain basement pricing at The Coast is Clear."

It took Zoe a second, but then she made the connection and
realized LeBlanc was referring to the name of his camp. "You don't
need to worry about my client's ability to pay."

He squinted at her a moment, studying her face then said,
"Good enough. Enough business for now. Let's save all that for after
lunch."

"Okay," Zoe said, even though she had plenty of questions. She
was on his turf, and she supposed a half hour or so wouldn't make
any difference.

"Grand Isle is an interesting place," LeBlanc said. "It's not just a
fishing community." He pointed with his beer to the east. "Fort
Livingston is over on Grand Terre." He gave the words a rolling
French pronunciation. "It's abandoned now, but before they built
the fort there, it was a bolt-hole for Jean Lafitte, the pirate. Lots of
smuggling in these waters."

"That's fascinating," Zoe said, noticing that he didn't use the
past tense.

The breaking waves raced farther up the beach and splashed
over LeBlanc's feet. He walked on. "People try to take the lawlessness away, but it will never go away from Grand Isle."

"Why is that?"

He grinned. "Location. Location. Location." He took another sip
of his beer. "We should get back. That chicken will be ready soon."

---

Other than the chicken, they had cornbread and huge bowls of red beans and rice, which was seasoned hotter than Zoe could imagine beans could be. She was glad of the cornbread and had another bottle of water. Zoe and LeBlanc sat across from each other at a picnic table. Phil sat to one side a little away from them and consumed his second lunch as quickly as he put away the sub sandwich. He didn't contribute to the conversation, but spent the time staring at his cell phone.

Since business talk was off the table until after the meal, Zoe asked LeBlanc about the island. He raved about the fishing. "It's the best deep-sea fishing you'll find, bar none."

As Zoe finished off her lunch, she wiped her fingers on a napkin and asked, "And how long have you lived here?"

"My family has always had a camp here." He tilted his head to the left. "A little fishing camp, down the beach a bit from here. We came out here every summer, and most holidays, but we lived in a little town not too far from New Orleans."

"So do you live here year-round, or just come out occasionally?"

"I'm here most of the time. I got family here. My aunt lives close-by, and my cousin works in the police department, which is good for business, if you know what I mean."

Zoe had a feeling that she did know what he meant—that his "business" wasn't always on the up-and-up. The mention of a connection to the police department wasn't an accident. And he wasn't just making conversation when he talked pirates and smuggling and lawlessness. Or maybe she was just feeling skittish. Was she reading too much into his words? Did Phil's hop-to attitude mean he was a good employee, or was he afraid of getting on the bad side of his boss who happened to have a gun on him while he cooked out and strolled on the beach?

LeBlanc pushed away his paper plate. "I've got some bad news for you about the butterfly painting."

A feeling of dread landed on Zoe's shoulders like a heavy weight. "Something's happened to it? Is it damaged?"

## 15

"Nothing like that," LeBlanc said. "No, the painting was fine when I sent it off this morning."

"Sent it off?" Had she misunderstood what he said? "Sent it off where?"

"To the buyer."

"To the buyer! But—*I'm* the buyer. Or potential buyer." Was this his idea of a joke? Zoe searched his face, which was now an even brighter pink after their walk, but she didn't see a trace of humor.

"That's right. You're a potential buyer," he said. "An *actual* buyer edged you out."

"But, I came all this way. And just now, on the beach, you said you had it."

He shook his head slowly. "No, I said I brought it with me earlier this week. I never said I had it in my possession at this moment."

Phil slowly extended his bony arm across the table like he was reaching into a lion's cage and gathered their empty plates then scuttled backward and melted away.

"But—how could...I mean—why would you do it? It doesn't make sense," Zoe said. "Why did you let me come all the way out here?"

LeBlanc laced his pudgy fingers together on the table and leaned closer. Despite his flushed face, his gaze was cold. All trace of southern hospitality was gone from his manner. "Because I'm a businessman. I had an offer for it last night after I spoke to you. The wire transfer came in this morning. Sadly, you were already on your plane. I figured since you'd come all the way to New Orleans"—he pronounced it 'Naw Lens'—"that the least I could do was feed you lunch." He lifted a shoulder. "And maybe we can find something else to make the trip worth your while."

Zoe ignored his last comment. No way would she buy something else from him after his bait and switch. She rubbed her forehead, stunned at his nerve. "You knew I was making a special trip out here—flying in from out of state, even—and you sold it out from under me?"

LeBlanc's eyes narrowed and she felt a chill run over her despite the hot day as his tone turned aggressive. "I don't know you. You might not have showed up. You could have looked at the painting and walked away." He waved a plump hand at her. "You could even be some kind of cop, for all I know."

"Me?" Zoe couldn't help but laugh. "A cop?"

His gaze defrosted a bit and the corners of his lips turned up. "As I said, I didn't know you. Luis, now, he's an old friend. Established and always follows through with the money. His wire transfer came in, just as he promised. I follow through, too. What could I do, but ship him the painting? Bird in hand. You can't fault me for that."

Zoe blew out a breath to calm down. She needed to stay focused. *Forget about LeBlanc's sleight of hand.* "Where is the painting now?"

His eyebrows disappeared under the rim of his Panama hat. "You really are interested in it." He slapped the table. "I should have waited."

Zoe knew he was thinking he could have gotten a higher price, but she ignored the implication that she'd be easier to get money out of than the person who had bought it. "You said you'd dealt with this person—Luis, wasn't it?—before. Is he a dealer?"

LeBlanc said, "Yeah, he's a dealer. High class. I'll get his contact information for you. In the meantime, take a look at this." Zoe hadn't noticed Phil had returned, but he scuttled out of the shadows carrying a plastic grocery bag. LeBlanc took the bag and said to him, "Print out Luis's contact details."

"Sure, boss." He left, trotting up the exterior staircase to the main floor of the house.

"Since you came all this way, I hate for you to go away empty handed. I don't have another butterfly painting, but I do have this." He whisked the bag away, revealing a clear Lucite box with an enormous blue butterfly mounted in the center of it.

The bright sunlight behind LeBlanc showed off the iridescent quality of the wings, highlighting their vivid blue color. He shifted the box, and the shades of blue altered subtly. Martin Johnson Heade had captured the iridescent quality of the wings in his painting, and the real thing was incredibly gorgeous, but she wasn't buying a butterfly no matter how beautiful it was, especially not from LeBlanc. "It's pretty, but I'm after a painting, not wildlife."

"Are you sure? If your client is interested in a painting of a blue butterfly, it stands to reason he—or she—would be interested in this as well. It's quite an unusual specimen. Don't you see it?" LeBlanc asked, his tone hinting at amazing things. "Look again. I know you're mad at me, but take a second look."

Zoe leaned in and peered at the butterfly. That's when she noticed an anomaly. She wasn't an expert on butterflies, but her quick delve into lepidopterology as she researched the painting had refreshed her middle school science lessons. Butterflies have four wings—two sets. But this butterfly had more than that. "An extra wing," she said quietly. The small wing attached to the thorax had the same vivid blue coloring as the other wings. "That is amazing," she said. She didn't know Thacker that well, but she was pretty sure he would be interested in this.

"A five-winged morpho," LeBlanc said. "And in A-1 condition. Nothing like this exists in the world. It's truly one-of-a-kind."

Zoe pushed down her irritation at LeBlanc. A rare and exotic butterfly trumped her feelings about him. "I'll have to call my client."

LeBlanc smiled. "Of course."

Phil trotted down the stairs with a paper in his hand. He gave it to LeBlanc, who handed it to Zoe. It was a copy of a packing slip.

The painting was on its way to Luis Cabello at the Cabello Gallery in Madrid, Spain.

**16**

---

Saturday

"So what did you do?" Jack asked.

"I bought it."

After a pause Jack said, "Even though you couldn't get Thacker on the phone?"

Zoe shuffled forward in a long line that snaked through the gate area, her boarding pass ready. It was Saturday, and she was in line for the flight that would take her to New York where she'd change planes and then fly on to Madrid. She had called the Cabello Gallery and spoken with Luis Cabello, confirming that he had acquired a painting in the style of Martin Johnson Heade with a hummingbird and a blue butterfly and that it was being shipped to his gallery. Cabello had texted photos of the painting he'd bought to Zoe, and they matched Artie's photo and LeBlanc's photo. She thought it was ironic that she was gathering a collection of photos of the painting, but not the painting itself.

Zoe switched her phone to her other hand and grabbed her suitcase as the line moved forward an inch. "Thacker was in some sort of meeting that went on for hours. He'd left instructions not to be disturbed. Kaz said to go ahead and buy it, and talk to Thacker about it later. So that's what I did."

"And you haven't heard back from Thacker? Surely that meeting didn't go all night and into today."

"No. I'm just not at the top of Thacker's priority list. I suppose he'll get back to me when he can. And if he's not happy about the butterfly...well...then I guess we're the proud owners of a rare butterfly."

"You don't think LeBlanc would take it back?" Jack asked.

"I'm pretty sure the return policy at The Coast is Clear is less than generous." Zoe rubbed her forehead, thinking about the financial hit that they might have to take. "Kaz said it wouldn't be a problem, but Thacker hired me to find a painting. Now I'm wondering what will happened if he doesn't want it. I'll pay back our savings account if Thacker passes on it."

"I can't imagine he'd do that," Jack said. "But even if he doesn't want it, don't worry about the money," Jack said.

"You're a pretty awesome husband, you know that, right?"

"I know I'm a lucky guy. Instead of buying designer clothes, you're out browsing entomological specimens with mutations. I have a feeling you won't run across too many of those in the future, so I think we're okay. Does it really have five wings?"

"Yes. It's amazing. It looks like a regular butterfly—if you can consider an iridescent blue butterfly a regular-looking butterfly. It's shaped like a butterfly that we might see flying through our backyard, but it has a small extra wing."

"And you think it's genuine?"

"I don't see how someone could fake those wings. The extra one is exactly the same shade as the rest of the butterfly. LeBlanc said he has authentication papers proving it isn't a fake. Although, I bet he could have any sort of paperwork made. In the end, I decided I should just get out of there with as little trouble as possible."

"So how much did it cost?" Jack asked. "Do I need to consolidate some credit card statements or make a bank transfer?"

"Leblanc originally wanted twenty-five thousand for it."

A choking sound came over the line. Zoe went on quickly, "But I negotiated."

"Thank goodness."

"I had a feeling that the butterfly was a one-off payment someone had given LeBlanc for...something else..."

"Drugs would be the likeliest explanation," Jack said. "As LeBlanc said, he's in the perfect location. I bet he's moving a lot of drugs along with his art."

"It's the first thing that comes to mind, isn't it? All that chat about lawlessness and his connection to the police. I never saw anything to indicate that was what was going on, but..."

"It's a logical assumption," Jack said. "I'm glad you got out of there, even if you did have to buy the thing sort of on spec."

"Anyway, I had a feeling that LeBlanc wanted to get rid of it. He wanted to get as much for it as he could, but it obviously wasn't something that he valued highly, or it wouldn't have been wrapped in a plastic grocery bag."

"Don't keep me in suspense any longer," Jack said. "How much did you pay for this butterfly in its luxurious plastic grocery bag wrapper that might be ours by default?"

"I talked him down to five thousand."

"Not bad, considering the starting point."

"Of course LeBlanc said it was worth much more than that. He claimed it would bring closer to a hundred thousand at auction."

"But he wasn't at an auction," Jack said.

"Right," Zoe said. "Turns out, there is occasionally some bargain basement pricing at The Coast is Clear. A quick trip to the car for the cash, and I was a proud owner of the five-winged blue morpho butterfly. It's on its way back to you right now. Until I heard from Thacker, I figured I should hang on to it. It should arrive Monday."

"You shipped it?"

"Well, it didn't seem like a good idea to take it with me in my luggage to Europe. LeBlanc assured me that it's not on the list of forbidden insects that require a permit to ship—I checked that myself—and it's not, but I'd rather not tote it around Madrid."

"Okay, I'm back on Monday, so that should work out, but I'll have the neighbors watch for it just in case."

"That's right," Zoe said. "I forgot you're going to London today. Too bad we're not flying to Europe together."

"Well, Maybe you'll get the painting authenticated, and we can fly back together," Jack said.

"I'd love that, but I'm not getting ahead of myself. I have to actually get my hands on it first. I still can't believe LeBlanc let me go all the way to Grand Isle when he'd already sold it."

"As he told you, he's a businessman. He made a sale. You took a rare butterfly off his hands."

"That still annoys me." The gate agent scanned Zoe's boarding pass. "I'm boarding now. I'll call you after I land."

---

*Tuck05: Nothing on the newsfeeds here. I've been refreshing all day. Problem?*

*Rbn: Yeah, there's a problem. I went in to work today to get in a little "extra work" and I heard about a new super-secret project. Scary stuff. We're talking being able to crack the protocols we're using.*

*Tuck05: Not possible. And even if it's real, it sounds unicorny.*

*Rbn: We specialize in making the impossible possible. It works. It's real. They're using it now. I've seen it in action. I can't risk going digital—not now. With the tech they have, they'd be able to track it back to me.*

*Tuck05: What will you do? You're not going to drop it, are you?*

*Rbn: Can't. Not now.*

*Tuck05: Then get out of town and release it once you're out.*

*Rbn: Still have my watcher. I went to the airport to pick up a friend yesterday. The guy on my tail closed in. He backed off when he saw I was going to baggage claim, but I'm not sure I can get out of the city—if they'd let me leave.*

*Tuck05: Then send it to me.*

*Rbn: I told you, digital is not an option.*

*Tuck05: Mail it.*

*Rbn:* Ok, I've picked myself up off the floor and wiped the tears out of my eyes. I can't mail what I have. Way too valuable. Too many chances for it to go astray. Too many different hands on it.

*Tuck05:* I'm glad I'm not on your project team—you're hard to work with.

*Rbn:* Realistic! I'm realistic.

*Tuck05:* Easy, buddy. You're not about to go ALL CAPS on me, are you? I have an idea. Let me check something, and I'll get back to you.

*Rbn:* Check what? What's your idea?

....

....

*Rbn:* ?? Where are you?

*Tuck05:* You're a control freak, you know that, right? I'm *checking* stuff. I'll let you know.

*Rbn:* Make it fast. I think we should go dark soon. Too risky to keep this conversation going with the tech they have now.

*Tuck05:* Give me a day. I'll let you know. You could always walk. Take a train or something. Start over in some other place.

*Rbn:* That's sounding better and better. I've always wanted to see South America.

*Tuck05:* Good place to get lost.

**Sunday**

*Tuck05: You still there, or are you sitting on a beach getting sunburnt?*
*Rbn: Still here. And I'm going hiking, not to the beach when this is over.
What have you got?*
*Tuck05: A solution. You'll love it. It's old-school.*
*Rbn: Make it quick. I want to sign off.*
*Tuck05: Your nerves are shot.*
*Rbn: Yours would be too if you'd seen what I did at work. Not good, man.
Not good.*
*Tuck05: Sending the details now. Follow them to the letter, and it
will work.*
...
...
*Rbn: I don't know. I don't like it.*
*Tuck05: Got a better plan?*
*Rbn: No.*
*Tuck05: Then do what I listed, and get out of town.*
....
*Tuck05: Still there?*

*Rbn: Yeah. I'm thinking.*

*Tuck05: Don't think. I'm offering you a way out. Take it. It's too important not to.*

*Rbn: You're right. I can't go this far and not finish.*

*Tuck05: Ok. I'd say keep in touch, but—not a good idea.*

*Rbn: Right. Thanks for your help.*

*Tuck05: You did the hard part. I'm just running the ball across the goal line.*

*Rbn: ??*

*Tuck05: Sorry. Football analogy. You'd say scoring a goal or something like that, I guess.*

*Rbn: This hasn't worked out like I planned. I'll be off-grid for a while. Probably a long time.*

*Tuck05: You better be. I expect at least a postcard from Brazil.*

*Rbn: You got it.*

---

**Monday**

Zoe strode across the marble floor of the Hotel Premier lobby. She circled around the burbling central fountain, gave a nod to the doorman, and stepped into the bright Madrid sunshine. She set off at a brisk pace toward the *Puerta del Sol*, where she was meeting Gloria Espino, the authenticator who was going to look at the painting with her today.

She had arrived in Madrid in the wee hours of Sunday morning, exhausted, but glad that Kaz had overseen all of her travel arrangements, especially when she saw the hotel. It took some coordination with Kaz on Friday, but within a few hours she had a meeting set up at the gallery along with airline tickets and a hotel reservation in Madrid. Kaz had also put her in touch with Gloria Espino, the person Thacker preferred to work with in Europe when he had paintings to authenticate. Fortunately, Gloria was based in Madrid, and had just returned from Rome. Gloria had to rearrange her schedule, and she hadn't sounded thrilled about it. But she said, "Since it's for Thacker, I'll do it," with barely a trace of an accent coming through in her husky voice.

The luxurious lobby and gilt of Hotel Premier had surprised Zoe, but when she called to let Kaz know she had arrived and subtly double check that the reservation had been made at the correct hotel, Kaz said, "Mr. Thacker always stays in a Premier when he travels. He says his employees and business associates should stay in the same accommodations he does."

The hotel was only a short distance away from the *Puerta del Sol*, which was at the heart of Madrid. It didn't take Zoe long to walk to the huge square lined with tall buildings. Restaurants, shops, and hotels ringed the square at ground level. On this bright day, the open plaza was packed with people, some of them striding along while others paused to watch street performers. Zoe spotted the bronze sculpture of a bear with its front paws on the trunk of a tree, where Gloria suggested they meet.

Several people were gathered around the base of the sculpture, but she didn't think any of them were Gloria, who had been extremely abrupt during their phone conversation. None of the people gave off the buttoned-down businesslike vibe that Gloria had when they'd spoken.

A woman with a mass of chestnut hair in a formfitting blue shirt tucked into skinny jeans stepped forward. "Zoe?"

"Yes," Zoe said, wondering if this was some sort of psychic street performer who told people their names.

"I'm Gloria." A narrow gold belt with a rhinestone clasp encircled her small waist and purple stilettos increased her already impressive height. The top of Zoe's head only came to the woman's chin. "So nice to meet you," Gloria said with warmth that had been missing on the phone.

"Thanks for rearranging your schedule," Zoe said, still trying to figure out if it was really the same person she'd spoken to earlier. Mental pictures that form on the phone can sometimes be far off the mark. Zoe had expected a dried-up, pinched-mouth, impatient woman in a boxy suit. The stylish woman in her thirties in front of her was nothing like she'd imagined Gloria would be, but the trace of an accent was there in her words, and her voice with its husky quality matched.

"It was easier than I thought it would be to shift my schedule."

"That's good. Do you know where the gallery is?" Zoe pulled out her phone to bring up the address.

"Yes, it's not too far. We can walk, if you'd like."

"Sure, as long as you're okay with that." Zoe glanced at Gloria's heels.

Gloria led the way across the square, deftly threading through the crowd to a side street. "It's fine. I wore my low heels today." Once they were on a quieter street lined with more tall buildings with iron balconies and storefronts on ground level, it was less crowded and easier to talk. As they walked side-by-side, Gloria asked, "Have you been to Madrid before?"

"No, it's my first visit."

"What have you seen so far?"

"Only the Prado." Zoe had been surprised to discover that the museum was open on Sunday afternoon. She'd spent a happy couple of hours prowling around, looking at paintings by El Greco, Velazquez, and Goya. "And I had dinner last night at one of the restaurants in the *Puerta del Sol*. That's all I've had time to do."

"You have to get out of the *Puerta del Sol*. I love it—it's so vibrant —but there's so much more to see. I can show you later, if you like." Gloria paused at an ornately trimmed door on the ground floor of a salmon-toned building with wrought-iron balconies on the four stories above the rusticated ground floor. A small gold plaque engraved with the words Cabello Gallery served as the only sign for the business. "Here we are."

## 18

Zoe followed Gloria into the expensive hush of the gallery as the door closed behind them, shutting out the sound of traffic.

In contrast to the classic exterior of the building, the design of the gallery interior was bare and modern. A golden hardwood floor stretched across the open room. Pure white walls partitioned the narrow space into several smaller areas. Each wall or partition showcased a single piece of art, which were an interesting mix, ranging from Abstract to Impressionist to a few Old Masters.

Footsteps sounded on the hardwood and a tall man with salt-and-pepper hair and a Van Dyke beard came around a partition. He wore a gray business suit, a silver tie, and a yellow pocket square. Arms outstretched, he said, "Gloria." A string of Spanish followed, but Zoe's high school Spanish didn't help her much. She picked out a word here and there, but the ratio was about twenty unknown words to one that she caught. Gloria gripped his hands, and they exchanged air kisses on each cheek along with a few more sentences at a staccato pace.

Gloria looked Zoe's way and switched back to English. "Luis, this is Zoe Andrews."

Luis transitioned to an American greeting, a handshake, but

also leaned forward slightly in a bow. "Forgive me. I'm being rude. Gloria has just returned from Italy. I had to hear how Rome was. I always want all the news."

"All the scandal, you mean," Gloria said.

"The best news *is* scandalous." Luis cut a look toward Gloria. "And if you'd bothered to reply to my emails I wouldn't have to ask."

Gloria threw up a hand. "Guilty. I've been overwhelmed, but you know I would have gotten back to you...eventually."

"Yes, eventually. I'm not on quite the same level as Mr. Thacker," he said.

"Not many people are," Gloria said.

He placed a hand over the yellow pocket square. "You wound me." He turned to Zoe, and his manner became more serious. "Speaking of Mr. Thacker, I know you are more interested in seeing the painting than talking about rumors and email. It arrived this morning, right on time, and I have everything set up in the workroom."

Luis gestured toward the rear of the gallery, and Gloria led the way, the crack of her spiky heels ringing out as she crossed the hardwood floor. They were about halfway through the gallery, when an unusual piece of art caught Zoe's eye, and she slowed to study a small sketch of a horse and rider done in ink with letters incorporated into the drawing. The plaque to the right of the artwork stated that it was by Salvador Dalí. Zoe looked back at the sketch and realized the letters in the drawing spelled the name Dalí.

Gloria noticed that Zoe had stopped and came back to look over Zoe's shoulder. Gloria asked Luis, "One of his checks?"

"Yes, just a little something that came in the other day." Zoe thought he sounded slightly embarrassed.

Zoe said, "It looks more like a caricature than the other work of Dalí's that I've seen."

"It is," Luis said. "He was a bit of a...um...I think the word is cheapskate. He would invite a large party out to dinner and pay for the meal with a check, but before giving it to the waiter, he would flip it over and sketch a drawing on the back, knowing it would make the check too valuable for the owner to cash."

"He was a scoundrel." Gloria shook her head, but the corners of her lips were turned up.

"Clever," Luis acknowledged, "yet slightly underhanded."

"And he repeated the little trick often, according to the stories." Gloria tilted her head toward the drawing. "Every once in a while one of these comes on the market. Has it been authenticated?" Gloria asked, her eyes narrowing as she studied the sketch. A blue mat that matched the color of the ink surrounded the sketch. A wooden frame several inches wide enclosed the artwork.

"Yes. Pietro."

"Ah, well, then there's no doubt," Gloria said. "It's a Dalí." She looked at me. "Pietro specializes in Dalí. There are so many Dalí lithographs floating around that Pietro will never run out of work." Gloria returned her gaze to the check. "I think this is more interesting than one of the ubiquitous lithographs."

"It is a diverting novelty, but it will sell," Luis said, his tone defensive.

"You are in business," Gloria said. "It makes sense to show what sells. Thacker would like it," she added in an aside to Zoe.

Luis missed her quiet comment. "I would be a fool *not* to offer it for sale. Now, let us look at the painting."

At the back of the gallery, Luis guided them by a long white waist-high counter that hid a computer, phone, and other business paraphernalia, then opened a door set into the wall. The lines of the doorframe were flush with the wall and so faint that the opening was hardly noticeable. Luis touched a sliver of a metal plate with the toe of his dress shoe, and the door popped open.

The minimal aesthetic of the gallery didn't extend to the workroom. Shelves covered one wall with a hodgepodge of files and boxes. A scarred rococo desk filled one wall, while a utilitarian plastic-topped table stood in the center of the room. A painting was positioned on the table.

The three of them walked to it and peered down. Zoe caught

her breath. The painting was beautiful. The iridescent wings of the butterfly glowed. Unlike the butterfly painting Zoe had seen in Vail, this butterfly was in full sunlight, so both wings seemed to radiate with a brilliant shine. A hummingbird hovered, its wings a blur. The detail on both the butterfly and hummingbird was exquisite, yet the painting didn't look academic. The artist had captured the sense of motion. Both creatures looked as if they might flitter away in a moment. The background was densely tropical and full of plants.

"It's stunning." Gloria plunked down her large bag onto the table, then removed a pair of gloves. She took a deep breath, blew it out, then picked up the painting. Tilting it this way and that, she studied it from all angles. "Looks promising."

She replaced it on the table then took a contraption from her bag and fit it over her head. It mashed her full hair down, molding it to her scalp. She positioned the strap on her forehead, then slid a pair of magnifying lenses into place over her eyes, giving her a bug-like look. "Let's see what we've got."

She clicked on a light on the frame of the lenses then re-examined every inch of the painting in silence. She turned it over and gave the same careful study to the back. She murmured, "Good color," then tapped the back of the canvas, and gave a nod of satisfaction. She peered at a small label affixed to the bottom left-hand corner then glanced up at Zoe. "The label states it's from the collection of S. Carter. There's a date, 1866."

Excitement bubbled up in Zoe, but she wasn't going to celebrate until Gloria finished the examination.

Luis motioned to a tissue thin piece of yellowed paper with faded writing. "This was tucked into the back of the painting between the stretcher and the canvas."

Zoe had been so focused on the painting that she hadn't even noticed the paper. She leaned closer to read it. The old-fashioned cursive was a bill of sale, recording that Silvanus Carter had bought "one hummingbird and butterfly oil painting" from the artist in 1866.

Gloria skimmed the paper. "I'll examine it in more detail in a moment," she said and returned her attention to the painting.

The frame, tubular metal and contemporary in style, didn't quite fit with the lush, detailed painting. Gloria carefully pried out the clips that held the canvas in the frame, then she separated the frame, which came apart in four separate pieces. She shook her head and made disapproving noises. Zoe thought she was probably thinking how could you put such a nice painting in such a cheap frame.

Gloria placed the pieces of the frame on the table to one side then focused on the edge of the canvas. Luis caught Zoe's eye and tilted his head to the door. She followed him into the gallery.

"She will be a while," he said. "Feel free to look around, if you'd like."

"I will, but before I do that, I wanted to ask you if you've heard anything about a Canaletto and a Picasso that are missing from a museum." Zoe brought up the images of the artwork on her phone.

Luis handed the phone back to Zoe. "No, I haven't seen anything like that offered for sale."

"If you do hear anything about them, I'd be interested."

"Of course," Luis said smoothly, but Zoe thought it was more of a mechanical response than a sincere promise to get in touch with her. She moved through the gallery, figuring it would be good to give Gloria some space to work.

The door at the front of the gallery opened, letting in the sound of the street noise for a moment, then it cut off again. Luis went to the front of the store and engaged a customer who'd just walked in, while Zoe browsed. She found a beautiful painting of a Venetian canal that she loved, but the price made her eyes water, so she moved on. She made a slow circuit through the gallery and was about to return to the back room, when a young woman in a white shirt and black pencil skirt entered the gallery.

Her head was bent as she clacked across the floor in a pair of outrageously high heels that were even higher than Gloria's. Did women in this city not own flats? Zoe couldn't imagine walking the cobblestone streets in stilettos, but the idea didn't faze the professional women Zoe had come across so far. The woman caught sight of Zoe as she came around one of the partitions at the back of the gallery near the counter. "*Hola*," she said. Thick lines of mascara outlined her eyes, ending in a curved swoop at the corners, giving the effect of little wings at the sides of her eyes. She put her bag away under the counter. "*¿Puedo ayudarte?*"

"*Hola*," Zoe replied, but further description of what she was doing at the gallery was beyond her. Luis leaned around one of the partitions and spoke to the woman, a few rapid sentences, gesturing to the workroom door.

She came around the counter. "I am Pilar," she said slowly, obviously searching for the right English words. "Please tell me if you need help."

"*Gracias*," Zoe said and moved to the workroom door, thinking she should check on Gloria. She pressed the metal plate at the base of the door with the tip of her shoe, and it swung open.

Gloria had removed her headgear and was photographing the painting. "I'm almost finished." She snapped a few photos, then rotated the painting and took more pictures.

"And?"

"I've examined it with a UV light and see no evidence of retouching or repainting, but I haven't x-rayed it or done any pigment analysis, which I know Thacker will not want to wait for. He's impatient when it comes to acquiring art. He wants it when he wants it."

"Right," Zoe said. "He told me to have it authenticated, but said he didn't want to wait for scientific tests. He wanted an expert opinion."

Gloria nodded. "Yes, so I'm going on my observations and my gut." She placed her gloved hand over her stomach.

"Kaz says your gut is rarely wrong."

Gloria closed her eyes and tilted her head back and forth quickly, acknowledging the compliment. "That is true, yes."

"And what does your gut say about this painting?"

A smile broke across her face. "Thacker will be pleased. I think it is an original undiscovered painting by Martin Johnson Heade."

———————

"Lunch?" Gloria asked as they left the gallery and merged into the flow of pedestrians heading toward the *Puerta del Sol.*

"Good idea."

"What would you like?"

"It doesn't matter to me," Zoe said. "I'm so happy that I finally tracked down the painting and that you were able to authenticate it that nothing else matters to me right now."

After Gloria told Luis the good news, Zoe had contacted Kaz through the Eon Industries employee app. When she left for Madrid, Kaz had created an account for her and told her it was the easiest way to stay in touch when traveling internationally. Within a few minutes, she had a notification from the Eon app that payment was being arranged for the painting. Zoe had passed the word on to Luis, who said he would take it from there. Zoe still had her cash on her—well, technically it was locked in the safe in the hotel—but she could tell from the prices on the other art in the gallery that this transaction was far bigger than the cash she had access to—and it was in dollars, not euros. Thacker would have to wire the money. She had asked if Luis needed a down payment to hold the painting, but he had shaken his head and said there was no need. "Not when working with Mr. Thacker."

Zoe dodged around a woman with a stroller and picked up her pace to keep up with Gloria, who was striding along, weaving in and out of the crowd. "Then we'll go to a place close to here, the *Museo del Jamon,*" Gloria said. "It may be packed with tourists, but the service is fast, and the food is good."

A few minutes later, Zoe said, "This certainly isn't like any museum I've ever been to." The place was a combination deli and restaurant. They had ordered while standing at a counter that displayed more varieties of ham than Zoe had known existed. Legs of ham hung suspended from the ceiling over the entire length of the counter and along one wall. Gloria motioned Zoe over to seats at a bar that ran along one wall, and they squeezed in between a German couple and a group of men speaking Spanish.

The waiter brought them plates with ham sandwiches and their drinks. While Gloria had opted for wine, Zoe had ordered water. She knew that jet lag would crush her soon and didn't want to hurry the process along with alcohol. Madrid had so much she wanted to see.

"You can't imagine how relieved I am that the painting is authentic," Gloria said.

Zoe swallowed her bite of delicious ham that was tucked inside a flaky roll. "Oh, I think I can." She didn't want to go into the long and winding journey that had brought her to this point. She was just glad everything had turned out okay. It was only when Gloria authenticated the painting that Zoe realized how stressed she'd been. The worry that had been weighing her down had lifted, and she felt light and confident. The whole fiasco of Grand Isle still rankled her, but it didn't seem nearly so bad now that she'd actually tracked down the painting.

Gloria took a sip of wine. "Thacker is not a man you want to disappoint."

"He seemed easygoing when I met him."

"Then you haven't seen him when he's in the pursuit of something he wants. He can be intense—and demanding. Unreasonably so."

She pulled a paper napkin from the dispenser and wiped her fingers then pointed at Zoe. "You should tell him about the check, the one with the Dalí sketch. Thacker loves that sort of stuff."

"I did see a painting that I thought was by Salvador Dalí when I visited him."

Gloria shook her head. "In this case, it isn't the sketch that will appeal to him. I mean, he loves the surreal aspect of the Dalí paintings, but he's also drawn to Dalí's commercial instincts and his entrepreneurial spirit—that's what Thacker would like about the check. Not so much the art, but what it represents."

"Has he collected similar things?"

Gloria threw up a hand. "What *hasn't* he collected?" She leaned forward, lowering her voice as if someone might overhear them, even in the noisy restaurant. "He goes through phases. So far, he's hit Impressionism, Abstract, porcelains, and Surrealism. And those are just off the top of my head. He can't seem to decide what he wants to collect. He can't focus on one thing."

"Now that you mention it," Zoe said, "I did see the Dalí painting and another work by Martin Johnson Heade at his house. He has an entomological collection, too. They're all unrelated."

"Eclectic, is what he'd say." Gloria signaled to the waiter for another sandwich and asked if Zoe wanted another as well. "Sure, I'm celebrating."

"But, his eclectic taste—as varied as it is—helps pay my bills," Gloria said. "So he can accumulate as many different things as he wants."

Zoe's phone buzzed with a notification. *Transaction arranged. Pick up painting tomorrow and bring it back with you. Flight details to follow.*

## 19

Zoe had barely finished reading the text message when her phone rang. It was an unfamiliar number, but she recognized the Colorado area code. "I better get this," she said, and Gloria nodded her understanding.

A male voice said, "It's Thacker. Kaz is on vacation, so I'm...*minding the store*, you could say. Did you get the notification about the payment transaction?"

Even if he hadn't identified himself, Zoe would have recognized his speaking style with his pauses and emphasis. "Yes, it came through. The painting is beautiful. I think you'll love it. Gloria took several high-resolution photos. I'm sure she'll send them to you with her report." Zoe looked inquiringly at Gloria.

She mouthed the word *tonight*.

"She says you'll receive them tonight," Zoe relayed.

"Great. Excellent work, Zoe. I'm looking forward to seeing the painting. I've contacted the person who handles my travel. You'll receive notification about your airline tickets soon. Contact Kaz as soon as you're back in the States. You can hand it off to him."

Gloria waved her hand. "Tell him about the Dalí sketch."

"Before you go, Gloria says you might be interested in something we saw at the gallery today, a sketch Salvador Dalí did on the back of a personal check."

Zoe was about to launch into the explanation that Gloria and Luis had given to her in the gallery, but before she could continue Thacker said, "Oh, one of those that he used to get out of paying his bill—interesting. What was the sketch?"

"A man on horseback with Dalí's name integrated into the image."

"A Don Quixote sketch, then," he said, sounding more intrigued. "Contact Luis—have him send me all the details."

"I'll do that. Anything else?"

"Is that all Gloria pointed out to you that I might like?"

"Yes, that was the only thing she mentioned."

"Then, that'll do. See you in a few days. And now, I must go rustle up a late dinner. Mary is in New York at some fundraising dinner, so...I'm a *bachelor* tonight. Take good care of that painting on the way back. Don't put it in your checked luggage."

"I wouldn't dream of it. It will be with me the whole time. By the way, did you get the message from Kaz about the rare butterfly—"

"Kaz mentioned something about it," he said, interrupting her. "I'll get him to brief me on it when he returns. Call me when you arrive with the painting," he said and hung up.

Clearly, Thacker only cared about the painting right now. Zoe would have to remind Kaz to bring up the rare blue morpho butterfly.

Gloria said, "He wants the Dalí sketch, doesn't he?"

"I don't know. He asked me to contact Luis and have him send all the information," Zoe said.

"He wants it. He'll buy it."

Zoe dialed the number for the gallery and told Luis that Thacker was interested in the sketch.

"*Excelente*," he said, then switched to English. "I'll send the details right now. The butterfly and hummingbird painting should be ready to go for you tomorrow. Shall I send it to your hotel, or would you like to pick it up?"

"I'll pick it up. What time should I be there?"

"As long as the payment comes through this afternoon, you can pick it up first thing in the morning. We open at eleven."

Zoe ended the call. "I won't be in Madrid much longer." She glanced out the window at the busy thoroughfare, thinking of all the sites she would like to take in before she left.

"Then you'll have to make the most of the time you have. I have a few hours. I can show you a few things nearby, if you'd like."

"Sounds great," Zoe said, surprised that Gloria was being so helpful after her initial standoffishness, but first impressions—or phone impressions—could be wrong.

Gloria said, "Let's start with the palace."

"Yes, every good tourist wants to see the palace. And I'm a very good tourist."

Gloria laughed. "Then let's go."

Zoe slid off the barstool then stopped. "Oh, we haven't paid for our second sandwiches."

Gloria waved a hand around the packed restaurant. "They'll never notice." She pushed through the crowd waiting to order and made her way to the door. Zoe tossed several euros beside her plate and caught up with Gloria, who was again setting a quick pace. "On the way to the palace, we'll drop into the *Plaza Mayor*."

They navigated through streets lined with shops and café tables under umbrellas until they emerged into an arcaded square. "The buildings are eighteenth century." Gloria motioned to the three-story buildings with formal lines that enclosed the rectangular cobblestoned plaza. "But the actual plaza itself dates back to the 1600s. It's been the sight of bullfights, and heretics were put on trial and executed here during the Inquisition."

Zoe glanced around at the tourists strolling leisurely as they window-shopped and contemplated restaurant menus. She shook her head. "It's hard to imagine." Zoe moved toward a sculpture of a man on horseback for a better look.

"Philip the Third," Gloria informed her.

They rambled through the plaza, gazing in shop windows that

displayed dolls dressed as Flamenco dancers, jewelry, and clothing, including a shop dedicated exclusively to sombreros. Zoe had to go inside the store that sold Spanish fans. Its window was a rainbow of colors, displaying everything from fans in modern styles with purple polka dots to antique fans. Zoe bought several modern paper fans in jewel tones as souvenirs. Her friend Helen would love one.

As they went back into the plaza, Zoe said, "Okay, enough shopping. You better get me out of here, or I won't see any historic sites, only shops. On to the palace."

The palace was not far away. They approached a towering wrought-iron fence that closed off an open plaza that ended in the white façade of the palace. Gloria tapped away on her phone while Zoe admired the imposing building and took photographs. "It's not open today," Gloria said. "That's a shame. Inside is amazing—opulent, lavish, decadent—all that. An official event is scheduled for today, so no tours. But you can still see the cathedral." They crossed to study the church that was located directly across from the palace. "The *Catedral de Santa María la Real de la Almudena*," Gloria said. "It's a mishmash of architectural styles, neoclassical, neo-Gothic, neo-Romanesque...whatever you like, it's got it. Would you like to go inside or do you want to keep going? You can always come back later in the day."

"I'll come back later." Zoe took a close-up photo of one of the sculptures on the roof. "There is so much to see, and I appreciate the city tour."

They moved through the *Plaza de Oriente*, which was filled with sculptures of the Spanish kings and queens that Gloria told her were originally designed to be placed on the palace roof. Zoe gave a pair of policemen mounted on horses a wide berth as they walked down a tree-shaded path. "Isn't there an Egyptian temple in Madrid?"

Gloria stopped and tilted her head. "How did you know that? Most people are surprised to learn about it. That was going to be my grand finale."

"I've done some freelance copy editing for travel guides, and it was one of the things that I thought was so interesting about Madrid. I know lots of European cities have Egyptian antiquities, but I don't think anyone else has a temple. Is it far from here?"

"Not at all." Gloria said. " The *Templo de Debod* is just up the road." They continued through the park then took another busy road for a short distance until they came to another park. They followed the path up an incline through the trees until they came to the top and the temple came into view.

"It was moved from Egypt before the construction of the Aswan Dam, right?" Zoe asked.

"Sounds like you know more about the temple than I do," Gloria said.

"What I remember is that the temple was a gift from Egypt to Spain after Spain helped Egypt save some historic sites during the construction of the dam."

"Yes, that's right. It was dismantled, transported to Spain, and then reassembled," Gloria said.

A reflecting pool surrounded two stone pylons with rectangular openings that led to the temple, which was a square building with a flat roof and stone columns on either side of the entrance. Anachronistic glass windows behind the columns and a pair of glass doors had been added, and Zoe wondered if it was to protect the interior of the temple from the elements or from tourists who might try to get in after hours.

After seeing the royal palace and the cathedral, the temple looked small in comparison. But as Gloria and Zoe moved closer, Zoe realized it was a substantial structure in its own right. The pylons dwarfed the line of tourists waiting to enter the Temple. It was quite a contrast—the ancient stones paired with the ragged line of tourists, who were either posing with their selfie sticks or focused on the screens of their phones.

Gloria's phone rang, and Zoe caught sight of the image associated with the incoming call, a girl about ten years old with long brown hair and dark eyes, who was smiling at the camera as she held a watercolor painting. "Excuse me," Gloria said. "It's my daughter."

Gloria switched to Spanish and had a short conversation. Zoe couldn't understand Gloria's words, but the tone was familiar. It reminded Zoe of the conversations she'd had with her mom when she was pleading for something, but her mom remained immovable. After a quick burst of words spoken in a firm tone, Gloria's voice softened as she said, "*Te quiero.*"

She ended the call with a shake of her head and transitioned back to English. "Sorry about that. I have to pick up my daughter, even if she would rather stay with a friend a little longer." She lifted her eyebrows as she glanced at the temple. "Do you want to go inside?"

"No, the line is too long. I may come back tomorrow morning before I pick up the painting. I'm sure the line will be shorter then."

Gloria shook her head. "There's no need for that. I can help you get in quickly."

"Do you know someone who works there?" Zoe asked.

"No. All you need to do is find a handsome man near the front of the line. Smile at him and thank him for holding your place. I'll distract the guard while you do it in case the man makes a fuss."

Zoe caught Gloria's arm because she was already moving toward the temple to put her plan in action. "That's okay. I'd rather take some pictures out here. Thank you so much for showing me some of Madrid."

"I hate to leave you so soon. You haven't seen the *Plaza de Cibeles.* It's stunning with an amazing fountain at the center. Don't miss that. And then of course there's the *Gran Vía,*" Gloria said. "It's like..." she waved her hand in a circular motion as she searched for the right word, "...what's the name of the busy street in New York with all the restaurants and shops?"

"Broadway?"

"Yes. The *Gran Vía* is the Broadway of Madrid. You have to go there too."

"Too many things to see in one day. I'll just have to do the best I can, and come back and see other things later."

"And we haven't even touched on the food." Gloria looked pained. "Madrid is all about food. You must go to the *Mercado de San Miguel*. That's a wonderful food market not far from here. It's a great place to go for *tapas*."

"Don't look so upset," Zoe said. "I'll see what I can, then I'll have to return and see the rest. I appreciate you getting me started today."

"It was a pleasure." Gloria extended her hand. "I hope we get to work together again soon."

They shook hands, and Gloria departed.

---

Zoe decided that trying to check everything off the sightseeing list that Gloria had given her would be impossible in one afternoon, so she spent the rest of the day wandering around the city instead. She browsed shops and ate her way through Madrid, stopping to admire the beautiful architecture as she discovered it. She found the *mercado* that Gloria told her about, a large building that was a food lover's paradise. The market was crowded with shoppers, and Zoe made her way through the press of people admiring the displays. Pyramids of black and green olives stuffed with meats and cheese filled one stall. A cascade of different types of nuts filled the next stall in shades ranging from dark brown almonds to golden cashews. The seafood counter displayed octopus, eel, and sea urchins packed in ice around the head of a marlin with its spear-like bill extending in the air. The fruit stalls were bursting in vibrant primary colors with green apples, red tomatoes, purple grapes, and yellow bananas plus hosts of berries and melons that Zoe couldn't identify. And she hadn't even explored the beer, wine, and pastries.

Her phone rang and she covered her other ear so she could hear

Jack as he said, "I got your message. Congratulations on locating the painting."

"Thanks. Everything should be wrapped up by tomorrow, and I'll be on my way back. I'm in a food market right now, and I want something from every stall. I don't even know where to start. I'll send some pictures."

"Sounds great. I wish I was there."

Zoe sighed. "Me, too. It's another place to add to our travel wish list."

"Definitely."

"So how's London?" Zoe asked.

"It's a gorgeous day here. Unfortunately, I've spent most of it in a conference room. But we got a lot of work done."

They talked a bit more about Jack's meeting, then hung up. Zoe took a few photos and sent them to Jack as a feeling of letdown settled over her. The job was over, which was great. She was elated that the painting had been found, and she was happy that she was getting to see Madrid, but it just wasn't the same without Jack.

———

**Tuesday**

The next morning Zoe dragged herself out of bed, showered, and packed her suitcase. The jet lag had caught up with her last night. She turned in early and slept hard until her alarm went off. She hit snooze a few times and wouldn't be able to do any sightseeing on the way to pick up the painting.

She parked her rolling suitcase at the end of the bed, pocketed her room key card, and slipped her messenger bag over her shoulder. Thacker had contacted her late yesterday, and said he'd also arranged to purchase the Dalí sketch. She'd again tried to bring up the rare blue morpho that she'd bought from LeBlanc, but he'd again cut her off with instructions about taking care of the painting and the sketch.

She'd pick up both pieces of artwork at the gallery this morning then come back to the hotel and check out later. Her flight was in the evening and there was no need for her to drag her suitcase through Madrid.

The day was dazzlingly bright, and Zoe slipped on her sunglasses as she made her way through the busy *Puerta del Sol*, walking along the route that she and Gloria had taken yesterday. She stopped to have breakfast, a Spanish omelet, which was a simple recipe of eggs, onion, and potato that was served with a glass of fresh squeezed orange juice and a croissant.

As she came to the gallery door, Zoe checked her watch. It was only a few minutes after eleven, but the door was unlocked, so she stepped into the expensive silence. Unlike yesterday, footfalls did not resound on the hardwood floor the moment the door closed behind her.

She walked around the partitions toward the back. "Luis?"

The counter at the back of the store was empty, and she didn't see any package labeled with her name waiting for her.

Zoe rotated, scanning the quiet gallery. She moved to the door to the workroom where Gloria had examined the painting. She knocked, waited a moment, then tapped the metal plate at the base of the door with her toe.

"Luis? It's Zoe. Do you have the paintings—"

The door swung open to reveal Luis sprawled on the floor.

**20**

---

Rbn: *Everything's falling apart. It's not going to work.*

Tuck05: *What's happened?*

Rbn: *They made their move. I don't have time to explain. I'm leaving, getting out of here, but they know everything—the whole plan.*

Tuck05: *Whoa. How can they know that?*

Rbn: *I had to tell them.*

Tuck05: *You had to tell them?*

Rbn: *I like my legs and my fingers and my toenails. I wanted to keep them all intact, so I answered their questions.*

Tuck05: *I can't believe it! They actually threatened to beat you up?*

Rbn: *No. They did. I think my nose is broken.*

Tuck05: *I don't know what to say. I never thought they'd do that.*

Rbn: *Yeah, me either. But I'm out.*

Tuck05: *That's crazy. After all you've done? Just lie low for a while. It's already in process, right?*

Rbn: *I will be lying low, but in a place far away from here. And it's too late. They've already gone after it. They probably have it by now.*

Tuck05: *No, I heard from my contact. Everything went according to plan. It'll be out of the country in a few hours.*

Rbn: *You don't understand—they beat me up and I told them everything.*

*They'll go get it. They'll do whatever they have to. Sorry, man. It would*
*have been great, if it worked. Later.*
*Tuck05: Let me check and get back to you.*

...

...

*Tuck05: You there?*

...

...

*Tuck05: Hey, don't mess around. It's too important to give up now.*

...

...

*Tuck05: Ok. Fine. I'll follow up myself. Even if you bail, I won't.*

———

Zoe dropped to her knees beside Luis. He was stretched out on his stomach with his arms at his side and his cheek pressed against the floor. Zoe felt a wash of relief as she saw his shoulder blades flex slightly. He was breathing, at least.

"Luis?" She put a hand on his shoulder and gave it a gentle shake, but his eyes remained closed, and he didn't move or react.

Zoe didn't see an obvious injury, but she didn't want to attempt to move him. Was it a stroke or heart attack or some sort of seizure? A burst of noise from the street filled the air for a moment, filtering in through the door that Zoe had left open. The sounds cut off. Someone had come into the gallery.

Zoe hurried out of the workroom and saw the young woman with the dramatic eyeliner who had arrived yesterday when Gloria was authenticating the painting. She again wore a white shirt and a narrow dark skirt and high heels, obviously her work uniform. What was her name...Pippa? No, Pilar.

"Pilar, I'm so glad you're here. Luis is..." Zoe paused at Pilar's confused expression. Zoe tried to remember the word for injured, but her mind went blank. "He's hurt...um...*enfermo*," Zoe said, settling on what she hoped was the word for "sick."

Even though Pilar didn't seem to understand Zoe's words, her attitude must have conveyed the urgency of the situation because when Zoe pointed to the back room Pilar dropped her bag on the counter and followed Zoe quickly.

Pilar crouched beside Luis, exclaiming in Spanish. She tapped Luis's shoulder and when she didn't get a reaction, she looked up at Zoe, her eyes wide. She let out a string of Spanish. Zoe could tell from the inflection at the end of the sentences that they were questions, but that was all Zoe could grasp. She certainly didn't have any answers, and shrugged her shoulders. "Ambulance?"

Pilar nodded, jumped up and went back to the gallery and opened her bag. Zoe was glad she didn't have to attempt to make the call. Her Spanish vocabulary had shrunk under stress. Within seconds Pilar was describing the situation in a voice that shook. She returned to the workroom and said a few sentences in Spanish, then saw Zoe's blank look and switched to English. "Soon. Help, soon."

Zoe nodded and mimed that she would go to the front and watch for the ambulance. Since the gallery only had one entrance the paramedics—or EMTs or whatever they were called in Spain— would have to come in that way. It only took a few moments for them to arrive, and Zoe pointed the pair of young men to the workroom, then followed them.

They set to work, checking over Luis with an air of calm efficiency that reassured Zoe. Surely if Luis was in serious danger, their actions and attitude wouldn't seem so routine. One of the men asked Pilar a series of questions as they worked, which she answered, and then she began relaying questions to Zoe in broken English, asking if Luis had fallen and how long ago it had happened.

Zoe shrugged. "I don't know." They understood and stopped asking questions.

Pilar stood beside Zoe, her hand pressed over her heart as she watched the paramedics. Zoe asked her, "What do they think happened?"

She shook her head. "They don't know."

The tone of the conversation between the paramedics changed, drawing Zoe's attention back to them. The men were bent over Luis's neck, examining something under his ear. Luis had on a different suit today, navy with a thin pinstripe. Above the collar of his white dress shirt Zoe could see two small red marks about an inch apart on his neck. She couldn't follow the rapid pace of their sentences, except for one word that came through clearly—Taser.

## 21

"Why are you..." Pilar looked at the ceiling for a moment as she searched for the English word, then shook her head and seemed to give up "*aquí?*"

Zoe glanced from Pilar to the policeman who stood beside her. "Why am I here?" Zoe repeated back to Pilar. "I came to pick up the artwork, of course." Zoe was so frazzled that she didn't even attempt to translate her reply into Spanish. The words "painting" and "butterfly" had not been part of her vocabulary in Spanish class.

Two police officers had arrived a few minutes ago. After a hurried conversation with the paramedics, the police officers had taken charge. One officer had changed the sign on the door to "closed" and motioned for Zoe and Pilar to go to the back counter, where Officer Alina waited, pen poised to take down their information. When he realized Zoe didn't speak much Spanish, he had used Pilar's broken English along with a few words that he knew, to ask questions.

Zoe took out her phone. "Let me find somebody who can interpret for us." She dialed Gloria's number and breathed a sigh of relief when she answered. Zoe quickly told her what had happened.

"Luis is unconscious? *Terrible!*" She gave the word it's Spanish pronunciation.

"Yes, the police are here now and it's...well, we're not communicating very well. My Spanish isn't up to the task, and the police don't speak much English."

"I'm not far away. Let me ask my neighbor if she can stay with my daughter. I'll be there as soon as I can."

Zoe turned to Pilar. "Gloria will be here soon."

Pilar looked as shaken up as Zoe. Tears had glazed her eyes earlier when the paramedics transferred Luis to the ambulance, and now her elaborate eyeliner was smudged, giving her raccoon eyes. Before the ambulance left, Pilar had a rapid-fire discussion with one of the paramedics. When they closed the ambulance doors and drove away, Zoe asked what they thought had happened to Luis. Pilar touched her forehead. She mimed something hitting her head and pointed to the floor, adding, "*mal*," before closing her eyes.

Didn't "*mal*" mean "bad?" Zoe interpreted the pantomime to mean that the paramedics thought that after Luis was Tasered, he'd hit his head on the floor, which in the workroom was exposed concrete.

Pilar seemed to understand that Gloria was on the way. She sniffed and nodded as she tried to translate Zoe's reply for the waiting police officer. Officer Alina jotted something down in his notebook.

Zoe's phone buzzed with a text. She saw Jack had replied to the text she'd sent him a few moments ago with the news about Luis. *Changing flight reservations now. My meeting is over. Instead of flying home, I'm coming to Madrid.*

Zoe began typing a reply when another text from him came in. *Don't bother to tell me not to come. I'm halfway to the airport already. The first flight I could get arrives later tonight.*

The thought that Jack would arrive in a few hours was comforting. She texted back. *No way would I try to stop you. Glad you're coming.*

Officer Alina must have decided not to wait for Gloria because he was asking another question, indicating that Pilar should translate. Zoe slipped her phone into her pocket as Pilar said, "Where is the artwork?"

"I don't have it. I found Luis as soon as I arrived." Zoe looked over the counter again, but didn't see two packages anywhere.

Pilar spoke to Officer Alina, and after a short exchange between them, Pilar went behind the counter and searched the drawers and cabinets. After a few moments she turned back to Zoe. "Not here." Officer Alina must have picked up on the meaning of the words because his gaze immediately went to Zoe's messenger bag.

He said something to Pilar. She said, "He wants to look in your bag."

"I don't have the painting or the sketch." With a flare of anger, Zoe unfastened the clasps and opened the mouth of her messenger bag. "No artwork." The bag was getting heavier every day that went by. Right now, a sweater, a Madrid map, and one of the fans she'd bought yesterday were on top.

It was only after she tossed back the flap and stretched the bag wide that a conspiracy theory scenario flashed through her mind. What if someone had slipped something...like a Taser...into her bag as she walked through the crowded *Puerta del Sol,* and it had fallen to the bottom of the bag? Could someone have done that without her knowing? No, surely not. She gave herself a mental shake. The tension of the situation was getting to her, she decided. *Don't be silly*, she lectured herself. Her messenger bag had been fastened securely.

She shifted the contents around, and her heart rate drifted back into a normal range as it became clear that the next strata of the bag only contained her wallet, passport, lip gloss, and a pocket-sized guide to Madrid that she'd picked up at the airport.

The officer then turned to Pilar, his gaze going to her large handbag that sat on the counter. Her eyebrows crunched down, and she looked offended. But after Officer Alina said a few more words, Pilar picked up her bag. With her lips pressed into a narrow line, she opened it and showed that it did not contain either a Taser or two pieces of artwork wrapped for transport.

The gallery door opened, and Gloria swept in, her mass of brown hair bouncing around her shoulders as her heels clicked across the wood floor. Today she wore a bright yellow dress with a wide white belt and an A-line skirt that fluttered around her knees.

Officer Alina took a step forward, hand raised, clearly indicating that she was not to be on the premises, but Gloria turned up the wattage on her smile as she spoke to him in a torrent of Spanish. Within a few moments he nodded, his resistance melting away.

Gloria moved to give Zoe a quick embrace. She lowered her voice. "I've convinced him that I'm an old friend of yours, and he says I can stay to interpret, but only until the police interpreter arrives."

Zoe's heart sank. A police interpreter was on the way? She had hoped that she could convince Officer Alina that she had nothing to do with this attack on Luis—because obviously they were treating it as a criminal attack, but if a police interpreter was coming, then it didn't sound like it would be wound up quickly. And now it looked like it was a robbery as well.

The other officer was in the workroom and called for Officer Alina, who went over to the door.

"Quickly," Gloria said. "Tell me what happened."

"It looks like Luis was attacked," Zoe said. "I arrived to pick up the artwork this morning and found him unconscious in the workroom. The paramedics noticed some red marks on his neck that they thought were Taser marks. The blue butterfly painting and the Dalí sketch are missing."

Gloria's eyes widened. "Poor Luis. Is he going to be all right?"

"I don't know. He was unconscious when they took him away in the ambulance."

"And the artwork gone, too." Gloria switched to Spanish, and Zoe had the impression that her language was a bit on the colorful side.

Officer Alina returned to the gallery, and Gloria fell silent, giving him an attentive look. He seemed to thaw a bit more.

With Gloria by his side, Officer Alina quickly ran through his questions, and Zoe summarized how she'd found Luis on the floor this morning. Then Officer Alina asked a question with the word Taser in it.

Zoe was beginning to hate that word. Gloria had barely finished asking if Zoe owned one of the devices, when Zoe said, "No, I do not own a Taser. I've never used one. And I did not hurt Luis." Zoe looked directly at Officer Alina. "I want to contact the American Embassy. I've told you everything I know, and you have my hotel information if you need to get in touch with me."

Gloria's eyes flashed Zoe a warning as she translated for Officer Alina. Her "translation" went on for quite a bit, and Zoe thought she was probably modifying the statement—toning it down—but in the end Officer Alina gave a reluctant nod and only said a short sentence before pointing them to the door.

Gloria tucked her hand through Zoe's elbow. "We can leave now. But the police may have more questions for you later."

"What was that last thing he said? His frown was pretty intense."

"You're not to leave Madrid without speaking to the police."

## 22

G loria insisted on taking Zoe to eat lunch after they left the gallery, saying, "You need food and something to drink. And if you don't, I do." Zoe couldn't remember what restaurant they'd gone to or the name of the dish she had. All she knew was that it was fish and that the restaurant was quiet. They'd sat at a booth in the back and rehashed everything that had happened. When they parted outside the restaurant, Gloria promised to call her after she visited Luis in the hospital.

She felt dazed. She hadn't expected to find someone she'd met the day before unconscious. On top of that shock, the fact that the artwork was gone was still sinking in. She returned to the hotel and rescheduled her airline reservations and extended her room reservation at the hotel's business center.

As she rode the elevator up to her room, she thought about how she'd break the news to Thacker about the artwork. This news was definitely something that couldn't be done over the company app. She'd have to call him. She was considering various ways to tell him when she felt someone's gaze on her. She glanced around the elevator and saw a man with a closely cropped Brutus haircut and jug ears watching her. The doors opened and he gestured for her to step out first. As she neared her door, her phone rang with an unidentified number. She wanted to let it go to voicemail but, considering everything that happened within the last few hours, she decided she better answer it.

"¿*Señora* Andrews?" The voice was too deep to be Officer Alina.

"Speaking."

"I am Chief Inspector Munez. I'm investigating the incident at the Cabello gallery." His English barely held a trace of an accent. "I would appreciate it if you could come to my office. I believe we have recovered the artwork that was stolen earlier today."

Zoe had been about to unlock the door to her hotel room with the key card, but she paused. "That's wonderful," she said, stunned. She knew firsthand that the recovery rate for stolen art was extremely low. Thank goodness she hadn't contacted Thacker yet. Much better to call with the news that the art had been stolen but recovered than the news that it was gone.

"I am glad you are pleased."

"My client will be even more pleased than I am."

"That is Mr. Thacker, I understand?"

"Yes, that's right"

"Before you contact him, please come and see the artwork. The other gallery employee is unavailable this afternoon. We need to confirm that what we have is the missing artwork. Mr. Cabello is unable to help us at this point."

"I'll be there as soon as I can." Zoe got the address and returned to the lobby. She asked the doorman to get her a taxi. The taxi driver gave her a second glance when she gave him the address, but he put the car in gear and drove her without another word. Her phone rang again, and she was relieved to see that this time it was Jack. "I'm so glad to hear from you."

He asked, "Are you all right?"

"Yes. There's good news. The police have recovered the artwork." A car cut in front of the taxi, and the driver hit the horn in a sharp blast. "I'm in a taxi on my way to see it, as you can probably hear."

"Is Gloria going with you to the police station?"

"No need. A different officer, a chief inspector, called me. He speaks English fluently."

"I don't like you going by yourself."

"I'm not crazy about the idea either, but I think it would be worse if I didn't go. All they need me to do is identify the painting."

---

Chief Inspector Munez was probably in his mid- to late-fifties and had a tanned face with pockmarked cheeks. His dark hair was going gray at the hairline where it was combed straight back from his forehead, but the ends of his hair, which reached to his collar, were black. He closed the door to the small room where Zoe had been waiting for nearly an hour. "Thank you for coming in."

He carried a box and a folder tucked under one arm. He set the box at one end of the table, then removed the folder, and sat down across the table from Zoe. As he flipped open the thick folder, he took a pair of reading glasses from his pocket. Without another word to Zoe, he skimmed the paperwork. Zoe felt the tension inside her ratchet up a notch. She had that awful feeling you get in a doctor's office when you're waiting for test results. After what seemed to be about a quarter of an hour, he leaned back. "The officers who were on the scene today brought me up to date. I apologize that the interpreter was not there."

"My friend Gloria was able to help out."

"So I understand," Munez said, disapproval in his tone. Then his tone became brisk. "Let's go through it all to make sure I understand exactly what happened." He took off the glasses, threw them down on top of the file, and hooked his elbow over the back of the chair.

Zoe glanced at the box. "I thought I was here to look at the painting and sketch."

"All in good time. Just tell me what happened in your own words."

Zoe pressed down a spurt of irritation. If Officer Alina had brought him up to date, then he had all the information in front of him in the file, but Zoe knew the drill. He wanted to check her answers against what she'd said earlier. "I went to the gallery this morning to pick up—"

"No, start with your arrival in Madrid."

"That's a lot of boring tourist stuff, mostly."

"I love to hear about my beautiful city." He gave her a quick smile that seemed all surface with no sincerity to back it up.

"All right." You asked for it, she thought as she proceeded to detail her movements from the moment she stepped off the plane. She chronicled everything from the rambling city tour with Gloria to her breakfast on the way to the gallery. Then she described how she'd found Luis unconscious and Pilar's arrival. "Pilar called for an ambulance," Zoe said. "The rest, you know."

He picked up his glasses and tapped an earpiece against the file. "So what did Luis say when you spoke to him today?"

"I didn't speak to him today. He was unconscious."

Munez smiled. "Of course. And what prior contact with him did you have before you arrived in Madrid?"

"I called him to set up an appointment. "

"And this was?"

Zoe thought back, working out the day. Traveling always screwed up her sense of time, and she wanted to make sure she didn't give Munez any ammunition to accuse her of lying. She felt she needed to watch her step. While Officer Alina had a straight-forward manner and seemed to only be interested in getting the details down in his notebook, Zoe felt that Munez was carefully examining each word, searching for the slightest variable or incon-sistency. "It would have been Friday."

"And you contacted him because..."

"I learned he had purchased a painting that I was looking for."

He slipped on his glasses and consulted the file. "That would be the butterfly and hummingbird painting by Martin Johnson Heade?"

"Yes, that's correct."

"And the Salvador Dalí?"

"That was a last minute purchase. Gloria saw it and suggested that I mention it to Mr. Thacker. He was interested in it and purchased it as well. I was supposed to pick up both the painting and the sketch this morning."

"Mr. Thacker..." Munez held the glasses by the earpiece and twirled them in the air. "What can you tell me about him?"

"Not a lot. I met him once. He's semi-retired from the company he started. He's a collector, and he's expecting his art to arrive in the U.S. tonight."

"On that topic...while it will be impossible for you to return to the U.S. tonight, I do have good news for you."

Muniz closed the file, put his glasses on top of it, then shoved it out of the way with one hand as he drew the box to him. He took out a plastic bag and set it on the table between them. The glare of the overhead light prevented Zoe from seeing what it was for a moment, but the plastic bag was too small to contain the painting. A sick feeling settled her stomach. Had the painting been cut or damaged? Was it in pieces? She leaned forward and realized she had it all wrong.

"The Dalí sketch." Hearing the disappointment in her own voice, Zoe added quickly, "This is wonderful. Mr. Thacker will be grateful you've found it."

He took another plastic bag from the box and laid it beside the sketch. It was bigger and contained pieces of wood. "Are those..." Zoe pushed at the plastic, "...pieces of the frame?"

"Yes. It was broken—shattered, if you can use that word to describe wood. Completely destroyed."

Munez didn't reach back into the box. Zoe stretched and peered into the box. It was empty. "I don't understand. You said you had recovered the artwork. This is just the Dalí sketch."

"Which is artwork, no? Mr. Thacker was willing to pay quite a bit for the sketch, I understand."

"Yes, of course," Zoe said, but wasn't about to be drawn into a "what is art" discussion. "What about the painting? The one with the blue butterfly and the hummingbird—where is it?"

"Still missing, I'm afraid. Let's return to the sketch." Munez gestured to the larger bag with the bits of wood. "Why was the frame destroyed?"

Anger bubbled inside Zoe. He'd deliberately misled her. His term "artwork" had been intentionally vague, and she had jumped to the conclusion that both the sketch and the painting had been recovered. But it wouldn't do her any good to vent her frustrations. She drew in a deep breath and then said, "I have no idea why someone would do this to the frame."

"Was the frame valuable?"

"As I said, I have no idea. I thought the value was in the sketch, not in the frame—at least that's what I picked up from listening to Gloria and Luis discuss it. Gloria could tell you more, I'm sure. Where did you find it?"

"In the trash a few blocks from the gallery."

"That's impressive detective work," Zoe said grudgingly, thinking of the tangle of busy, twisting streets around the gallery.

Munez pressed a finger against the plastic bag, pushing one of the pieces of wood away from the others. It had a dark spot on it. "The fool who stole it set it on fire before tossing it in the trash, and the smoke drew attention. A business nearby had a fire extinguisher. Because they acted quickly, the fire did not spread over more than the corner of the thick frame. The wrapping paper with the address of the gallery on it had also been discarded. It had been separated from the frame and was not damaged."

"Do you think they burned the painting?" Zoe asked, alarmed as she envisioned the edges of the canvas blackening as flames closed in on those amazing iridescent wings. Surely someone couldn't destroy something so beautiful. But it had happened before. She could only hope that the value of the painting, which she knew was more than the sketch, would ensure it wasn't damaged.

"I have no evidence at this point that indicates that," Munez said.

Zoe pulled at the plastic around the sketch. Except for a bent corner, it had escaped damage. "Why steal the sketch only to destroy it?"

Munez didn't answer. Instead, he picked up both plastic bags. "I will let you know if we have further information about the painting." He put them in the box and closed the flaps. "Now, if you'll come with me, we need your prints. Then you're free to carry on with your day."

"You want my fingerprints?"

"For elimination purposes only."

Zoe noticed the man with close-cropped hair and jug ears on her way back to the hotel.

Since she had to wait another hour to have her fingerprints taken, it was after six when Zoe left the police station, and Madrid was waking up from its siesta. Not wanting to be cooped up in a taxi, and with questions spinning through her mind, Zoe had decided the long walk back to the hotel was exactly what she needed.

She had paused to check her map when the man caught her eye, his gaze focused on her. The second he realized she'd noticed him, he looked away. The quick, jerky shift of his gaze worried her. If you caught someone staring, most people at least acknowledged the social faux pas with a brief smile or faint nod. He focused on a street sign and tugged at the lobe of his oversized ear.

Hadn't she seen him in the elevator at the hotel this afternoon? She glanced back. Yes, it was the same guy. He wore a blue dress shirt with the cuffs rolled up and dark pants. His Brutus-style haircut was combed down over his forehead. The short haircut only emphasized his large ears. It was odd that their paths had crossed again in a city the size of Madrid. If she'd been hitting the tourist sites, it might be understandable, but she was returning from a police station.

She walked on, slowing at the next corner to look at the map again. A tilt of her head showed the man a few paces behind her on the other side of the street. He was walking at a leisurely pace, checking his phone.

Zoe's phone rang, and she answered it before crossing the street.

"Zoe?" Thacker's voice reverberated over the line. "What the hell is going on out there?"

"I'm not sure. Let me bring you up—"

"I'm away for a couple of hours, and I come back and hear the painting's stolen? You'd think *buying* the painting would be the simple part. Once you found the damn thing, bringing it back should be easy."

Zoe let him vent as she made her way down the curving cobblestone street, which was lined on both sides with tall apartment buildings. She glanced over her shoulder a few times—discreetly, the way Jack had taught her. She found a napkin in her pocket and half turned back to toss it in a trashcan. A few steps later she used the large window of a store to check the area across the street. Both times, she saw the man with the prominent ears as he took the same path she did, but on the opposite side of the street, his movements echoing hers. That couldn't be a coincidence, could it?

Thacker's angry words tapered off, and Zoe said, "Let me tell you what I know." She increased her pace as she summarized everything that had happened. She darted to the right down a short street, then turned left at the next narrow street. As she hurried along she noticed the street was getting more crowded. Some people strolled and looked like tourists, but others seemed to be natives of Madrid with their wheeled shopping carts and briefcases.

Zoe spotted an arcade entrance that people were filtering toward, the *Plaza Mayor*. Of course the pedestrian traffic was thicker around the plaza. "I do have good news," Zoe said. "I've just come from a meeting with a chief inspector." Zoe was sure that Munez would characterize their meeting in another way—an interview with a suspect, most likely—but Zoe liked the word "meeting" much better.

"The Dalí sketch has been found," she continued. "I've seen it. The sketch itself is undamaged, as far as I can tell. The frame...well, it's not in such good shape."

Thacker muttered an obscenity and said that he couldn't care less about the frame. Zoe hustled on, skimming around the edge of the plaza. A quick glance over her shoulder showed the man, Jug Ears, as she was beginning to think of him, had followed her into the plaza, but he lingered at the entrance.

Maybe she was being paranoid. The plaza was a huge pedestrian crossroad. Perhaps it wasn't so strange that Jug Ears had also entered the plaza after her. Perhaps his path was simply the same as Zoe's, and it was a coincidence.

"So you have the sketch in your possession?" Thacker asked, and Zoe noticed that his typical speech pattern, which was usually layered with pauses, silent beats, and the emphasis of certain words, had disappeared. He was focused and all-business. The mischievous undertone of teasing that had come through when she met him in Vail had evaporated from his manner.

Zoe drew in a breath and braced herself for a renewed burst of anger from him. "It's part of a police investigation, and Chief Inspector Munez says that it will be released when the investigation is complete." Another string of obscenities flowed through the phone, but Zoe barely listened as she moved to a restaurant's menu board and watched Jug Ears out of the corner of her eye.

He took a few steps in the same direction then paused to look at a display of paintings.

Zoe focused on the conversation as Thacker said, "I'll take care of getting the sketch released." His voice had a weary why-do-I-have-to-do-everything quality. "I'll make a few calls. You should be able to bring it home in a day or two. What about the painting?"

"No sign of it, so far. I'll call Gloria tonight. She said she would visit Luis in the hospital to check on him. Hopefully, he'll be awake, and he might be able to tell us something about who took it or what happened."

"Keep me updated." The line went dead.

"Well, goodbye to you too," Zoe muttered after checking to make sure the call had disconnected. Gloria had been right about Thacker's personality. When things were going well, he had a playful and accommodating nature, but when things didn't go his way, he could be quite ugly.

A couple hovered at Zoe's shoulder, trying to read the menu so she moved on. She browsed the windows of a few shops, then slipped inside a sombrero store. She watched Jug Ears through the store's front window as he meandered along in her wake, then paused at the same restaurant menu display that Zoe had studied.

Who was this guy? Had Munez sent someone to follow her? Had the police been keeping an eye on her before Munez called her? Even if he was a police officer—which was better than some other scenarios that she could come up with—she didn't like it. Her instinct was to slip away. No matter who the guy was, she didn't want someone following her.

Zoe admired some hats near the window and kept an eye on him. He checked his watch a few times, but didn't seem to be interested in the sombrero shop. Zoe purchased a straw hat with a wide brim and told the woman that she wanted to wear it out of the store. The woman removed it from a large bag and clipped the tag, then offered her the large empty bag. Figuring it would add another layer to her disguise, Zoe took the empty bag.

Zoe twisted her bright hair into a knot, and shoved the hat over it. She used the mirror positioned on the counter to check and make sure all her hair was tucked up under the hat, then timed her exit from the shop so that she joined a group of three women as they left.

Zoe saw Jug Ears still lingered beside the restaurant menu. She didn't glance over her shoulder as she kept pace with the three chattering women. She stayed on the far side of the group, making sure they were between her and Jug Ears. The women were making for one of the arcaded passageways on the far side of the plaza. Zoe stayed with them until they left the plaza.

She turned down the first street that she came to, then slipped into the nearest shop. This one was selling T-shirts, key chains, and shot glasses, all with images of bulls, matadors, and the Madrid skyline. Zoe browsed the two crowded aisles, keeping an eye on the street. When Jug Ears didn't appear, she left the store.

A quick glance up and down the street showed that Jug Ears had not followed her. The road was less crowded than the plaza, and it was easy to see that he wasn't lurking. Zoe set off again at a brisk pace, working her way to the *Puerta del Sol*, which was filling up with the evening crowd, but she didn't stop.

She entered the hotel and breathed a sigh of relief, but she waited until she was in the elevator before she took off the hat and shook out her hair. When Zoe inserted her key card into the lock on the door of her hotel room, a small red light blinked at her. The handle wouldn't move.

"Typical, for today," Zoe said to herself and returned to the elevator.

As she walked across the lobby, she heard her name over the sound of the splash of the lobby fountain.

"Over here," the voice called again, and Zoe saw Gloria waving to her. She was near the entrance to the hotel restaurant with her daughter at her side. As Zoe crossed the lobby to her, Gloria leaned down and said something to her daughter, who shot by Zoe on her way to the fountain.

"I called you earlier but you didn't answer so I left you a message," Gloria said.

"I must've missed it. Sorry about that," she said. "How is Luis? Did you get a chance to go see him?"

"Not so good. He did wake up, but he's in and out of consciousness, and can't remember a thing about what happened. The doctor says that's common, and his memory will probably come back later."

"I'm glad he's doing better, but that doesn't help us figure out what happened. I had a call from the police this afternoon. Did Chief Inspector Munez contact you, too?"

"No."

"I'm sure it won't be long." Zoe told her about the Dalí sketch and her chat with Munez.

"That is amazing. I'm so glad they found—Sophia," Gloria called, "throw your coin and come back." Gloria made a tossing motion with her hand. Sophia, who had been examining the fountain from every angle, squared her shoulders and tossed the coin. It landed on the top tier with a plop, and Sophia raced back to Gloria's side, chattering in Spanish.

Gloria murmured to her, *un momento*, and turned back to Zoe. "Have you spoken to Thacker?" She brushed Sophia's hair off her forehead as she spoke, a soothing gesture to calm the girl who was clearly impatient to either throw another coin or move on.

"Just now. He's not happy."

She grimaced. "You can't blame him. Two pieces of art stolen before he has even seen them."

Sophia tugged Gloria's arm, her voice pleading as she asked a question. Gloria replied with a firm negative then rolled her eyes at Zoe over Sophia's head. "She just ate two plates of *tapas*, and says she's still hungry. More like *aburrida*, I'd say." Gloria smiled at Sophia. Sophia grinned back at her and swung her arms back and forth.

"I remember that word," Zoe said. "It means bored, doesn't it?"

"Yes, that's right," Gloria said. "I should go. I'll call you if anything changes."

Zoe said goodbye and went back around the fountain, threading her way through the chairs and couches scattered around the lobby, passing the business center on her way to the front desk. She was sure the snafu with the key card was because of the change in her hotel reservation.

She had almost reached the front desk when she saw a man in a blue shirt with short dark hair and protruding ears. A large tour group streamed into the lobby, cutting off her view. They gathered around their pile of luggage with bright yellow tags. She slowed her pace as she moved through the tour group, scanning the lobby, but she didn't see the man again.

Could it have been Jug Ears? Was she just hyper-aware of men with short hair and conspicuous ears? She wished she'd seen his face, but even though she spent a few more minutes looking around, she didn't see him again.

At the front desk, Zoe explained the situation to the clerk, a middle-aged man with a narrow face and a mustache, who spoke perfect English.

"I apologize, *Señora* Andrews. We have an electrical outage in several rooms on the seventh floor, and your room is affected. We've arranged to move you to a room a short distance away, just across the hall and down a few doors. Will this be acceptable?"

"That's fine. Have you already moved my things?"

"No. I will help you." He picked up two key cards.

"It's fine," Zoe said. "If you'll just give me a key card that will unlock the door to my original room I can handle it myself."

"But there is no light in your room. It is a safety issue. I apologize for the inconvenience. We also have a package for you. Would you like to take that with you now?"

"A package?"

"Yes, it came in this morning." He consulted the monitor in front of him. "We left a message on your room phone this morning to let you know."

"I haven't been in my room all day. I'll take the package now," she said.

He disappeared through the door behind the counter then returned, carrying a rectangular package wrapped in brown paper. "Here you are."

Zoe took the package and stood motionless. Her heart thumping, she flipped it over and looked at the back. A small sticker with the name Cabello Gallery was affixed to the paper.

## 24

"Is there a problem?"

Zoe's head snapped up. "No," she said to the desk clerk. "Not at all. Who brought this, do you know?"

"Let's see..." The man looked at the monitor. "A courier brought it this morning about ten. No note of the name or the company that delivered it, though."

"Okay. Thank you." Zoe stood for a moment, her hands suddenly sweaty as she tried to work out what had happened. For some reason Luis must have sent the painting by courier. Why would he have done that without notifying her? She had told Luis she would pick up the painting at the gallery. Had his plans changed? Had he forgotten? Did someone else from the gallery send it without Luis knowing? She fought off the impulse to rip into the paper. She wanted to be alone when she opened the package, and she couldn't do that until she was in her new hotel room. If it really was the painting, then she'd decide what to do with it.

The desk clerk cleared his throat and transferred the flashlight from one hand to another. "Sorry. I'm ready." Zoe pressed the package close to her chest and followed him to the elevator.

He apologized again for the inconvenience as he used the new key card to open Zoe's hotel room door.

"Believe me," Zoe said, "It's the least of my worries today."

The room was dim but not completely dark. The desk clerk entered first, using the flashlight. As soon as Zoe crossed the threshold she caught a whiff of a distinctive aroma. She sniffed and recognized the faint scent was cigarette smoke. The desk clerk didn't seem to notice. The curtains were partially closed, and he had moved across the room to pull them open, letting in the evening sun.

A bright red light blinked on the room phone. "Let me check that message," Zoe said, still holding the package.

She had two messages. The first was from Luis. "Zoe, I am sorry, but I have had a change in plans. I have to close the gallery this morning—another urgent appointment—and I will not be here when you arrived to pick up the packages. I'm sending them by messenger to the hotel—" He muttered something in Spanish, his tone irritated, then he switched back to English, "I must apologize a second time. I just noticed that the sketch was not packed properly."

He broke off again, and Zoe heard a few muffled words of Spanish, then his voice came back on the line. "The courier has arrived. I will send the painting to you now, repack the sketch the correct way, and then call for another courier to pick it up. Hopefully, this message will catch you before you leave your hotel. I do not have your mobile number with me, or I would contact you that way. Again, I apologize for the inconvenience, and thank you for your patience with this change of plan."

The second message was the desk saying that a package had arrived for her.

"Can the messages be forwarded to my new room?" Zoe asked as she tightened her one-handed grip on the package, which must contain the blue butterfly painting. Luis must have been attacked after he sent the painting off, but before he could call for a second courier for the Dalí sketch.

The desk clerk said, "Of course." Zoe saved the messages, then handed the receiver to him. He made a call, spoke to someone briefly, then said, "It's done. They will be on the phone in your new room. May I help you pack?"

"No, it will only take a second. I don't have much." Zoe carefully set down the package on the bed. She was itching to open it, but wasn't about to do that until she was safely locked away alone in her new hotel room. Zoe's suitcase sat on the luggage rack, the lid tossed back as she'd left it. She wasn't an extremely neat person, but she did remember that she'd decided the day was warm enough that she wouldn't need to bring her black sweater to the gallery. She'd tossed it on top of the stack of clothes in her suitcase before she went out the door. Now the sweater was squished to the side under her white shirt.

Before she bundled her clothes into the suitcase, Zoe paused, her gaze running over the room. The desk clerk was twitching the bed cover straight, smoothing out several wrinkles.

It hadn't looked like that this morning when Zoe left the room. The maid had arrived early, and Zoe had gone down to get a coffee while the maid cleaned the room. Zoe had returned to the room before she headed out to eat breakfast on the way to the gallery. When she left the room, the bed didn't have a single ridge or furrow. Someone had been in her room, and she didn't think it was one of the hotel staff.

It only took Zoe a minute to rearrange the clothes so they fit more neatly in the suitcase. She placed the package on top of the clothes then zipped the suitcase. "Now I only have my things in the bath."

Zoe rolled the suitcase into the bathroom with her. She wasn't about to leave the package unattended in the hotel room, even though the desk clerk looked nice. At this point, Zoe wasn't letting it out of her sight. Because the bathroom didn't have any windows, it was pitch black. The flashlight came in handy as Zoe tossed her makeup, hair clips, and toothbrush into her small flowered bag. "Okay, that's all."

The desk clerk insisted on checking the closet and every drawer in the dresser before leading her down the hall. He opened the door to her new room and flipped on the lights, demonstrating that they worked in this room. He insisted on doing a quick inspection of the room, checking that the temperature was acceptable to Zoe and demonstrating how the heated towel rack worked. Zoe declined his offer to help her unpack and hustled him out of the room.

She threw the deadbolt, unzipped her suitcase, and removed the package. She held it in her hands a moment, studying the brown wrapper.

She knew she should call Chief Inspector Munez, but he had manipulated her earlier today, letting her think that he had recovered both pieces of artwork when he only had the sketch and a mangled frame. She wasn't feeling too charitable toward him.

Once she called him, the package would be sealed away in a plastic bag. She wouldn't get to examine it closely—probably not even touch it. She debated with herself for about two seconds, then ran her finger under the tape at the edge of one of the seams. The painting wasn't even stolen property—not really. It had only been misplaced. They had assumed the thief had taken both pieces of art, but this package had been delivered to her here at the hotel.

As the paper and layers of padding fell away, she sucked in a breath. There was something almost magical about art. It stopped you in your tracks. Even in the midst of the craziness of this day and everything that was going on, Zoe had to take a moment to appreciate the shining wings on the blue butterfly and the blur of the hummingbird's wings. It was indeed the missing blue butterfly painting—still in its ugly metal frame too—completely unharmed.

## 25

"What is it about you that's so interesting?" Zoe murmured as she paced back and forth in front of the dresser where she'd propped up the blue butterfly painting.

The whiff of cigarette smoke along with her mussed suitcase and the rumpled bed in her former hotel room made her think that she wasn't paranoid. Jug Ears *had* been following her today, and it was probably a good assumption that he'd searched her room. It seemed more and more likely that Jug Ears wasn't with the police. With the painting sitting in the room behind the hotel reception desk, it had been safe, but he must have assumed that either she had it with her or that she would lead him to it.

That train of thought was worrying in its own way. Had he been following her since she arrived in Madrid but she'd only noticed him in the elevator today? Zoe shook off those thoughts. She was safely locked in her new hotel room. She couldn't answer any questions about Jug Ears right now, but she could focus on the painting.

Zoe looked over the paperwork that came with the painting again. She'd already glanced through it once. The packaging contained a packing slip with a list of contents, a bill of sale from the Cabello Gallery, and a slim unsealed envelope with the original bill of sale from 1866. Everything with the documents appeared to be in order. The bill of sale showed the sales price, which made Zoe's eyebrows fly upward, but she supposed that for someone like Thacker the amount, which seemed exorbitant to her, was only pocket change.

Gloria had authenticated the painting, declaring it was a genuine Martin Johnson Heade. Could she have been wrong? Was there something else about the painting itself that she had missed? Perhaps there was another painting underneath? Was that why Jug Ears was so interested in her?

Zoe dropped the paperwork on the bed and picked up the painting, gazing intently at it from every angle. Gloria said she'd examined it with ultraviolet light, which didn't show anything unexpected, but she hadn't x-rayed the painting or performed any other tests. Thacker hadn't wanted her to.

Did Thacker know that there was something about this painting that made it so valuable that he didn't care about—or need—the high-tech tests? He'd said he didn't want the scientific reports and didn't rely on them, but maybe he knew something else about the painting. Was he pursuing it with a collector's passion or was there more at work?

If there was something underneath the painting, it might explain his insistence on tracking it down and purchasing it without a full battery of authentication tests. Zoe sighed. Without some advanced technology she could stare at the painting all day long and never know what was under the top layer of paint....unless there was some telltale pigment of a completely different color on the edge of the stretcher that she could see with the naked eye.

It wouldn't be conclusive, of course, even if she did find something like that. Zoe had learned that painters often reused canvases, so it might not mean anything except that Martin Johnson Heade recycled his materials, but she couldn't think of anything else to do.

"Let's just take a quick peek," Zoe murmured. She went to the bathroom, got one of the large white towels, and spread it on the desk. She flipped the painting over and carefully removed the clips that held the metal frame in place. Zoe had only looked at the edge of the painting briefly when Gloria examined it, but now she figured she had time. She could go over the whole canvas millimeter by millimeter.

The metal frame separated into four pieces. Three of the pieces came away easily, but one stuck. Zoe frowned. She had watched Gloria take the frame apart, and she hadn't had any trouble with it.

Zoe took a deep breath—the last thing she wanted was to damage the painting—and carefully applied more force as she pulled. As the frame piece came away in her hand, a small plastic tube tumbled out of the hollow space in the frame. It bounced onto the white towel. It was a tube of lip balm.

"Well no wonder it was stuck," Zoe said, as she examined the thick piece of tape that had held the lip balm in place. An edge of the tape must have folded back and been caught on the canvas, which made it hard to remove the metal frame.

She picked up the lip balm and removed the cap. Instead of a waxy column of ointment, a rectangular piece of metal protruded from the tube. Zoe twisted it around. It looked like the exterior portion of a flash drive, the part that plugs into a computer port. The inside of the tube had been filled with some sort of substance that held the rest of the flash drive securely in place.

As she pulled the tape off the outside of the tube, she kicked herself for not bringing her laptop. She only had her phone and a small computer tablet that didn't have any ports for a flash drive, so she had no way to see what was on the device, unless she went down to the business center—and she wasn't leaving her hotel room right now. Jug Ears might have returned. He could be camped out in the lobby, waiting for her. Jack would have his laptop. He usually traveled with it, when he went to a business meeting, so she was almost sure he would have his computer.

She checked her watch. Jack's flight should have landed, so it wouldn't be that long before he arrived. She'd texted him her hotel information, and he'd said he would meet her here.

She felt like a kid looking at wrapped Christmas presents weeks before the holiday. She hated waiting to open gifts, and she had that same itch to know what was on the flash drive. Reluctantly, she recapped the lip balm and put it down on the towel then returned her attention to the painting.

She examined every section of the canvas where it had been pulled around the wooden stretcher. She went slowly and methodically, but she didn't see a trace of a paint color that wasn't on the surface of the canvas.

A sharp knock at her door startled Zoe, and she nearly dropped the painting.

"Room service," a voice called in English, but with a Spanish accent.

A flare of guilt traced through her as she looked at the dismantled frame scattered over the towel. She put the painting down and flipped the edge of the towel up to cover the painting and the tube of lip balm.

"There must be a mistake," she called as she went to the door. "I didn't order anything." She looked through the peephole and sucked in a breath. It was Jug Ears. The glass in the peephole distorted his face, enlarging the dome of his head and one ear to Dumbo-like proportions. He held a silver ice bucket containing a green bottle pressed against the burgundy blazer he wore. It looked similar to the blazer uniform that the desk clerks wore, but instead of a white shirt, he had on the blue shirt she'd seen him wearing earlier.

He glanced at the elevator. "It's complimentary. A bottle of champagne for you."

"Thank you, but I don't want it. You must have the wrong room."

He leaned close to the peephole, which magnified one eye and his nose like a fun house mirror. "No, it is for you...because of the inconvenience of the room change."

"Thanks, but no."

He stepped back, and Zoe got a glimpse of a white key card that dangled from a cord around his neck. Did he have a passkey to the room? Zoe knew she'd put on the safety lock, but she felt it again, making sure it was pushed into place.

"We insist. It is our gift."

"But...I..." Zoe reached for an explanation of why she wouldn't accept free champagne. "I...uh...I don't drink."

That stopped him. "You don't drink?" His tone said that was an incomprehensible concept.

"Yes," Zoe said firmly. "No alcohol. Just give it to someone else."

They were dancing back and forth. He was pretending to be a hotel employee, and she was pretending to not recognize him. If she could convince him to go away that would be best. Once they shifted away from the pretense, things could go downhill quickly.

He shook his head. "I'm required to deliver it to you." He removed the cord with the key card from around his neck.

No more pretending. He was coming in the room. "I'm calling the front desk right now," Zoe said, "and telling them that you're harassing me."

The faint ding of the elevator arriving on the floor sounded. He darted a quick glance over his shoulder. Zoe raised her voice. "And that a man is impersonating a hotel employee and trying to get into my room."

Jug Ears stepped hurriedly away from her door. Zoe shifted to the side and caught a glimpse of him as he gave a nod to a group of people coming down the hall. A bellboy trudged by first, pushing a luggage trolley loaded with suitcases and tote bags with the distinctive yellow logo of the tour group Zoe had seen in the lobby. A middle-aged couple followed on the bellboy's heels.

She waited, leaning against the door, her eye to the peephole until the group passed. The elevator chimed again and another luggage cart with more yellow tags lumbered into view. Jug Ears eased his way toward the elevator, nodding and smiling as people passed him. The distant metallic whir of doors unlocking, and the chatter of couples as they walked down the hall, sounded wonderful to Zoe.

She had a few seconds before the hallway cleared. Zoe spun away from the door and reassembled the frame around the painting with shaking fingers. She felt like a sitting duck in the hotel room. If

Jug Ears had some sort of passkey, could he get into the hotel room, even if she had the safety lock on? She didn't know, and she wasn't going to wait around to find out. She didn't doubt that he would be back after the tour group were in their rooms. He obviously had some sort of connection at the hotel. He'd known her new room number and seemed to have a passkey.

Her phone buzzed with a text. It was from Jack. *I'm off the plane. Should arrive at the hotel in 30 minutes.*

Zoe paused, her breathing coming quickly from the stress of thinking Jug Ears was about to come into her room. She thought for a moment, then texted back. *Change of plan. Meet me at the Mercado De San Miguel.*

Zoe wrapped the packing paper with its layers of padding in place around the painting, then she covered the whole thing in the hotel towel and shoved it in the bottom of the large shopping bag that she had gotten earlier in the day when she bought her hat.

Her instincts told her to get out of the hotel, and she was going to do it as stealthily as possible. She took a change of clothes and added them to the shopping bag. She put the lip balm tube in the bag with her makeup. She zipped the flowered bag closed and tucked it into the shopping bag.

She changed into a pair of jeans and a black shirt with a scoop neck. Her last maneuver was to scrape her hair into a tight bun on top of her head. She positioned the hat over her hair, tilting the brim down so that it covered most of her face. She slipped her messenger bag over her shoulder and picked up the shopping bag. The brim of her hat bumped against the door as she checked the peephole, but she was able to get close enough to see that there was still one luggage cart parked outside a door on her side of the hall. Another trundled by and she slipped out, following a pair of tourists as they trailed behind a bellboy.

She took the stairs down and emerged into the lobby near the front desk. The open lobby area stretched between her and the central fountain. The bank of elevators stood on the other side of the fountain. The splash of the fountain, the chime of the elevators, and the murmur of conversation—all so normal—steadied Zoe.

She surveyed the lobby as she walked briskly to the main door. Her steps faltered when she saw Jug Ears sitting in one of the over-sized club chairs turned three-quarters away from her. He'd removed the hotel blazer. He had a view of both the elevators and the front doors. An elevator chimed. He looked up from his phone, studied the family that poured out, then went back to his phone.

Zoe reversed course and went into the hotel's restaurant, which kept her from crossing Jug Ear's line of sight. When the maître d' greeted her, she motioned to the patio. "I'm meeting someone."

She breezed by him, striding through the tables to the far side of the restaurant, which had outdoor dining on the sidewalk in front of the hotel. She stepped out into the warm night. The patio was alive with the chatter of conversation, clinks of silverware, and the movement of waiters.

She darted through the tables until she reached the edge of the patio, where a row of topiaries in stone urns shielded tables from the foot traffic on the street. "So sorry," Zoe said to the startled couple dining near the edge of the patio as she squeezed between two of the potted plants. She glanced back once and saw their startled faces staring after her.

## 26

The *mercado* glowed, lighting up the cobblestoned street as crowds bustled in and out of the wrought-iron and glass building. Zoe squeezed inside, but it was so packed that she had to take off her hat because she kept bumping into people with the brim. She paused to stuff it in the shopping bag then continued to work her way through the press of people. She'd asked Jack to meet her at the market because she thought it would be an ideal place to lose Jug Ears, if he managed to follow her from the hotel. Fortunately, she hadn't seen him as she made her way to the market, but she was still glad that it was so incredibly jam-packed. She inched her way around a group of boisterous men that she thought must be out for a bachelor party celebration. One of the guys was wearing a dress over his shirt and slacks and had a short veil hanging from the back of his head.

If anything, the press of people around her made her feel more secure. She'd much rather be in the overcrowded market than on a deserted street. She moved with baby steps to the café where Jack was waiting. She'd received a text from him a few minutes ago telling her where he was in the market.

When she reached the café area, she spotted Jack's broad shoulders and dark hair. He was at one of the standing tables, his rolling suitcase parked beside him, and he had two plates on the table in front of him. He saw Zoe and stepped away from the table. She kissed him, and then pressed her face into his shoulder, giving him a tight hug and breathing in the scent of laundry soap and his citrus shaving cream.

He asked, "Are you okay?"

She leaned against his solid chest a moment more, enjoying the feeling of his arms around her. "No, but things are better now that you're here." She stepped back. "I have so much to tell you."

Zoe tucked her shopping bag next to his suitcase, and he pushed a plate with olives, cheese, and croquettes so that it was positioned between them. "So, bring me up-to-date. How did it go with the police?"

"Before I start, first check and see if there's a man with a Brutus haircut—short with the hair combed down onto the forehead—anywhere in the crowd behind me. He's wearing a blue shirt and has jug ears."

Jack's expression didn't change, but Zoe could sense a serious-ness settle over him. He was always an observant person, but he had switched to his hyper-aware mode. She popped an olive in her mouth while Jack discreetly surveyed the crowd behind her.

"No, I don't see anyone like that, but it's pretty crowded in here. He could be lingering at one of the exits." He raised an eyebrow at her. "You were followed?"

"Not from the hotel, I don't think, but I was earlier. It was when I left the interview with Chief Inspector Munez this afternoon." Zoe described how she had lost the man in the *Plaza Mayor*. "He might have been following me all day—I'm not sure. I didn't notice anyone. I'm not quite as good at picking up on things like that as you are. I thought it might be a coincidence or," she lifted a shoul-der, "maybe I was imagining things. But then I could tell someone had been in my hotel room, and I immediately thought of the guy who was following me—Jug Ears, as I've been thinking of him. I had to switch rooms because the electricity went out, which made me feel better. I thought whoever had been in my room wouldn't know I'd moved—but Jug Ears showed up later at my new room and tried to talk his way in."

"So it definitely wasn't your imagination." Jack ran his gaze over the crowd again. "Do you think he took the paintings?"

"Possibly, but there's more to that story, too." Zoe recapped her meeting with Munez, describing how it had only been the Dalí sketch that had been recovered with the frame destroyed, and then she told him about the package waiting for her at the reception desk. "So I took the package upstairs." Zoe speared a square of cheese. "It was the blue butterfly painting."

Jack smiled. "I know that was a relief for you."

"Yes, I was thrilled to see it. I know Thacker will be as well. I haven't called him, though. And I haven't contacted Munez either." Zoe described the phone message from Luis about sending the painting to the hotel and the delay with the sketch while he repackaged it. "I think whoever took the sketch didn't realize the painting was already gone and stole the sketch, thinking it was the blue butterfly painting."

"Could be," Jack said.

"I thought that there might be something about the painting that was...off, so I took apart the metal frame to examine the sides of the canvas, but when I did that, I found a flash drive inside a modified tube of lip balm."

Jack paused, olive half way to his mouth, and gave her a long look.

Zoe shook her head. "No, it wasn't there when Gloria examined the painting at the gallery—at least, it wasn't there when she took the frame apart to examine the sides of the painting. I was with her when she did that."

"What about when she reassembled it?"

"I didn't see her do that. But I can't imagine why she would hide something in the frame."

"Money or blackmail, to name just two reasons."

"You have such faith in humanity."

Jack shrugged. "It's true."

"I know, but..." Zoe shook her head, thinking of the glamorous, confident image Gloria projected. "She just doesn't seem the sort to be involved in something underhanded like that. Maybe I'm wrong. Maybe I'm letting the fact that she came to my rescue and interpreted for me with the police color my view of her. But she did take the time to walk around Madrid and give me a tour. She seemed to enjoy showing off the city to me."

"I'm not saying she put the flash drive in the frame." Jack leaned forward, his arms crossed on the table. Zoe could tell he was already ticking through possible scenarios. "But she is a possibility," he said. "It sounds like the flash drive had to have been placed in the frame between when Gloria examined the painting and when it was sent to the hotel the next morning—unless someone at the hotel tampered with it."

"Let's not go there." Zoe grimaced. "Do you know how many unknown variables that adds to the equation? The whole front desk staff to begin with, and I have no idea how big a group of people that is. Let's take that option off the table, for now."

"Okay. Since it sounds like Luis's decision to send the painting by messenger to the front desk was a last-minute thing, let's go first with the assumption that the person who could have tampered with it was someone who had access to it in the gallery. That must be a shorter list."

Zoe put a piece of croquette back on the plate, her appetite fading. "Besides Gloria, there's only Luis and Pilar. Gloria and I ate lunch together after she interpreted for me with the police. Gloria said the police officer questioned Pilar about who had keys to the gallery. Pilar works there part-time and doesn't have a key. Luis is the only one with a key."

"Pilar could have gotten Luis's key and made a copy," Jack said as his gaze swept around the market then came back to Zoe. "Unless someone got in. Was there any evidence of a break-in?"

"No, and the police checked the place over pretty thoroughly after they took Luis away in the ambulance. The door hadn't been forced or broken open, and nothing else had been disturbed in the gallery. They had Pilar check everything. The only thing that she could find that was missing was the artwork—the sketch and the painting."

"So what do you think is on the flash drive?" Jack asked Zoe.

"I have no idea." Zoe glanced down at the shopping bag. "I brought it with me along with a couple of extra things. I didn't feel comfortable staying at the hotel."

Jack nodded. "Good call."

"I hope you brought your laptop."

"Never leave home without it."

"Good. Then let's see what's on the flash drive."

## 27

The stairs creaked under their footsteps as Zoe and Jack climbed to the top floor of the small hotel where they'd taken a room. Jack used an old-fashioned key with a huge tassel attached to it to unlock the door, and Zoe followed him into the no-frills room. It was quite a step down from the luxury of the Hotel Premier.

No thousand-count sheets on the bed here. Two single beds had been pushed together to form a make-shift queen-size bed, but from the divot in the covering, it was clear the bed sagged in the middle. A dresser filled the wall opposite the bed. The only other piece of furniture was a battered desk that sat under a television mounted on the wall. The room did have a connecting bathroom with two thin towels about the size of Zoe's kitchen towels.

When they left the *mercado*, Zoe and Jack had taken a rambling route through the streets of Madrid, keeping an eye out for anyone who might shadow their steps. After strolling for about half an hour without a sign of anyone behind them, they stopped at a small hotel tucked away on a quiet street several blocks away from the royal palace. The hotel didn't have an actual lobby downstairs, only a small tiled entranceway with a dusty plastic plant and a window set in one wall where the night clerk had dispensed the old-fashioned key and taken their passport details.

Jack closed the curtains over the window that looked out onto a tiny square. "It's not quite in the same league as the Hotel Premier. More like one-star instead of five."

"Just what I was thinking, but it does have one big bonus—no Jug Ears hanging out in the lobby." Zoe dropped the shopping bag along with her messenger bag on the bed.

Jack pulled out his laptop, and Zoe retrieved the lip balm from her flowered makeup case and removed the cap. Jack inserted the drive in one of the ports on his computer. He clicked away on the keyboard. "First, let's scan this for viruses." After a few minutes, the program ended, and Jack said, "It looks okay."

He angled the screen so they could both see it and selected the external drive. He scrolled through the list that popped up. "Looks like about twenty files."

The filenames were strings of numbers and letters that didn't make any sense to Zoe. "Too bad they're not named with something we can understand," Zoe said as Jack clicked on the first file.

The screen filled with a document. Zoe stared at the text for a bit. "I can't read it. Can you figure it out? Is it code?"

"Yes, it's definitely code." Jack clicked through the various documents, taking a quick look at each one. "But not all of the files are programming code."

"That one looks like a manual of some sort," Zoe said. "I can actually understand some of the words." The page listed commands in an orderly fashion, but also contained strings of words and letters that Zoe couldn't decipher.

Jack clicked back and forth between a few of the documents. A stillness went over him.

"What is it?" Zoe asked.

"Give me a minute," Jack said. "Let me look again." He went back to the documents, scrolling and reading, then he stood and walked around the room, his hand over his mouth.

Zoe wanted to hop up and demand he tell her what he was

thinking, but the room was too small for two people to be pacing, and Zoe had learned that Jack liked to work out his thoughts before he spoke. She always liked to talk things through, but Jack was the opposite.

Finally, he turned to her and dropped his hand. "If that's what I think it is, then..." He shook his head and waved a hand at the computer. "That's some scary stuff."

"What do you think it is?"

"A zero-day."

"Your tone is ominous, but I don't know what that means."

"It's a vulnerability in software. The reason it's called a zero-day is because the flaw has been there from the moment the software was released. The developers weren't aware of it, and so every copy of the software contains the vulnerability. It's a gap in the software that hackers can exploit to get access to all sorts of stuff—computers, phones, routers, and even televisions."

"So you're saying it's a hack," Zoe said. "All these files are instructions and code to...exploit the vulnerability, as you phrased it."

"Yes, and it's worth a lot of money, if it's what I think it is."

It took a lot to ruffle Jack, and he truly looked shaken up. The tension she'd felt all day increased, settling into a heavy knot in her stomach. "How much do you think?"

"If it's what I think it is...then we're talking millions."

Zoe looked at the lip balm tube, which stuck out from the computer port. It looked like something you'd buy at a novelty shop, a gimmick. It was hard to imagine that it could be worth so much. "I guess that explains why the sketch was stolen, and why Jug Ears followed me around Madrid. He must be after the info on the flash drive. If you're right about it being a—um—zero-day thing —then it's worth a whole lot more than a painting by Martin Johnson Heade—even an undiscovered one."

Jack said, "Zero-days are big business. Remember that hacking competition I told you about at the conference? The money the winner of that competition got would be chump change compared to what a hacker could get for it on the open market. And that wasn't a zero-day hack."

"Open market?"

"Black market—or, technically gray market—would be a better term. All sorts of groups will pay for that type of information—criminal gangs, legitimate businesses, and even governments. In fact, governments are the number one client for these zero-day hacks."

"Clients?" Zoe said. "That makes the whole thing sound kind of corporate."

"Some of the interested parties are definitely corporate. Some businesses search out these vulnerabilities and then sell them to corporations and governments."

"You don't mean legitimate, publicly-known companies?" Zoe couldn't keep the skepticism out of her voice.

"Yes, I do. Some of them even have venture capital funding."

"That's amazing."

"And lucrative. But we don't know if that's what we have for sure." Jack's frowning gaze went back to the computer screen. "I'm still learning about all this stuff. We need an expert."

"Fortunately, we know someone like that."

---

Zoe pounced on the phone when it rang. Carla had not been in when Zoe called, and Zoe had to leave her a message, which left her feeling irritated and worried. She'd paced back and forth inside the tiny hotel room, wishing she had gone with Jack to do "a little shopping," as he called it.

Carla's voice, breezy and relaxed, came through the line. "Sorry I missed your call. I was at yoga."

With her sunny smile and her golden blond hair, Carla was the opposite of what most people thought of when they heard the word *hacker*, but she was excellent at it. She refused to give Zoe the full story on how she'd made her living before she put on a white hat and went to work for major corporations that relied on her to check their cybersecurity.

Zoe gave Carla a quick summary, describing what had happened over the last day.

"Of course I'll take a look," Carla said. "You know I love stuff like this."

"We're not one hundred percent sure what it is." Zoe switched the phone to her other ear. "It might be something...illegal or dangerous."

"Even better."

"Okay, well, in that case, Jack will be back any minute, and you can talk to him. He thinks it may be—"

"Don't tell me what Jack thinks," Carla said. "It's better I go into it without any preconceived notions."

Zoe heard the key in the lock of the hotel room door. "There's Jack now. How do you want to look at the files? Do you want me to email them to you?"

She laughed. "You are an innocent at this stuff, aren't you?"

"I think I should be offended," Zoe said.

"Don't be. You haven't had a need to know this."

"Until now."

"You better put Jack on," Carla said. "He's brushing up on cyber-security, isn't he?"

"Yes, he can speak your language. Or at least a little bit of it."

Jack tossed several plastic shopping bags on the bed, and Zoe handed the phone to him. "It's Carla. She's in to help us, but says she needs to talk to you."

Jack said, "Hello, Carla." He cut his gaze toward Zoe as he listened. "Yes, she does have a way of getting herself involved in... interesting situations."

Zoe rolled her eyes. "It's not my fault someone put that flash drive in a painting I was picking up."

Jack smiled back at her, then his face turned serious as he said to Carla, "Okay, I'll call you back in a moment."

Zoe opened the shopping bags that Jack had tossed on the bed. "*Three* burner phones?"

"You can never have too many burner phones."

A few minutes later, Jack used one of the new phones and called Carla. He tucked the phone next to his shoulder and hitched the rickety chair closer to the desk as he tapped on his computer. Jack's conversation drifted into discussions about proxies, tunneling, secure areas, and other jargon with acronyms that Zoe didn't follow.

Zoe paced a circuit around the room, her thoughts going to the many questions she didn't have answers to. She'd been so wrapped up in figuring out what was going on that she hadn't thought about why the flash drive had been in the frame. Was it to get it back to the States? To Thacker? His company focused on high-tech home security. Was it something for his business...? A look at a competitor's technology or something groundbreaking that would give him an advantage in the market? But why would someone send digital information on a flash drive? Surely it could be sent through one of those secure connections, like the one Carla and Jack were using now.

Zoe walked to the window, and peeked through the slit in the curtains. The street below was empty, which should have made her feel better, but the knot of tension she felt didn't ease.

Jack called to Zoe, "We have a verdict," and put the phone on speaker. She let the curtain fall back into place.

All the teasing and lightness had gone out of Carla's voice as she said, "You guys need to be extremely careful. This is dangerous. Zero-day stuff always is."

Jack blew out a breath. "I thought that's what it was."

"But this one is really tantalizing—it's for mobile devices," Carla said and went on to name the top-of-the-line phone. "That's like the holy grail. Criminal gangs would pay... I can't even tell you how much."

"And governments even more," Jack said, his voice somber.

"Right. It would allow them to unlock any phone, anywhere,

anytime. Passwords, credit card data, birthdates, internet browsing, phone calls, contact lists, you name it, they'd have access to it."

"And we do everything on our phones now," Jack said. "It would be complete access to someone's life."

"Stocks, investment portfolios, banking information," Carla went on. "The possibilities are endless."

They were all silent for a few seconds. Zoe felt as if a new weight had settled on her shoulders.

Carla's voice came over the line again. "I don't need to tell you again to be careful, do I?"

"No," Jack said. "Already on it."

"What will you do?" she asked.

Jack ran his hand over the back of his neck and shook his head. "I don't know yet."

"I can contact a friend, see if I can get in touch with a developer connected to the company," Carla said, her voice tentative.

"Do that."

"Okay, I'll let you know."

"Good. I'm going to destroy this phone," Carla said. "I recommend you do the same for that one."

"In five minutes," Jack said, "this one won't exist either."

## 28

J ack headed for the door with the cell phone. "I'll be right back."

Zoe went back to her pacing routine until he returned, his hands empty. "It's gone?"

"Yes." He went to the bed and picked up one of the two remaining burner phones and removed it from the packaging. "See. Told you we'd need more than one." He flashed a quick grin, which made the burden weighing on her seem not quite so bad. At least they were dealing with this together.

"I'll always buy my burner phones in multi-packs," Zoe said, then turned serious. "So Carla is trying to get in touch with the developer so we can give them the hack?"

"Yes."

"You don't think the police would do that?" Zoe sat down on the bed and removed the rest of the items from the shopping bag, several packages of flash drives along with lip balm in the identical brand that the flash drive was packaged in. "You know I'm a fan of doing things the unconventional way, but this seems like a situation where we should drop everything in the lap of the police and high-tail it home—with the blue butterfly painting, of course."

"So, full disclosure, except for the artwork."

"Something like that."

"It won't work." Jack switched on the phone, then went to work opening the next burner phone. "This is bigger than the local police, bigger than art theft."

"Harrington would cringe at that description," Zoe said. "Art theft is as bad as any other kind of theft." They'd had many discussions about the sliding scale police forces used to prioritize their investigations. Resources usually went to solve crimes against people, not property. "So you think we should go bigger? What would that be?"

Jack worked to free the phone from the encasing plastic. "The embassy."

Zoe was surprised. It wasn't like Jack to suggest they go to his former employer for solutions. He knew firsthand how much red tape was involved in dealing with government agencies. "But you don't like that idea either," Zoe said. "I can tell from your tone."

Jack tossed the second burner phone on the bed and sat down beside her. "Once we turn the zero-day over to anyone connected with any branch of government—the police here, the U.S. Embassy, whoever—it goes into a black hole. It will disappear. The government won't contact the developers and let them know about the flaw so it can be fixed."

"You're saying they'll exploit it for themselves."

"Right. It will be another tool for spying on foreigners and maybe—probably—their own citizens."

"Really? You think the government—our government—would do that?"

"I know they do. Just look at the leaks coming out of the NSA and the CIA. They'll hack anything they can and keep the info about the vulnerability to themselves."

"Then I hope Carla comes through with a contact for us."

"I do, too."

**Wednesday**

Carla's call came late the next morning. "I'm sorry, guys. I tried everyone I could think of and no one will return my calls."

"I guess it's Plan B," Zoe said. Jack gave a nod. They didn't have to talk about it. They'd already rehashed their options for half the night and all of the morning.

A Metro ride and a short walk brought them to the U.S. Embassy, which was located in a blocky rectangular building that felt unimaginative and bland after the Neo-classical and Baroque architecture that Zoe had seen in Madrid.

"How are you doing? Still having second thoughts?" Zoe asked as the embassy came in sight. A soldier armed with an automatic weapon patrolled the sidewalk in front of the entrance, distracting her from noticing anything else about the building or neighborhood.

"More like fifth or sixth thoughts," Jack said.

Zoe stopped walking. "We don't have to keep the appointment, if you're still worried."

"No. We've been around and around on this. It's too dangerous to keep it to ourselves." Jack reached for her hand and they started walking again. "We have to at least float the idea that we have it, and see what their reaction is."

Jack's quasi-diplomatic background had come in handy. He'd made a call that morning to his friend Ash Hawker—"that is his real name," Jack had sworn—who Jack had met years ago while working in Naples. Ash was now assigned to Madrid and had pulled some strings. Zoe and Jack had an appointment with Mr. Gerald V. Clement at two o'clock.

After making their way through several layers of security, Zoe and Jack finally reached Mr. Clement, who turned out to be a middle-aged man with thinning brown hair, a pallid complexion, and a stooped posture that stayed with him even when he stood, as if he spent so much time hunched over a keyboard that his body was permanently stuck in that position.

His hand shake was sweaty, and Zoe had to resist the urge to dry her palm on the skirt of her dress as she and Jack took their seats in the narrow space allotted for two chairs, their backs pressed against the fabric cubicle wall. A gold nameplate sat at the edge of Mr. Clement's desk facing them. It was the only impressive thing in the tiny space.

He turned and positioned his hands on his keyboard as he asked in a voice only slightly louder than a whisper, "Now, which one of you has lost your passport?"

Zoe and Jack exchanged a glance, then Jack said, "I think there's been a misunderstanding."

"Oh, you've *both* lost your passports." He made a *tsking* sound and began typing. "It does happen occasionally. Most unfortunate..."

Jack spoke over the clatter of the keyboard. "Neither one of us has lost a passport. I think Zoe should tell you what's happened. She's had a bit of trouble here in Madrid."

Mr. Clement turned back to them and reached for a pen, which he knocked off the desk. He bent, disappearing for a moment, then popped back up. "Trouble?" he asked in his soft voice. "To do with your passport?"

"No, it's about a painting," Zoe said. "I arrived in Madrid on behalf of Mr. Fredrick Thacker, who was interested in a painting that was for sale at the Cabello Gallery. The painting was authenticated on Monday, and I arranged to pick it up the next day—"

The phone on Mr. Clement's desk rang. He held up a finger. "One moment, please." He answered in his quiet tone, then listened a moment. "But I emailed it last week..." He twisted his chair to his computer and opened his email program.

The conversation went on for a few moments. Jack said to Zoe in a low voice, "Not what I expected. Maybe I don't have quite the same pull with the embassy that I thought I did."

"Maybe it's your friend Ash who doesn't have the pull—"

"Sorry about that." Mr. Clement replaced the receiver and

clasped his hands together, his gaze fixed on Zoe. "You were saying?"

"When I went to pick up the painting at the gallery—"

The phone rang again. Mr. Clement held up his finger. "One moment, please." He listened. "Right, yes... Well, here, I can tell you." He swiveled to his computer again.

Jack's gaze bored into Mr. Clement's temple, but he chattered away, unaware of Jack's increasing irritation.

The conversation went on quite a while, but finally Mr. Clement hung up and turned back to Zoe, completely missing Jack's intense stare. Zoe picked up her story where she'd left off, hurrying through it, describing the attack on Luis and Jug Ears following her through Madrid.

Mr. Clement held up a finger. "Have you informed the police about this?"

"They know about the attack on Luis, but not about the guy who followed me. You see, there's something else that's happened that we felt moves it out of a local police jurisdiction. It's connected to the painting, but it's not about art. It's programming code. We've come across a hack, a zero-day hack."

Zoe glanced at Jack, indicating he should pick up the story, but Mr. Clement spoke, his voice growing slightly stronger. "Oh, no. That's not right at all. Anything of this sort you should report to the police. Especially since you already have a contact there, this Chief Inspector Munez. You must take it to him. There's nothing we can do at this point. No crime has been committed against *you*. And you have your passports, correct?"

Zoe felt her shoulders sag. "Yes, we have our passports. But there's more—"

Jack said, "We need to speak with your supervisor."

What little color there was in Mr. Clement's face drained away. "My supervisor?" His gaze darted to the cubicle opening and then back to Zoe and Jack. "Why? Why would you need to do that?"

"Because we have information that is sensitive in nature and needs to be passed on to the correct authorities," Jack said. "You handle lost passports, correct?"

"Yes," Mr. Clement said, relief in his voice. He reached for his pen and knocked it off the corner of the desk again. He bobbed down and reappeared with the pen.

"Then we need to see a supervisor," Jack said. "They can pass this on to the correct person."

Mr. Clement licked his lips. "I don't think—I mean—that's not how it's done."

"That's how we need to do it today. Time is of the essence with this."

Mr. Clement's face suddenly flushed. "I will be happy to pass your name and information on to my supervisor," he said in a shaky near-whisper as if the words shouldn't be spoken aloud. "I have all your contact details here." He tapped the computer screen. "She will be in touch with you later today. She's in a meeting—she has a meeting every week at this time—and can't talk to you right now."

"We'll wait," Jack said.

"I'm afraid that's not possible. That's not how we do things here. In fact," he glanced at his watch, "you have to leave now." Mr. Clement scribbled a note, muttering "zero-day" under his breath then said, "Since you don't have an issue with your passports, I have to move on to the next appointment." He stood and flapped his hand vaguely toward the door.

Zoe stayed seated. She looked at Jack, eyebrows raised. "What do you want to do?"

"We'll get nowhere today. It's no use. We might as well leave."

Zoe got up and followed Mr. Clement's stoop-shouldered figure.

A few moments later as they walked away from the building, Zoe said, "Why did we give up?"

"Because I know how bureaucracy works. Mr. Clement is never going to be able to help us with what we need. By the time our situation gets to a person who *can* help us, days—weeks, even— will have gone by. We could wait around there all day, and nothing will happen. It'll be better if we work this issue from another angle."

They came to an intersection and stopped as the traffic surged by them. Zoe took her map out of her messenger bag and checked where they needed to turn to get back to the Metro. "What other angle? I thought we'd covered them all."

Jack sighed. "We do have one other option."

Zoe looked up from the map. "Something not great, apparently."

"It would be radical." The light changed and several pedestrians around them stepped into the crosswalk. Zoe and Jack followed a few paces behind. "We could post it online."

Zoe stepped onto the curb at the other side of the street, and slowly refolded the map. "You mean...just put it out there...where everyone can see it."

"Yes. Once a zero-day is in the public domain...it's done. Worthless. Problem solved."

"Unless the people who wanted it find out that we were the ones who posted it and come after us for—revenge?"

"That might happen, but I think we're safer publishing it than keeping it secret."

"That *is* radical." Zoe considered the thought of posting the hack on the internet for a moment, then gave a nod. "Okay, let's do it."

Jack laughed. "Come on, Zoe, stop lollygagging and make a decision."

"Why should we drag it out? We've already been through our options countless times. Every other choice has been blocked, so let's release it—set it free." She tucked the map into her messenger bag and picked up her pace with a nod. She felt the coil of tension inside her ease. "Whew. I feel better—lighter."

"Yeah, you're right. No reason to draw it out. That's what we'll do as soon as we get back to the hotel."

"This street will take us back to the Metro—oh look, there's a sign for the *Plaza de Cibeles*."

"Always the tourist," Jack said.

"Hey, you have to work in sightseeing when you can, and it's on our way back."

One corner of Jack's mouth turned up. "The world has gone this long without knowing about the zero-day, so a few more minutes shouldn't matter."

When they arrived in the plaza he said, "That's quite a ride," as they studied the fountain's sculpture of a Greek goddess who commanded a chariot pulled by lions.

"See, I knew you'd like it. Move over a bit and I can get you in the picture." Zoe had already taken several photos of the sculpture, the fountain, and the impressively ornate buildings that surrounded the plaza. "This place is supposed to be gorgeous at night. The whole thing is lit up," she said as her phone rang. "It's Gloria. Maybe she has some news about Luis."

Zoe had barely said hello before Gloria started talking. "Zoe, is that you? Where are you? I went to your hotel but you weren't there."

Zoe pressed the phone closer to her ear to hear over the traffic. "We're out—at the *Plaza de Cibeles*, in fact. Is something wrong? Is it Luis?" Gloria's voice was shaky and had a frantic tone.

"Luis?" Gloria said as if Zoe had asked about some unrelated topic. "No, this isn't about Luis." Gloria breathed deeply. "No, this is much more important. I'm not too far from where you are. Can you meet me? I know a café close to where you are. I have to talk to you. I can't tell you this over the phone, but I *must* see you."

With the phone still at her ear, Zoe said to Jack, "I suppose we could make a detour? Gloria wants to meet. She says it's urgent."

"We—who is we?" Gloria said sharply. "Who are you with?"

"My husband, Jack. He came out when...well, when everything went wrong with the painting."

"Oh—I suppose that's okay."

Zoe felt a little miffed. Gloria had no say at all in whether her husband joined her in Madrid or not.

Gloria's voice shifted back to pleading. "Please meet me. It's about the butterfly painting."

"What was the name of the restaurant again?" Zoe asked. "We'll go straight there."

## 29

W hen Zoe and Jack arrived at the café, Gloria was seated in the back at a small table. She jumped up the moment she saw them. Mirrors lined one side of the narrow restaurant, and for a second Zoe thought that she was seeing double as Gloria and her reflection raced toward her and embraced her.

Engulfed in Gloria's mass of hair, Zoe couldn't see anything for a second as Gloria clung to her, her fingers digging into Zoe's shoulders. Gloria released Zoe and latched on to her hand. "Thank you for coming."

"Of course. What's wrong?"

"I'll tell you all about it," Gloria said, squeezing Zoe's hand as they went back to the table. Gloria's mascara was smudged and, instead of the confident stride that Zoe had to race to keep up with on their tour of Madrid, Gloria moved slowly as if the sprint to the front of the restaurant had drained her energy. "First, I have to know—do you have the painting?"

"The Heade painting with the butterfly and the hummingbird?" Zoe glanced at Jack. Her instinct was to keep quiet about the discovery of the painting, but Gloria tightened her grip on Zoe's hand, crushing her fingers. "Please say you have it. Otherwise—"

She pressed her free hand to her lips for a moment, "...it doesn't matter."

Zoe wavered...Gloria was so distraught. Zoe looked at Jack to see if he agreed with her quick mental reversal. He had taken a seat to the side of Gloria and gave a small nod that only Zoe noticed. With his typical shuffling and deft maneuvering, Jack arranged it so that he was seated at the far side of the table with a good view of the whole café. Zoe was on his right by the restaurant's main aisle, and Gloria was on Jack's left with her back against the mirrored wall.

"We do know where the painting is," Zoe said.

Gloria launched into a mumbled string of Spanish that Zoe couldn't understand, but the tone conveyed gratitude. She dropped Zoe's hand and made the sign of the cross, then switched to English. "Wonderful. That is wonderful." She blew out a breath and seemed to finally notice Jack. "Oh, hello. I'm sorry I was so rude. It's just been so stressful. Here, let me make some room." The small café table was crowded with Gloria's cell phone and enormous leather handbag as well as a half-eaten churro and a cup of the thick hot chocolate so popular in Madrid, which reminded Zoe more of pudding than a drink. As Gloria moved her purse to the floor, Zoe introduced Jack.

Gloria acknowledged Jack with a small nod, then turned back to Zoe. "You can't imagine how worried I've been. He said you had the painting, but I thought that if he was wrong—if you *didn't* have it— well...that would be too awful." She shifted her cup of chocolate and cell phone to the center of the table then leaned toward Zoe. "Where is it?"

At the intensity of her posture, Zoe instinctively leaned back an inch. "The painting? It's in a safe place."

"Do you have it with you?" Gloria's gaze dropped to the messenger bag Zoe held in her lap.

"No, I learned that lesson the hard way," Zoe said, thinking of an incident that happened in Salzburg when a thief cut the strap of her messenger bag while she was wearing it.

They'd hidden the painting in the hotel room, and Zoe knew it was in a good place. But even with the precautions they'd taken she still felt a twist of worry. She'd only feel better when they were able to get back and check everything.

"Are you sure it's safe, though? And how did you get it?" Still leaning over the table, she fixed her attention on Zoe with a concentration that made her uncomfortable. Was this how a mouse felt when a cat stalked it?

Jack inched his chair forward. "That's a long story." Gloria shifted her attention to him as he asked, "How did you know we had it? Who is this 'he' that told you we had the painting?"

Gloria pushed her hair behind her ears as she straightened. "I don't know who he is, but he's the man who has Sophia."

"A man has Sophia?" Zoe said. "Your daughter?"

"Yes." Gloria's eyes turned glassy, and her lips wobbled. "He kidnapped her. He—" She took a moment and got her emotions under control then continued. "He came to my apartment this morning. I left Sophia alone when I went out to get a coffee. When I came back, she was gone. It was only a few minutes. She should have been fine. She's stayed alone in the apartment before. I'm only ever gone for a few minutes—maybe five at the most. She must have opened the door to him even though she *knows* not to do that. She probably thought it was her little school friend who lives on the other floor."

"I'm so sorry," Zoe said, amazed that Gloria could even put together coherent sentences after something like that.

Jack asked, "What did the police say?"

Gloria jerked as if she'd been shot, her gaze going around the quiet café. "He said not to call the police." She lowered her voice to a whisper as she said *police*. "He threatened to—" She swallowed and shook her head. "I can't even repeat it. It was horrible—what he said he'd do—if I called the police, so I didn't. He said you had the butterfly painting and that I had to talk to you."

"How did he contact you?" Jack asked, and Gloria seemed to shrink a little at his tone.

Zoe sent Jack an ease-off look and said, "This is terrible, and we'll do everything we can to help you. So how did he contact you?" She wasn't sure Gloria had made a smart move when she avoided calling the police, but she couldn't ignore Gloria's distress. "Did he call you?"

Gloria nodded as she sniffed. "My phone rang as soon as I walked into the empty apartment. It was this man with a gruff voice who said he had her, but if I got the flash drive back from you he would make sure she was returned safe."

Zoe and Jack exchanged a glance at the word *flash drive.*

"So it's the *flash drive* that you want, not the painting," Zoe said.

"Yes, that's right." Gloria's hair fell forward over an eye as she bobbed her head again. She swiped her hair behind her ear. "The flash drive is inside the frame of the painting. It's in a tube. You have the painting, so you have the flash drive."

"But how did you know that the flash drive was in the frame of the painting?" Zoe asked.

"Because I put it there."

## 30

"You put the flash drive in the frame of the painting?" Zoe asked Gloria.

"It seemed like such a small thing." She lifted a shoulder. "It was so easy to slip it in during the authentication. It only took a second. Five hundred euros seemed like so much for," she flexed her fingers, opening her hand wide, "for doing hardly anything..." She closed her eyes for a long moment and whispered, "And now I wish I had never done it."

"So someone paid you to put the flash drive in the frame of the painting. Was it the man who called you?" Zoe asked.

"It wasn't him. The man who called me today spoke Spanish. No, it was Kaz who asked me to hide the flash drive."

"Kaz?" Zoe asked, trying to follow Gloria's explanation. "He works for Thacker?" There couldn't be too many people with that name.

"Yes, Kaz Volk," Gloria said. "You've met him, right? He's geeky and a little awkward, I think. No, it wasn't him on the phone."

"Okay," Zoe said, "Let me make sure I've got this straight. Kaz asked you to put the flash drive in the frame of the painting?"

"Yes," Gloria said. "I've worked with him a couple of times when

I authenticated artwork for Thacker. Kaz is the one who handles everything." She fiddled with her cell phone and focused on it as she spoke. "He called me and asked if I'd do him a favor. It was so easy. Just put something in the painting that I would be asked to authenticate. He would pay me five hundred euros. I just needed to make sure it was in the painting or the packaging." Her tone turned defensive. "That's quite a lot of money."

"Yes, it is," Zoe said doing a quick mental calculation, transferring the figure into dollars. There had been many times in Zoe's life when even a figure as small as fifty dollars would be tempting, especially when it involved something so simple as what Kaz had asked. Zoe figured that Gloria was a single parent—she'd never mentioned a husband and surely he'd be on the scene now, if there was one. So maybe Gloria had a tough time making ends meet, which made Gloria's willingness to do what Kaz wanted more understandable. Zoe sympathized with Gloria, but the financial angle wasn't what was important here, Zoe reminded herself and refocused. "So the painting...is it really an authentic Martin Johnson Heade painting?"

"Yes! Of course it is. I would never compromise myself and say it was real if it wasn't."

"I had to ask. Thacker will want to know."

Gloria rolled her eyes. "Yes, of course. It's always about the artwork with him."

"So you're saying if the painting hadn't been by Martin Johnson Heade, you would have told me?"

"Certainly. And I told Kaz that, too. I wouldn't deceive Thacker."

Zoe tilted her head. "That's why you suggested I should tell Thacker about the Dalí sketch," Zoe said. "It was your backup."

Gloria shifted in her chair and brushed some crumbs from the table. "In case the painting wasn't legitimate I had to have some other way to send the flash drive, so I suggested the sketch. Fortunately, I didn't need it, but I knew that Thacker would want the sketch anyway. And he did," she said with an I-told-you-so lilt.

Jack asked, "Did Kaz tell you what was on the flash drive, or why he needed you to send it to him?"

She leaned back in the chair. "I didn't want to know. I didn't care."

"He didn't tell you anything about it?" Jack asked, clearly skeptical.

"He said a friend had some information he needed to get into the United States. His friend wanted to do it in a way that there could be no possible link to him."

"No link to Kaz?" Jack asked with a frown. "That doesn't make sense. You'd be able to link the flash drive with Kaz."

"No," Gloria said. "No link between Kaz's friend and the information he was sending to Kaz."

"And Kaz didn't tell you anything about why or how he came to be receiving this?" Jack pressed.

"I only know that he said it would change everything, that it would serve them right."

"He said those exact words 'serve them right?'" Jack repeated.

"Yes. That and something about charging up the people."

Jack's forehead wrinkled, then cleared. "Power to the people?" Jack asked.

"Yes, that was it." Gloria said. "That's all I know. It arrived in the mail one day. No note or explanation, no return address, just the flash drive. I was watching for it and knew exactly what it was."

"What about the postmark on the envelope?" Zoe asked, thinking of their own mysterious package that had arrived unexpectedly. "Where did it come from?"

"I didn't look."

Zoe raised her eyebrows. "Seriously? You weren't the least bit curious?"

"No. I didn't care. I was going to make sure it got into the packaging with the painting—luckily, it fit into the frame—and collect my money. There's nothing wrong with that."

"You didn't think that it might be something a bit shady?" Jack asked.

"No, I got the feeling that it was something personal...how would you say it..." she stared at the ceiling a moment, "...a point of pride for Kaz and his friend. But I was wrong. Obviously. I should have walked away. But it seemed like such an easy thing to do for the money."

"It always does," Jack said under his breath as Gloria's phone, which was lying face down on the table, rang. She snatched it up, and Zoe caught a glimpse of the image of the caller's dark eyes and hair, reflected in the mirror behind Gloria before she sent the call to voicemail. "Not him." Gloria put the phone down. "He said he would call with instructions."

"The man who has Sophia?" Jack asked.

Gloria said, "Yes. He said he would call. He *should* have called by now." She checked the time on her phone. "He said he'd call within the hour."

Zoe felt Jack's gaze on her. She'd been staring at Gloria, telling herself she couldn't have seen what she thought she had on Gloria's phone. Zoe's gaze traveled over the tabletop as she processed that glimpse, looking at the cup of chocolate and the churro with new eyes.

Jack lifted an eyebrow, seeming to ask, *what's wrong*? She pulled herself together. If she was right, she didn't know what game Gloria was playing, but she instinctively felt she shouldn't let Gloria know what she'd seen. What had they been talking about? That's right, Kaz. Zoe asked Gloria, "So have you heard from Kaz since the sketch was stolen?"

"After Luis was attacked, I called him and told him the painting was missing. He was frantic." Gloria's lips pressed together for a second. "That's when I began to understand that this was not a simple thing."

"Have you talked to him since then?" Zoe asked.

"No."

"When I spoke to Thacker the other day, he said Kaz was on vacation."

Gloria frowned. "That doesn't sound right. He was so upset—"
Gloria's phone trilled again, and she grabbed it. This time, the
reflection didn't show a photo, just a blank screen with a phone
number. She pressed the phone to her ear and listened. "*Sí...sí.*" She
nodded her head, and Zoe caught a few Spanish words she could
understand. Gloria said they had it.

She listened a moment, then tilted the phone away from her
mouth and translated what was said to Zoe. "He wants you to bring
the flash drive to..." She frowned and brought the phone back to
her mouth. "*¿Está seguro? Pero...*" She jumped a bit, and Zoe could
hear the sharp words coming through the phone speaker.

Gloria said hurriedly, "*Sí, lo entiendo,*" then said to Zoe, "He
wants you to bring the flash drive to the Temple of Debod at nine
thirty tonight." She listened to what Zoe assumed must be more
instructions, then she asked something in Spanish.

Jack said, "You should get proof of life."

Gloria's eyes widened. "What?"

"Proof of life of your daughter—I know it's hard to even think
about asking—but you need to know she's okay," Jack said in a
low voice.

"Oh, right." She said something in Spanish, the skin on her
fingers whitening as she squeezed the phone. She listened for a
moment, then her voice went soft as she said, "Sophia!" She asked a
couple of questions as her eyes filled with tears. She murmured a
soothing tone, then she said sharply, "Sophia? Sophia?"

She dropped the phone onto the table and covered her eyes
with her hands as she gathered her composure, then straightened
and took a thin paper napkin from the dispenser on the table. "I'm
sorry. It was so good to hear her voice." She wiped her eyes. "He
said I'm to go back to my apartment and stay there until tonight.
We're to meet at the corner of *Calle Ferras* and *Calle Luisa Fernanda*
at nine twenty-five. I'm supposed to wait on the street while Zoe
goes to the temple—alone—he was very specific about that—no
one else." She looked at Jack. "You should wait with me on the

street." She shifted to look at Zoe. "When you give the man the flash drive, he says he will check it, and then Sophia will be dropped off at the corner where I'm waiting."

Jack asked, "Is that close?"

"Yes, *Calle Luisa Fernanda* is across the street from the park where the temple is." Gloria turned to Zoe and fastened her hand around Zoe's wrist. "You can do that, can't you?" Her grip was like a steel band. "The flash drive is somewhere nearby, right? You can bring it tonight?"

Zoe looked at Jack. She could see the question in his eyes. She gave a slight shake of her head and hoped he understood she had something to tell him, but she couldn't do it now. He lifted his chin in a "go ahead" gesture.

Gloria noticed the nonverbal communication flying back and forth between them. "What? Is something wrong? You can bring the flash drive tonight, can't you?"

Zoe said, "Looks like we'll have to."

"Are you sure you don't want to go to the police?" Jack said, "It's not too late."

"No." Gloria shook her head so strongly that her hair whipped back and forth. "He said no police or that would be..." she swallowed "...the end of it. I believe him."

"Well then," Jack said. "We better go get it."

"Yes. Good. Oh, thank you. You can't imagine what this means to me. Let me know when you have it, won't you?" Gloria dropped her mascara-stained napkin on the table and picked up her phone. "It will make me feel so much better."

"Of course," Zoe said.

Gloria stood and hooked her enormous bag on her shoulder, then leaned in to give Zoe another shoulder-crunching hug as she murmured, "Thank you. Thank you. Thank you. I can't say more than that." She drew in a deep breath, turned to Jack, and held out a hand. "Thank you."

The three of them left the coffee shop together, but at the first corner, Gloria pointed to the right. "I'm going home, just like he said for me to do. I'll wait for your call."

Jack waited until Gloria was out of earshot, then said, "So what's going on?"

"I don't buy it."

"The kidnapping story? You thought something was off, too?"

"So many things," Zoe said. "But the clincher was the phone call she sent to voicemail. Did you see the image of the caller?"

"No."

"I could. It was reflected in the mirror behind her. It was her *daughter*, Sophia. Who would send a call from their 'kidnapped daughter' to voicemail?"

"No one." Jack shook his head. "Even if it wasn't her daughter calling her, it might be whoever had her, using her phone."

"Right. That's one call you'd never send to voicemail. There's definitely something odd going on there. And who would order churros and chocolate after their daughter had been kidnapped? Who could eat at a time like that?"

Jack tilted his head back and forth. "I suppose some people stress-eat."

"True, but not going to the police, devouring a sweet snack while she waited for us, and sending her daughter's call to voicemail? No, I don't believe some mystery man has her daughter. I think she's lying about...well, probably all of it, except maybe the request from Kaz to place the flash drive. The question is, what do we do?"

Jack squinted as he stared down the street, where Gloria's dark cloud of hair was still visible. "I think we should follow her and gather all the details we can. Probably best if it's only one of us."

"I agree. Less chance of her noticing." Gloria's figure was getting smaller and smaller, but Zoe knew Jack could catch up. "Of the two of us, you're the best one at tailing people. You should do it. I'll go back to the hotel and see what the situation is there."

"Okay, I'll meet you there in a little while."

Although Zoe and Jack had been careful to make sure they weren't followed after they left the *mercado* and went to their new hotel, Zoe hadn't been able to shake the uneasy feeling she had about leaving the painting. They'd learned the hard way that toting around art wasn't the safest thing to do, so Jack had said, "Then we'll hide it and leave a trap for anyone who comes searching for it."

## 31

The hotel room was a mess—and it wasn't because the maid hadn't been in yet.

Zoe paused at the door, her gaze skipping over the disorder. Crumpled sheets lay in a tangled pile on the floor. The mattresses and box springs had been tossed against a wall. Jack's suitcase was open, and his clothing littered the floor. Zoe's hat, the crown flattened, sat discarded under the desk.

She took all of the chaos in with a quick glance. It was the small dresser that interested her the most. The drawers had been removed and stacked around it like oversized blocks. "So far so good," she murmured as she closed the door. Her phone rang with a call from Jack.

"How's it going?" he asked.

"The trap's been sprung."

"Really?" Jack said. "I didn't expect that. I was sure we weren't followed. I must be getting rusty."

"I wouldn't say that. You're pretty high on the situational awareness scale, I think. You're always tracking what is going on around us. Whoever got in our room must have found us some other way. Let's see if they took our bait." With the phone pressed to her ear, she kneeled beside the dresser and reached in through the opening where a drawer had been removed. She patted the underside of the dresser's top. Her fingers encountered a sticky surface where the tape had been. Only the tacky residue remained. Zoe sat back on her heels. "It's gone."

"I hope they enjoy their oil painting of the *Plaza Mayor*."

"I wonder if they will even notice it's not the right painting?"

Last night after they figured out what was actually on the flash drive, they decided they needed a decoy. Zoe had read that Madrid was famous for its vibrant nightlife that carried on until the early hours of the morning at full steam, but she had still been surprised to find the *Plaza Mayor* bustling with people and laughter as if it was seven o'clock at night, not after midnight.

They had no trouble finding an artist with her paintings on display. They'd found an oil painting about the same size as the blue butterfly painting and bought it. Once they returned to the room, they removed the metal frame from the blue butterfly painting, popped a new tube of lip balm into it, then enclosed the new painting in the metal frame. They wrapped the whole thing in the packaging from the gallery and hid it. Jack had said, "We want to make it a challenge to find, but not impossible." They settled on taping it to the underside of the dresser top.

Zoe got to her feet and crossed the room. "You were right. They checked the dresser."

"Anyone doing a decent search should check there. It's only logical. A hotel room doesn't have that many places to hide something."

"Thank goodness our searcher was logical."

"Everything else okay?"

"Checking right now." Zoe went to the TV that was mounted on the wall and stretched. She let out a sigh of relief as her fingers connected with the package taped to the back of the TV. The blue butterfly painting still sat snuggly between the back of the TV and the wall. "Still here. I'll just check to make sure." She could feel the thickness of the wooden stretcher of the canvas through the layer of padding. She tugged, pulling the tape away from the back of the TV until the package came free. Holding the phone to her ear with her shoulder, she unwrapped the towel that they'd used to protect the painting, revealing the iridescent butterfly, the hummingbird, and the jungle background. "It's all good." Zoe quickly rewrapped the painting and returned the painting to its hiding place. "I guess I better call Gloria and tell her we have the flash drive. That will hold her off while we decide what to do. So how's it going for you?"

"Gloria didn't spot me. She went to an apartment building. A man was waiting there for her, and they went inside together. I managed to get a photo of him. Did you get it?"

"Let me put you on speaker while I look at it. I got a notification that a text came in as I was coming up the stairs, but I haven't looked at it yet." As Zoe opened the text, Jack said, "It's a little blurry."

"No, it's fine." Zoe sat down on the bed and rubbed her forehead. "That's Jug Ears." Things were happening so quickly. She felt like they were on a roller coaster that had been slowly climbing uphill until last night when she found the flash drive. Since then, they'd been racing down the slope, twists and turns coming at them so fast that she couldn't keep up. Did this mean that Gloria's mystery man, the one who supposedly had her daughter, was Jug Ears? Were they working together?

Jack said, "Another resident went into the building behind Gloria and her friend with the big ears. I caught the door before it closed and followed them up the stairs. They were talking a mile a minute, all in Spanish, of course, so I wasn't able to understand anything. I saw which apartment they went into on the third floor. I waited around the landing as long as I could to see if they came back out, but there was nowhere I could watch the apartment unobserved from inside the building, so I left. I was on my way out when the woman who lives across the hall from Gloria left her apartment. Fortunately, she spoke a little English. I walked down with her, and we had a nice little chat."

Zoe said, "I bet you did." She could imagine Jack turning on the charm, helpfully holding open the street door for the woman and drawing her into a conversation. "And what did you find out?"

"I managed to convey that I'd been up to see Gloria, but had missed her. The woman said she'd last seen Gloria early this afternoon when Gloria sent her daughter off with someone named *Abuela*."

"That's not a name, it's a title. *Abuela* means grandmother." Zoe went to the window and checked outside, half-expecting to see Jug Ears poised on the corner, but she only saw a smattering of tourists. "So Sophia is with her grandmother. Gloria made up that whole kidnapping story." As her suspicions of Gloria were confirmed, a surge of anger rose inside Zoe. "Can you believe she did that—" Zoe was so upset that she couldn't finish her sentence. The tears, the distress. It had all been an act.

Jack's voice, cool and calm, cut through her haze of anger. "I'll stay here for a few more minutes—I'm in the bookstore across from the apartment."

"I can't believe you're not more upset," Zoe said. "She lied to us, which is terrible, but to spin a story about her daughter being kidnapped..."

"Don't think that I'm not outraged. But now we know exactly what sort of person we're dealing with."

"Someone who lies and manipulates. I should have picked up on it," Zoe said, thinking of how Gloria had skipped out on paying for their extra food the first time they had lunch and how ready Gloria had been to put a plan in play to help Zoe skip the line at the temple. Granted, they were small things, and Zoe had discounted them. Instead, she'd focused on Gloria's willingness to show her around Madrid and her help later with the translations. "No wonder she showed up so quickly to translate when I called her after Luis was attacked. She was probably thrilled to have an excuse to see first-hand what had happened to the precious flash drive."

"Let's worry about all that later," Jack said. "Right now we have bigger issues."

"Yes, you're right," Zoe said and moved to the desk. "What's happening now?"

"I've already told the clerk here in the bookstore twice that I'm just looking. I think I'll have to buy something before I leave to keep my cover as a shopper intact. If Gloria doesn't come back out in a few minutes, I'm heading back your way. Have you checked the video yet?"

"Getting ready to do that right now. What do you bet it shows that it was Jug Ears who tossed our room?"

"Gloria kept us at the café while he searched? It's a possibility."

"Although, I didn't smell any cigarette smoke when I came in."

"Maybe he's given up smoking—at least for today. Oh, here comes the very helpful clerk. I better get that book."

"Okay. I'll let you know what I find out."

Zoe searched through the debris from the desk that was scattered over the floor until she found the charging cord. She connected her phone to the charger that was plugged into the outlet on the base of the desk lamp. Jack had plugged it in before they left to go to the embassy, and the person who tossed their room hadn't been interested in it. It was a handy gadget that Jack had brought along. It did charge a phone, but it also had a video camera in it. He'd said they might as well go ahead and set it up to record while they were out of the room, just as a precaution.

With the location of the desk in one corner of the room, it should have recorded the whole room during the entire time she and Jack were away. Zoe downloaded the camera's info to her phone and found the video, labeled with today's date. She hit play and an image of the hotel room filled the screen. She put it on fast-forward.

After several minutes of video of their empty hotel room, the maid arrived and tidied up. She left, and then Zoe watched some more unchanging footage of the empty hotel room.

Finally about an hour in, another figure entered the room, and Zoe switched to regular speed. It wasn't a man with oversized ears.

The man who stealthily entered their room was lean and young with a swath of dark curly hair and glasses with wide frames like blinders, Kaz Volk.

## 32

J ack looked around the trashed hotel room. "Kaz did all this and took the decoy painting?"

"I couldn't believe it either. I had no idea he was in Madrid." Zoe handed him her phone with an image from the video. "This is what he looks like—in case, he pops up unexpectedly again."

Jack studied the image for a few seconds. "Kaz being here in Madrid raises a lot of questions."

"Like how long has he been here? And did he have anything to do with the attack on Luis?" Zoe paced to the window and looked outside at the increasing foot traffic along the street. It had been fairly quiet when she arrived back at the hotel, but now siesta was over.

Zoe let the curtain fall back into place. "It doesn't make sense that Kaz would attack Luis. I was all set to bring the painting to Kaz. Why would Kaz need to attack Luis? Thacker even told me to contact Kaz when my plane landed. I would have delivered the painting to Kaz so he could pass it on to Thacker. Kaz could have arranged it so that he had some time to remove the flash drive before he handed the painting off to Thacker."

"Then Kaz must have some other reason for being here in Madrid," Jack said.

"Thacker said Kaz was on vacation," Zoe said. "Maybe he just happened to come to Madrid?"

They both shook their heads. Jack said, "Too much of a coincidence, I think."

"I agree," Zoe said. "If Kaz planned to be here for vacation, why wouldn't he just offer to pick up the painting for Thacker in the first place? They didn't need me, if Kaz was scheduled to travel here." Zoe paced across the room, stepping around the debris of sheets and scattered clothes. "And what are we going to do about this meeting tonight? Gloria thinks we're going to show up and hand over the flash drive to someone. After you sent me the picture of her and Jug Ears, I assumed it was Jug Ears who would be at the handoff tonight, but now that we know Kaz was looking for the painting, I'm not sure what's going on."

A knock at the door startled them both. Zoe was closest to the door and looked out the peephole, her heart suddenly pounding along in time with the repeated thumping on the door. "It's Chief Inspector Munez."

Jack twitched the curtain. "A police car just parked in front of the hotel." Jack ran his gaze over the window. "These windows don't open, and even if they did, there's no balcony or decorative moldings to hold onto. It's a straight drop."

"You're not just saying that so we don't have to go out the window?" Zoe said with a quick smile.

"I promise my dislike of heights has in no way impacted my analysis of the situation."

"And the bathroom window is tiny. I could probably get my foot out, but nothing else."

The banging sounded again. "¡Policía!"

Jack said. "I'm sure the manager will open the door soon, if we don't."

"Okay." Zoe cast a quick glance over the trashed room. There was no way Munez would think they were just messy, but they couldn't make it presentable in a few seconds either. "Cover story for this mess?"

"The truth is always the best—an intruder got in and ransacked the place. Must have been looking for valuables. No need to say what valuables."

"Somehow, I think Munez won't forget to ask that, but maybe we can convince him it was just a run-of-the-mill incident. It looks like it's our only option." Zoe took a deep breath and opened the door.

A uniformed police officer accompanied Chief Inspector Munez, but as soon as Zoe opened the door, he stepped back and waited in the hall. Munez said, "Mrs. Andrews—" He scanned the disordered room. "It appears you have had a little trouble."

"You could say that."

"Then it is fortunate I'm here," Munez said. He looked expectantly toward Jack. "And who is this?"

"My husband, Jack Andrews," Zoe said.

Munez inclined his head. "Pleased to meet you." He waved a hand around, indicating the hotel room. "When did this happen?"

"This afternoon while we were out."

"Yes, you went to speak to your embassy," Munez said. "I can see you are surprised that I know of your movements, but you shouldn't be. They told you that your message would be passed along to the appropriate person. *I* am the appropriate person to speak to about the issue you brought to them—the hack."

This wasn't how the conversation was supposed to go. Zoe had figured it would take quite a while to get past the state of the hotel room, but Munez had skimmed right over it as if it didn't matter. Had the U.S. Embassy really been in contact with Munez? Had Mr. Clement actually passed their information on to someone with authority? And that someone had contacted Munez?

Zoe glanced at Jack, who was standing at ease, his hip propped against the desk, and his hands in his pockets. Zoe was sure she didn't look as relaxed as he did, but forced herself not to grip her hands together. Jack lifted one shoulder a millimeter, a movement that only Zoe saw, but she knew it meant Jack wasn't sure about Munez either.

"The hack?" Zoe asked. "What do you mean?"

Munez said, "Please, let's not waste time. I know you have come into possession of a valuable piece of...computer programming, shall we call it? Your actions of going to your embassy have convinced me that you are not on the criminal side of the equation in this situation. You talked with a Mr. Gerald V. Clement. He passed on the information that you'd found a zero-day hack. His supervisor handed it 'up-the-chain' I believe you would say. A colleague of mine received it. He contacted me because we have information regarding a zero-day hack that's related to a current investigation. I hope we can cooperate so that this situation is resolved quickly. Then you can enjoy our lovely city and return home."

Zoe glanced at Jack then back at Munez. Jack was studying Munez with an intensity that would make most people squirm, but Munez seemed to be completely unaware of Jack's blistering gaze. Before either of them could say anything else, Munez went on. "Perhaps you're wondering why the U.S. Embassy would contact me about your...ah...concerns? The answer is simple. I did not give you my full title when we met. I work for the UDYCO, which is the drugs and organized crime section of the National Police. My specialty is cybercrime. We are working with a group of agencies— an international group—including some from your country. I believe the word you would be familiar with is *task force*."

Zoe asked, "Then why were you investigating the art theft? That's pretty far from cybercrime."

Munez took his phone from his pocket, tapped on it a few times, then turned the screen to Zoe. "Because a security camera caught this man disposing of the artwork after the theft."

"That's Jug Ears."

The corners of Munez's lips twitched. "An appropriate nickname. He works for a criminal organization, the Trullas gang. I have been monitoring them for several months. Anything he does interests me. I didn't mention it to you because...well, rarely do I disclose *all* information in my possession to someone I am interviewing. But I also had to determine if you were connected with him and his criminal network, or if you were an innocent and had stumbled into something accidentally. At first, I thought that you were simply inadvertently caught up in this situation, but then..." he transferred his glance to Jack, "I received information about your husband's background. Those facts, coupled with his arrival here..."

Munez shrugged. "I began to have more questions and had to rethink my assessment. But when I learned you'd contacted your embassy about turning over the computer program, I decided to drop by for a chat. The fact that you moved hotels without informing us delayed me slightly. But now that we are here together, we should make the most of the time, no?"

Zoe and Jack had used their passports to check into the new hotel. They were hiding from Jug Ears, not from Munez. It had probably only taken him a few minutes to search some sort of database to find them.

Zoe wasn't sure they should trust Munez. What he said made sense, and he did know about their trip to the embassy—names of who they'd spoken to and everything—but with so many surprises in the last few hours, Zoe felt skittish. Although, she did know Munez was with the police. She'd spoken to him at the police station. What Zoe wasn't so sure about was the cybercrime task force thing. She raised an eyebrow at Jack. Cybercrime and all things diplomatic were his department.

Jack got the signal. He said to Munez, "I'm sure you understand that we'd like to verify your identity."

"Of course. May I suggest you call your friend? Mr. Ash Hawker, wasn't it? He helped you get your appointment at the embassy, correct? He's been fully briefed and can pass you along to a Ms. Montclair, who will tell you all about me."

## 33

Jack spent about twenty minutes on the phone. Munez was in the hall speaking to the police officer when Jack ended the call. Zoe hadn't been able to pick up much from the few words she heard on Jack's end of the conversation.

He slipped his phone into his pocket. "Ash vouched for Munez and then transferred the call to Ms. Montclair, who backed up everything Munez said. He's working with an international task force, and the embassy would appreciate our complete cooperation with him."

"Really?" Zoe asked. "That seems odd to me, that they'd hand us off to Munez."

"Munez has authority to investigate and arrest—something that the embassy personnel can't do here in Spain."

"But what about the government wanting the information on the flash drive for themselves?" Zoe asked.

"That's perplexing to me, too."

"Allow me to explain," a voice behind them said. Munez had returned to the room.

"Any information the task force recovers will be shared jointly among all members."

*So all sorts of governments will be able to spy on their citizens, not just one country*, Zoe thought. She could see disapproval trace over Jack's face. Munez must have seen it too, because he said quickly, "I assure you, the information you have is small compared to the scope of the investigation into the Trullas organization, which is linked to Russian organized crime. We are very close to bringing down the whole operation. They are involved in cybercrime—identity theft, ransomware, hacks such as the one you've discovered, and even child pornography—but other branches of the gang move drugs and smuggle people across borders. Several of the members of the group are also linked to known terrorists." Munez had taken out his phone and tapped on it as he spoke. He handed it to Jack. "As you can see, just a search of the term 'Trullas gang' shows how extensive their reach is."

Zoe looked over Jack's shoulder as he scrolled down the list of links to stories from well-known news outlets with headlines about drugs, cybercrime, and human trafficking.

Jack's mouth quirked down on one side. She knew that face. He wasn't any happier with the situation than she was. "And this is why I left 'diplomacy' and went into security," he said as he looked at Zoe, his face resigned.

She knew what he was thinking. It wasn't an ideal situation, but it was what they had. Jack was all about working with the options that were available. He was practical and thought that they should work with Munez, despite the drawbacks. Zoe gave Jack a small nod to let him know she agreed. It wasn't ideal—nothing about this situation was ideal—but being mixed up with Russian organized crime went way beyond anything they could deal with themselves. Jack seemed to suppress a sigh, then said to Munez, "We'll do what we can to help you."

"Excellent." Munez looked into the hall where the police officer nodded to him. "I've arranged for us to use the manager's office while your room is cleaned." He waved a hand toward the door. "Shall we?"

Downstairs, the three of them barely fit into the cramped manager's office. Munez ignored the flickering overhead light and the cold cup of tea alongside a stack of papers on the desktop. He focused with a single-minded concentration on Zoe and Jack as they told him everything that had happened.

When they finished, Munez dialed a number on his phone. While waiting for the call to connect he said, "First, we must make sure the child, Sophia, is with her *abuela*."

He spoke into the phone in Spanish for a few minutes, then ended the call and placed his phone on top of his notepad, which was now covered with his handwriting. He'd slipped on his glasses as he made notes, but now he removed them and rubbed his eyes. "Next, we must consider the alliance of Gloria and Fossa."

"Fossa?" Zoe asked.

"The man you call Jug Ears—he is Tomás Fossa."

"It will be hard for me to think of him as anything but Jug Ears," Zoe said.

"I imagine so," Munez said. "Fossa is one of several people from the Trullas gang that we have been 'keeping tabs on,' as you would say. I studied at a university in your country. That is where I learned your expressions." He smiled briefly, then turned grave. "While Fossa is not the top man, he is one of the most important people I'm tracking."

"Because of who Fossa takes orders from?" Jack asked.

"Exactly. I could have arrested Fossa many times, but he is not my goal. I am after Izydor Mato, a man who is careful to stay clear of the police. He sends his people to carry out his orders, and Fossa is one of his most trusted lieutenants. We have been tracking Fossa closely."

He tapped his glasses against his notebook. "You have been open. I will return the favor, so you understand the situation. The day of the theft at the gallery, Fossa was in another part of Madrid. Neighbors reported an altercation in the morning, but my people could not intervene—to do so would have revealed to Fossa that we were watching him. When police officers who cover that area arrived, they found an empty apartment, which was in the same state as your hotel room. My people followed Fossa when he left, so we do not know what happened to the man who lived there, Robert Novall. He's vanished. My people saw Novall leave his apartment after the altercation. He slipped away before the police officers arrived. Novall was bleeding from his nose and walking slowly as if in pain, but when a neighbor offered to help, he refused and left. He was last seen heading for the Metro station. We assume that he has disappeared to stay out of the way of people like Fossa. One lead places him in South America, but..." Munez gave a little shake of his head, "...it will be difficult to track him. And, frankly, I have larger criminals to focus on."

"But why would Fossa attack him?"

"Oh, didn't I mention it? Robert Novall, or Rob as his friends call him, is a computer programmer—a very talented one by all reports. He's been working for Val-tech."

Jack blinked. "Val-tech? That's one of the corporate hacking companies."

"Yes, the premier one, I'd say. Novall left a job at a similar firm in France ten months ago to work for Val-tech. Novall has been 'out sick' since Tuesday."

"The day Luis was attacked and the sketch was stolen," Zoe said. "Then maybe this Robert Novall is the person who emailed Kaz? Yes, that's got to be it, doesn't it? That's why you were so interested in Kaz," Zoe said to Munez. "You think Robert Novall is the person who was trying to send the hack to Kaz."

When Zoe and Jack were bringing Munez up to date on everything that had happened, Munez had been particularly interested in Kaz and had asked several additional questions about him after Zoe described how Kaz had searched her second hotel room. Munez had even asked for Zoe to send him a copy of the video footage of Kaz in the hotel room.

"That is correct," Munez said. "We have confirmed that Novall's main project at work involved a zero-day and that Novall and Kaz Volk were working together to release the hack. When we searched Novall's apartment, we did not find much. His computer had nothing of significance on it regarding any hacks or exploits, and he left no physical evidence of what he'd been doing. He covered his tracks well except for one small thing. He had not signed out of a discussion forum where he is quite active. He expressed his opinions about surveillance quite openly in many detailed and passionate posts. He believes in privacy rights, and that surveillance —especially cyber surveillance—shouldn't be done either by corporations or governments."

Munez folded his glasses and put them in his pocket. "Another user on the forum—Tuck05 was his forum identity—was Novall's most frequent supporter. This user hid his identity, but I suspect it is Kaz Volk. I believe they made plans to distribute the zero-day. Those discussions would have taken place in a secure way, not on a public forum. It seems that Novall took the job at Val-Tech so that he could obtain and then release this hack. That seemed to be his goal, to find the most valuable piece of information he could, and release it to the public. His previous employer is tight-lipped about Novall, but I've heard rumors that he left under a cloud. It's possible he attempted something similar before coming to work at Val-Tech. We're still tracking that down."

"Sort of a digital Robin Hood," Zoe said.

"That's how he saw himself," Munez said. "He even employed a variant of it, almost an abbreviation of it, as an identifier in some communications, Rbn."

Jack shifted in his chair. "Robin Hood and Friar Tuck. They did see themselves as righting the world's wrongs."

Munez said, "He's a hacktivist."

Zoe glanced at Jack, eyebrows raised. He said, "Someone who uses their computer programming skills for political ends."

Munez nodded. "I'm sure Novall thinks he's doing the right thing. But to his employers, Novall is a traitor. And when the criminal world heard of the possibility that this hack might be active and circulating, well...then Novall became a target."

"And Jug Ears—er, Fossa, I mean—was sent to do the dirty work of getting the hack," Zoe said.

"Yes," Munez said. "We can now make some connections. We

know from what Ms. Espino told you that Novall had already sent her the hack, so Novall must have told Fossa that. I'm sure Fossa made it clear to Novall that he would make it extremely painful for Novall if he didn't tell him what he wanted to know. Novall was lucky to escape with only a bloody nose and some bruises. Novall must have disclosed the plan to send the flash drive to Ms. Espino and for her to put it in the painting, which led to Fossa's attack at the gallery."

"But how would he know where I was? Or where to find Gloria?" Zoe asked.

"Fossa would wring every piece of information from Novall." The flat way Munez said the words sent a chill through Zoe. Violence was a given with Fossa, it seemed.

Munez went on, "Fossa would not leave without all the details on where Novall had sent the flash drive, which would include Ms. Espino's address as well as the name of the gallery. I believe that once Fossa realized his mistake of taking the wrong painting, he returned to the gallery and spotted you with Gloria. You said you ate lunch together after the police interview, no?" Munez shrugged. "It would be easy to follow you back to your hotel. He did not need to follow Ms. Espino. He would have already extracted her address from Novall."

Zoe rubbed her forehead. It was a lot of information to take in, but at least the pieces were beginning to fit together. Kaz and the computer programmer, Robert Novall, were connected. He sent the hack to Gloria to put in the frame, but another detail troubled Zoe. "But if Novall and Kaz were coordinating with each other to distribute the hack, how did anyone else know about it? You said word got out about it in the criminal world. How did that happen?" Zoe asked. "Did they discuss it online in a way that could be traced?"

"It was simpler than that," Munez said. "The downfall of so many—arrogance."

Jack said, "Novall must have bragged about it to the wrong person."

"Exactly," Munez said. "One of our confidential informants heard that Novall hinted to a work associate about his plans to release the information in a way that left little to the imagination, at least for someone in the same line of work. Novall's colleague saw an opportunity to make some money and put the word out that the hack was 'in play,' which attracted the attention of Fossa's employer, Izydor Mato, who would be eager to have that sort of hack. Mato sent Fossa to get it. Fossa wouldn't want to return empty-handed. That's why he didn't give up. After his failure to get the flash drive from the gallery, he followed you."

"And searched my hotel room, and then tried to talk his way into my new room."

Munez chuckled. "I'm sure you frustrated him. When you disappeared, he contacted Gloria Espino to get her to convince you to produce the flash drive."

"More of your close surveillance of Fossa?" Zoe asked.

"Yes, our observation methods are quite...advanced, yet still imperfect. We were not able to follow exactly what was said, but we do know they met. Fossa is holding a threat over Ms. Espino— perhaps revealing her part in the release of the hack—or he's provided an incentive that she can't resist."

"Money," Zoe said. "She admitted to us that the cash was what convinced her to help Kaz in the first place."

"Her involvement does complicate the handoff of the flash drive," Munez said, his gaze fixed on Zoe. She shifted in her chair, uncomfortable with his observation. "If the instructions were for you to simply drop the flash drive at a location and leave, then we could find someone to go in your place. It would involve a wig and makeup, but it could be done. However, you said Fossa rode in the hotel elevator with you. Was he close enough to get a good look at you?"

"Yes," Zoe said, her heart sinking. "He stared. It bothered me."

Munez's lips turned down in a grimace. "That changes things. We have fewer options. If he didn't work for Mato we could forget about the handoff and send police officers to arrest him at the temple in connection with the gallery robbery. Unfortunately, we can't do that. We are at a sensitive point in an operation to bring down Mato and the Trullas organization. I can't risk Fossa becoming suspicious and relaying his concerns. It could ruin the plans to close in on the Trullas gang."

"Then there's only one thing to do, I think," Zoe said as she looked at Jack. "I have to take the flash drive into the temple."

Worry flickered in his eyes. "I don't like it. If someone has to go, I'd rather do it." He sat with his ankle propped on his knee and one hand resting on his ankle, but Zoe could see the skin whiten around his knuckles. "I'll make an excuse—you got sick or something."

"I appreciate that you're trying to keep your wife out of danger, Mr. Andrews, but with your training you know a substitution is not a good idea."

"You were going to try it," Jack said.

"But only if Fossa hadn't come into close contact with your wife. He has, so that plan is off the table," Munez said. "And unless I am mistaken, Mrs. Andrews has been in some tight spots before and handled them well, no?"

Jack looked at Zoe out of the corner of his eye. "I do have to concede that point."

She put her hand over Jack's. "I appreciate that you want to protect me, but I can do something as simple as drop off the flash drive. I'll be in and out of the temple in less than a minute. And we've already called Gloria and told her we're bringing the flash drive tonight. If someone else shows up, she'll be suspicious."

"That's true," Munez said.

Jack blew out a breath. "I can see I'm not winning this argument." He turned his hand under hers and linked their fingers. "You've got to wear a wire, though." He looked to Munez. "You can do that, right?"

"Oh, yes. In fact, I'm adamant on that point. We may even pick up something useful."

Jack leaned forward. "The temple is a horrible place for the handoff."

"I agree," Munez said. "Not a smart move on Fossa's part, but a lucky break for us. With only one entrance, and the temple's position at the top of the rise of land, it will be easy for us to keep track of him."

"Could it be an initial meeting point?" Jack asked. "Then instructions will be given to go on to another location?"

"No, I don't believe so. Fossa's cousin is a guard at the temple. He's scheduled to work tonight. I'm sure that in Fossa's mind, it's a good out-of-the-way location where he can check the flash drive in privacy while his cousin provides external security, preventing anyone from approaching the temple after hours—except the one person who is expected." Munez tilted his head toward Zoe, and she felt a flutter in her stomach. Despite her confidence that she could handle the drop off, the thought of meeting someone linked to a gang of criminals was frightening. Add in the element of a two-thousand-year-old Egyptian temple at night, and Zoe liked the idea even less.

Munez's phone rang. He asked a few questions in Spanish, then hung up, a small smile on his face. "It is good news. The little girl, Sophia, is indeed with her grandmother. She is fine." He tucked his phone into a pocket and pressed his hands to his knees as he prepared to stand. "We must prepare." He checked his watch. "We have an hour until the meeting time."

---

Zoe closed her hand more tightly around the tube of lip balm with the flash drive inside it as she and Jack made their way to the meeting with Gloria. The night pulsed with activity. Traffic whizzed along the road. Pedestrians filled the sidewalk. Laughter and conversation spilled out of the packed sidewalk cafés.

"How are you doing?" Jack asked.

"My palms are sweaty, my heart is racing, the tape holding the microphone in place is making me itch, and I'm wondering why in the world I agreed to do this." Not words to inspire whichever police officer was listening to her conversation through the wire, but she wasn't going to lie to Jack.

With every step, the tape that held the microphone in place under the neckline of her dress pulled against her skin. How could something so small be so irritating? Not even the size of a tiny button, the device lay flat against her skin. It wouldn't be obvious if Fossa insisted on patting her down. Her stomach roiled at that thought—much better to think about the itchiness instead. She clenched her free hand so she wouldn't scratch. They'd had enough trouble just getting the wire to stay in place in a way that would let the sound come through clearly. "Once you're in there, try not to move too much," the female technician had said a few minutes earlier. "This type of fabric causes a lot of interference."

Jack reached for her free hand. "Sounds like a typical under-cover operation. You're on high alert, which is good." Although Jack still didn't like the idea of Zoe handing off the flash drive, once he'd realized Zoe was set on it, he hadn't tried to talk her out of it. She was sure she was the only one who noticed the strain around his eyes and the slight tension that underlined all his words.

"There's Gloria." Zoe blew out a long breath, coaching herself to forget everything she'd learned about Gloria's lies. Zoe couldn't let her knowledge of that come through in her attitude.

Gloria stood a little farther down the street. The light from a restaurant window behind her created an aureole around her head. She was pacing back and forth, nibbling on her thumbnail. The moment she saw Zoe and Jack she hurried toward them. She gave Zoe another crushing hug and then gripped both of Jack's hands. "I'm so relieved to see you. I was worried that something had happened. Do you have it?"

"Yes, everything is fine." Zoe marveled at Gloria's acting ability. If Zoe didn't know that Gloria's daughter was safe, she would have believed that Gloria was a genuinely distraught mother. Gloria checked her watch. "Right on time. You go on, I'll be here."

Jack said, "Remember, I'm waiting with you."

"Oh, yes, I'd forgotten that," Gloria said with a trace of irritation in her tone.

As Zoe reached up and gave Jack a kiss on the cheek, he whispered, "Break a leg," so softly that only she could hear.

She set off for the corner and moved across the street in a crowd when the light changed. Once on the other side, the cluster of people continued down the street. Zoe was the only one who moved into the park and headed up the incline to the temple. A distant playful shout carried through the air from the street, but the only sounds immediately around her were her own muted footfalls. Not even a breeze stirred the leaves on the bushes that lined the path.

Munez had said he would put a ring of officers around the park. They would encircle the temple and prevent anyone from entering except her. She searched the shadows for hidden figures as she walked, but she didn't see anyone.

When she reached the temple, the pool of water reflected back the lit pylons without a ripple. The rest of the park stretched out dark and quiet. Beyond the black outlines of the park's foliage, the skyline of Madrid glowed, a study in contrasts that ranged from blocky streamlined modern architecture to the elaborate façade of the royal palace.

Zoe made her way around the pylons, feeling as if she were on stage instead of in a deserted park.

## 34

Zoe half expected a guard to stop her, but no one blocked her way as she walked toward the quiet temple. She approached the modern double glass doors that reminded her of a supermarket entrance. The doors swooshed open, and Zoe started at the sound, which seemed extremely loud in the dim and silent surroundings. After a second of hesitation, she stepped over the threshold, and the doors closed.

The scent of cigarette smoke filled the air. A narrow, high-ceilinged corridor lined with hieroglyphic reliefs ran from the main entrance to a square cut doorway directly ahead. Panel displays about waist high with educational descriptions and graphics about the hieroglyphics lined both sides of the corridor. About halfway down the corridor, a halogen lantern sat propped on one of the panel displays. It leaned against the stone wall, its glow lighting the display and throwing the etchings on the wall into sharp relief.

Fossa—Zoe realized she had stopped thinking of him as Jug Ears after the conversation with Munez—stood beside the halogen lamp, a cigarette in the other. A small laptop sat beside the lantern. "Thank you for being on time. Very considerate." A Spanish accent flowed through his words, but Zoe was able to understand him. The low angle of the light shining up from below him highlighted his nose and large ears and threw his enormous shadow onto the corridor wall behind him.

He wore a sport coat over a dark button-down shirt with black dress pants. His attire and his courteous statement almost made Zoe feel like she was at a business meeting. She'd been prepared for a confrontation or even anger, not this straightforward manner. He took a deep drag on his stub of a cigarette and blew the smoke toward the top tier of hieroglyphics. Zoe was pretty sure smoking was not allowed inside the antiquity, but she kept that thought to herself. He dropped the cigarette butt to the floor.

"You're welcome." Zoe matched his professional tone, but her heart was beating hard. Yep, just chatting with a gangster—that's me, she thought as a bubble of panic rose inside her as she thought of everything that could go wrong.

"You have it?"

"Yes." Zoe fought down the giddy almost out-of-body feeling. Just hand off the flash drive, she coached herself, and get out. She took two steps forward and held out the lip balm.

His dark eyebrows went up at the sight of the tube. The lantern's shadows carved extra-deep lines in his forehead.

"It's the flash drive," Zoe said. "This is what I found in the frame."

His eyebrows snapped down, and he jerked it from her hand, then ripped off the cap and exposed the end of the flash drive. As soon as he took it from her, she stepped back toward the double glass doors.

He rolled his eyes, and muttered, "Amateurs. Always trying too hard." He dropped the cap on the floor beside the cigarette butt. He looked at her out of the corner of his eye as he put the flash drive into the slot on the laptop. "Please do not leave until I have verified it."

Zoe swallowed. "Of course."

The seconds seemed to stretch out as he waited for it to load. A faint scraping, barely a whisper of noise, floated through the air.

Fossa lifted his head and went completely still as he listened, his gaze probing the deep shadows at the edge of the lantern's circle of light.

Zoe looked behind Fossa to the dark inner sanctuary. She had found a layout of the temple on her phone and given it a quick look before she and Jack left to meet Gloria. She knew there were several rooms beyond the entry corridor, including a sanctuary room, a staircase, and what had once been the temple's storage rooms.

They both listened for a few moments, then Fossa said, "Rats."

That thought didn't make Zoe feel any better. She licked her lips. "Yes, probably."

The light from the computer shining on Fossa's face shifted to a different shade, which drew his attention to the screen. Zoe fisted her hands so she wouldn't scratch at the tape holding the microphone. Almost done. A few minutes and she'd be back outside in the fresh night air.

He gave a small nod, then a grunt of satisfaction. Zoe let out her breath slowly—it wouldn't do to hyperventilate—and moved another inch closer to the door.

A change in air pressure tugged at Zoe's skirt as the doors swept open. Something slammed into her back between her shoulder blades, and suddenly she was gasping for air, her face on the dusty ground.

Someone was shouting, but the words didn't matter. She couldn't breathe.

She managed to suck in a dusty breath that seared her nasal passages. The air burned into her lungs as she struggled up onto her hands and knees. After another painful breath, the shouting resolved into words.

"Keep your hands up! Where I can see them."

The words reverberated in the small space. Zoe, still stooped over, lifted her quivering arms, but then saw that the words weren't directed at her.

In the glow of the lantern, Fossa stood with his hands in the air shouting in rapid-fire Spanish. Even though the other man was in the shadow beyond the circle of light, Zoe recognized the lanky figure with curly hair and thick-framed glasses. Kaz yelled, "Stay where you are! Don't move." He pointed a gun shakily at Fossa's chest.

The laptop had fallen to the ground between the two men, and Kaz squatted down, inch by inch, extending his free hand to the laptop while he kept his trembling gun hand trained on Fossa.

"I know you can understand English," Kaz yelled. "Stop shouting!" He punched the gun toward Fossa as he said the last few words.

The wild dipping and bobbing of Kaz's unsteady gun hand must have worried Fossa because he went quiet. Both men breathed hard for a moment then Kaz said, "I'm not going to let you mess up everything. Not when we've gotten this far." His fingers connected with the edge of the laptop, and he dragged it across the floor. The light from the screen reflected off his glasses as he divided his attention between the laptop and Fossa. The fingers of his free hand danced over the keyboard.

Zoe looked over her shoulder and out the glass doors, hoping to see Munez or some police officers closing in on the temple but the reflection of the lantern masked any movement near the ground and only a strip of black night showed at the top of the doors.

Somehow Kaz must have slipped through the ring of officers Munez put around the temple. Surely the plan to let Fossa walk with the flash drive was off? With Kaz in here, wouldn't Munez give the order to storm the building? Or was she on her own?

Zoe shifted her weight back into her heels and studied the distance to the doors. Two steps and she could be at the doors, but then she'd have to wait for them to open. Kaz wouldn't shoot her—would he? He only wanted the flash drive, right?

Fossa let out another volley of shouting, and Zoe tensed.

"I told you, shut up!" Kaz moved his free hand away from the computer and made a slicing motion across his throat. The energetic movement caused his hand with a gun to flicker off point for a moment.

Fossa lunged at Kaz.

At the same moment a high-pitched stinging sound pierced the air. Fossa fell to the side, clutching his right arm. A second whine split the air, and Kaz jerked backward with a yelp, crashing into the display along the wall of the corridor, his gun falling to the floor.

A red line appeared on Kaz's thigh. He stared at it a moment, clearly confused. The line widened, and it was only at that moment that Zoe realized Kaz had been shot, grazed by a bullet. Kaz must have realized it too because the color drained from his face as he let out a cry and gripped his leg.

Zoe hadn't had time to move from her huddled crouch, but now she sprang up and darted for the door. Another shrill whine sounded. A circle appeared on the glass door in front of Zoe, a spider web of cracks radiating out from it.

She jerked to a stop. The door vibrated with the impact of the bullet, but didn't open.

A female voice said, "Don't go anywhere yet, Zoe." The voice came from the door to the sanctuary beyond the glow of the lantern.

The sharp tap of heels sounded, then Mary Thacker stepped into the light of the lantern, which was still sitting on the panel display. "As you can see, I have no qualms about shooting anyone." She held a gun with a silencer attached, which she kept trained on Fossa, but the corridor was so narrow that with a movement of a few millimeters she would be lined up to fire at Zoe again.

Zoe remained motionless—mostly because of the gun—but she was also rooted to the spot as she stared at Mary. She looked the same, yet different. Her hair was still bouffant and blond, and her face was again perfectly made up, but something about her expression had changed. Her gaze had a hardness, a detached coldness, as she looked over the two men. Her clothes were different, too. Instead of the flowing flowered top and chunky jewelry Zoe had seen her in before, Mary now wore a tight red tank, black slacks with high-heeled boots, and a black leather jacket that fit her rounded figure perfectly. A little tab collar flapped back and forth at her neck as she leaned over Fossa and expertly removed a gun from a shoulder holster under his jacket. She kept her gun with the silencer trained on his face the whole time.

Fossa, one hand clasped to his upper arm, was breathing hard. His gaze locked with Mary's, but he didn't move as she took his gun.

"Good choice, not fighting me," she said to him as she put his gun in the pocket of her leather jacket. "You'll notice that I shot you in your right arm. Consider that a compliment on your skills. I respect you enough to make sure you're not a threat to me. Unlike this one." She tilted her head to Kaz. "Him, I shot in the leg. I know he's no good with a gun."

Kaz didn't seem to have heard her. He was leaning forward, groaning as he pressed his hands on his thigh. "Don't be such a baby," Mary said. "It's barely a scratch. You'll be fine." Zoe still couldn't see any movement through the glass doors. She shifted a bit so she'd have a better stance and could lunge at the door at her first opportunity. Mary was keeping watch on all three of them, and Zoe had no doubt that Mary would shoot her if she made a dash for the door. And judging from the state of Fossa and Kaz, Mary could hit a target.

As Zoe altered her position slightly, she felt the pull of the tape holding the microphone in place. It was still there. Was it still working? Had being thrown to the ground damaged it? Surely if the microphone went silent, the police would move in. Because the reflection of the lantern was masking any movement from outside the temple, Zoe thought she'd probably hear something outside before she saw anything. She tensed, ready to move at the first moment she heard the whir of the motor opening the doors.

In one smooth movement, Mary squatted and picked up Kaz's gun, which lay in the middle of the corridor. "Stop whimpering." She tilted her head and gazed pointedly at Kaz's leg. "That's what happens to people who go behind my back."

Kaz had been focused on his leg, but at her words, he looked up. "What? What are you talking about?"

She shook her head, her gaze bouncing between Kaz and Fossa then occasionally over to Zoe. "You think I don't know you've been poking around in my email and on my computer?" Mary said to Kaz. "I know what you were doing—looking for something to blackmail me with."

"No! It was nothing like that."

Mary narrowed her eyes as she watched him for a few extra beats. Kaz scrambled backward, wincing as he jarred his leg. "I thought someone had been in the system—I had to check it out. It's my job. I believe in privacy. I'd never snoop around just to see what I could find. I had to check to make sure no one had breached the system."

Mary's lips thinned. "I half believe you. You do have a streak of the do-gooder about you."

Kaz let out a shaky breath. "But how did you know?"

"That you'd been nosing around?" Mary laughed. "You've seen my bio—it's on the company website. You know I was one of Freddie's first employees." She shook her head in a disappointed manner. "You thought I was his secretary, didn't you?" She shot a quick conspiratorial look at Zoe, who had begun to think that maybe Mary had forgotten about her.

The quick look hit Zoe like a punch in the gut. Was she about to swing the gun her way? No, Zoe took a shuddery breath that matched Kaz's uneven breathing as Mary said, "Gender can be such an advantage." She leaned toward Kaz and spoke slowly. "I was Freddie's first programmer at Eon."

"You? But you're not interested in programming. You didn't know what hashing was or TOR or man-in-the-middle attacks—oh. You were playing me."

"Exactly." Smugness layered her words. "And you were so busy making sure no one was paying any attention to *you* at work, you left your own phone wide open." She glanced at Zoe again. "Isn't it surprising that the people who truly know how vulnerable we are to a hack often overlook the most basic security precautions themselves? Using the same password for your phone at work and your personal phone—so lax! But of course I was careful. You'd have to look quite deeply to see what I did to your phone, which has worked out so well. With you tracking Zoe through *her* phone, I had all the details on both you and her. So efficient. It saved me so much time."

Mary caught Zoe's look. "Yes. I'm afraid it's true. You downloaded the Eon company app that Kaz sent you. It had a bit of special code, didn't it, Kaz?" Mary shook her head at him. "You're such a hypocrite, spouting about privacy, but planting a hack on poor Zoe's phone so that you could track her."

"I didn't like doing it," Kaz said, "but it was for the greater good." He looked at Zoe. "I wouldn't have done anything with it. I didn't even look at your email or your bank or anything. Once you brought back the zero-day, I would have disabled the tracking."

Zoe closed her eyes briefly. Jack was right—burner phones were the way to go.

"Kaz always knew where you were." Mary smiled brightly. "And so did I. That tracking app and a look at your search history showed me everything I needed to know."

"That explains so much," Zoe said, and hoped the microphone was still working—that Munez was getting all this. In case it was working, Zoe said to Mary, "And I suppose you want the flash drive so you can sell it."

"Of course." Mary sent a withering glance at Kaz. "I can't believe someone would be so stupid to literally throw away millions of dollars."

"But if you take the hack, you can't go back to the U.S. after this," Kaz said. "We'll know it was you who took the zero-day. Not even Thacker can protect you." He trailed off as if he just realized it wasn't a good idea to remind Mary not to leave any witnesses.

"Go back to Thacker?" Mary laughed. "That's the last thing I want to do. I've had my fill of his silly games, like that stunt with the ballet dancer." Mary rolled her eyes at Zoe. "Forget the elaborate story Thacker told you at lunch about the 'mix-up' with the packages. He planned it all to reel you in. He wanted you to look for the blue butterfly painting—why he picked you, I don't know—and he didn't think just picking up the phone and calling you would do the trick. No, he had to go overboard with the whole lost sculpture and misdirected package scenario to get you interested. And to test you," she added.

"The whole thing did feel a little off," Zoe said, forcing herself to keep her gaze away from the glass door in case someone was sneaking up to it. She *hoped* Munez's officers were moving stealthily outside.

"Tell her, Kaz," Mary said, gesturing with the gun toward him.

His Adam's apple bobbed as he swallowed. "Mr. Thacker thought of sending you the ballet dancer as an evaluation," Kaz said to Zoe. "He wanted to see what you'd do with it. If you contacted the authorities, he figured he could trust you, and he'd hire you."

"What was he going to do if I didn't contact the police or the FBI?"

"He said he'd call them himself and say he had a tip that you had the sculpture. Either way, he'd get his ballet dancer back, and he could vet you at the same time. 'Win-win' he called it."

Zoe thought she should be more upset than she was at hearing that news, but being manipulated paled in comparison to being trapped in a small area with a woman wielding a gun. Mary held the gun with the silencer in her right hand in a comfortable grip. In her left, she held Kaz's gun.

Suddenly her forehead wrinkled. She bounced Kaz's gun up and down as if her hand were a scale, and she was weighing the gun, then her face cleared. She chuckled. "A toy gun, Kaz? Only you would bring a plastic gun to threaten an international criminal."

She dropped the gun on the floor. It landed with a hollow bounce instead of a weighty metal thud. "I suppose it would be difficult to get a real gun on short notice in a foreign country. You certainly couldn't bring one on the plane, could you?" She smiled in a superior way. "Having a private jet is so nice. So much less scrutiny. And if anyone does seem interested...a few thousand dollars—or euros—does the trick."

She swiveled her attention to Fossa. "And it's amazing what people will let you do for a few hundred euros. The guard on the day shift will let you in with the last group of tourists viewing the temple and conveniently overlook you when he does his final round of the building before closing up and going off his shift. He was such a nice man. He even let me bring in a camp chair, so I wouldn't have to sit on the hard floor while I waited for your meeting."

She scooped up the laptop, which was at Kaz's feet. "Now, let's see what we have here." She propped the laptop on the display near the lantern, but kept her body turned so that she had everyone in her view.

"Cute," she said with a glance at the lip balm tube that extended from the side of the laptop.

She held the gun with a casual confidence, but never let the barrel of the gun waver from Fossa. Zoe wondered how Mary could be so calm—she'd just shot two people. But she was navigating the laptop's keyboard one-handed with fingers that didn't even tremble.

With her blood zinging through her body and her erratic heartbeat, Zoe felt like she'd overdosed on caffeine.

Mary said, "Okay, Zoe, let's see if I have to shoot you, too."

## 35

That weak, shaky-leg feeling that comes on after a bout with the flu swept over Zoe as Mary's gaze darted back and forth between the code on the laptop screen and her three captives. Thank goodness Jack had insisted that she bring the original flash drive with the authentic code. Zoe had no doubt that if Mary didn't like what she saw, she'd be quick to switch the aim of the gun to Zoe. She certainly hadn't been stingy with her bullets so far.

Mary gave a quick nod. "Very good. I'm glad to see you're smart enough to bring the real thing." She yanked the lip balm tube out of the port, and the computer pinged at the unapproved removal. At that same instant, Fossa shifted closer to Mary, kicked out one of his legs in a lightning movement, connecting with the back of her knees. Her legs buckled as Fossa rolled to the side so that he wasn't under her. Zoe ducked as the gun went off again with a sharp ping.

Zoe uncurled enough from her crouched position to see Mary flat on her back, gasping for air. Both her hands were empty. She must have dropped the gun and the flash drive when she fell. Mary lay motionless for a second, her raspy breathing the only sound in the corridor. Then she rolled onto her side, her hands already sweeping the floor as she continued to wheeze.

Fossa was already on his feet, his gaze scouring the floor.

Zoe saw Mary's gun first, which had landed only a few feet away from Zoe. The lip balm tube had rolled farther. Fossa had seen it and was already moving.

He scooped up the lip balm tube and sprinted for the glass doors, a grimace of pain on his face as he clamped his injured arm to his side. The doors swished open, and he shot through the doorway at an all-out run.

Mary was on her feet now. Zoe scrambled forward and gave the gun a solid kick, sending it straight down the corridor. It whizzed by Mary before she could react and disappeared through the doorway into the dark recess of the sanctuary.

Mary made for the door, giving Zoe a look of such intense hatred that Zoe was sure Mary would have liked to stop and strangle her with her bare hands if only she wasn't so intent on chasing Fossa and getting back the flash drive.

The doors had swished shut behind Fossa, but they whisked open again too soon for Mary's approach to have set the sensor off. Suddenly the entrance was like an elevator at a busy hotel with people pushing and shoving as Mary surged forward and several police officers, Munez in the lead, pressed inside the temple.

Mary crumpled against the display. Her eyes welled with tears as she pointed a shaky finger at the crowded door. "He went that way. That man who ran out of here—he tried to kill me."

Munez shook his head. "No, Mrs. Thacker. We know exactly what happened. We heard your whole conversation."

Zoe was barely listening. The doors opened again, and Jack pushed his way inside the crowded corridor, his face pale as his gaze swept over the corridor. "Make way. Zoe?"

"Over here." Zoe waved her hand above the heads of the two police officers who blocked her path. They stepped aside as Jack reached her.

At Zoe's elbow, Munez, his hand in a firm grip around Mary's bicep, frowned. "Mr. Andrews—you were not to enter—"

Jack ignored him and caught Zoe's shoulders, his gaze roving over her. "You okay?"

She nodded. "All good now."

Munez sighed. "Highly irregular," he said, then waved his hand, motioning them to the door. "But you did an excellent job staying calm and not moving around, Mrs. Andrews. We have the whole encounter recorded."

Jack squeezed Zoe's shoulders. "You didn't do anything. I'm so proud of you."

"Not my usual way. It was killing me! And this wire thing has to come off. It's so itchy, it was all I could do not to scratch away like I had chicken pox."

"You're sure you're okay?" He stepped back another few inches and ran his gaze from her head to her feet. "Those shots—" He swallowed.

"I'm fine. Not a scratch. She shot Kaz and Fossa. Mary didn't even see me as a threat—oh!" Zoe spun away from Jack to Munez. "She's got a gun—another one. In her pock—"

But it was too late. Mary had jerked her arm away from Munez. Fossa's gun was already in her hand, the barrel aimed at Zoe and Jack. The bustle and movement in the temple cut off instantly. Jack shifted Zoe so that she was behind him.

Above her mascara-stained cheeks, Mary's gaze was steely. "I'm walking out of here. No one touches me, or I shoot the lovebirds."

Munez made a pressing down motion with his hands, and his officers remained still.

Mary took a step to the door, and Jack shifted position to keep himself between Zoe and the gun, then took a step toward Mary. She fired at his chest.

Zoe screamed—or at least she thought she did. The report of the gun without the silencer was deafening in the tiny space.

Ears ringing, Zoe watched unbelievingly as Jack doubled over for a second, then straightened. Mary's eyes widened in shock.

Before she could react and move to the door, Jack grabbed Mary's wrist, twisting it with both his hands. Zoe heard Mary yelp, but it was a fuzzy, muffled sound as if she were far away instead of only across the room. The gun fell to the ground, but the droning sound in Zoe's ears silenced any sound of impact.

The second after the gun fell, Jack disappeared into a scrum of uniformed officers as they closed in on Mary.

A burning smell filtered through the air, stinging her nose as the ringing faded a bit. Her ears felt less like they were stuffed with cotton, and she began to distinguish the voices of the police officers as Jack pushed his way out of the crowd.

"What? How?" She was probably shouting, but she didn't care. She gripped his arms, ran her hands over his chest, then stopped abruptly at the unfamiliar contouring. "A bulletproof vest? I don't know whether to slap you or hug you. You didn't tell me. What are you doing wearing that?" A singed area with bits of his shirt threads around the edges showed where the vest had stopped the bullet.

He caught her hand as she poked and prodded. Leaning close to her ear, he said, "Easy. I think I'll have a bruise," he said, then seeing her face, he added, "but that's all. I'm fine." He tapped the vest. "Munez insisted. Let's get out of here." He gripped her hand and they worked their way through the press of officers still gathered around Mary.

The doors swept open, and they stepped into the cool night air. Several more officers were spaced around the perimeter of the temple, but they weren't interested in Zoe and Jack. "That's better," Jack said as they moved down the steps. "How are your ears? Can you hear me?"

"Yes, it's getting better, but forget about my hearing. A vest? When did that happen?"

"While you were being fitted up with the wire, Munez had me put it on. Everyone had to wear one, except you, of course. It might have tipped off Fossa."

"You didn't tell me."

"There wasn't time."

"Jack—" She made an inarticulate sound, which she realized Jack probably couldn't hear, but he saw her face.

He said, "You're so upset you don't know what to say? Let's call it a draw. That's how I felt when you were in there."

"But you didn't have to move when Mary made for the door and draw her attention."

"I couldn't let her just walk out—not when she was only a step away."

"She was surrounded by police officers! And look at all these officers out here. She wouldn't have gotten far. Who knows how many more officers Munez has out here?"

"Seven," Jack said. "But I was right there. Seemed a shame to let her walk right by. She didn't think for a moment that I'd have a vest on. The element of surprise is the best weapon."

"Well, let's not wield that weapon again, okay?"

"Says the woman who just came through a confrontation with a member of an international gang and a gun-toting crazy woman."

"I don't know whether to slap you...or...or..."

"Kiss me?"

"That's not what I was thinking."

"Then hold that thought." Jack folded her into his arms. After a few seconds the tension went out of her, and she wrapped her arms around his chest, bulky vest and all.

## 36

**Thursday**

"In all the confusion I completely forgot about Gloria. What happened to her? Where is she?" Zoe asked.

It had been almost twenty-four hours since the encounter in the temple, and thankfully both she and Jack could hear clearly.

It had taken until three in the morning before Zoe and Jack had been able to return to their hotel room, which they were glad to find had been cleaned and the bed remade. Three in the morning was not actually that late by Madrid standards, but Zoe and Jack were both exhausted. Zoe had slept straight through sunrise and didn't wake up until afternoon. They had packed up and returned to Zoe's original hotel to claim the belongings that she had left there, then it had been a busy afternoon of tying up loose ends as they completed their statements for Munez and made new airline reservations. Now that all that was finished, they were celebrating their last night in Madrid.

Jack reached for one of the mushrooms on the small plate between them. "A few minutes after you left to go to the temple, Munez showed up and said one of his officers needed to speak to Gloria."

They were sitting at wooden tables with picnic-style benches in one of Madrid's oldest and most well-known *tapas* bars, *El Mesón del Champiñón*, which had an interesting interior design theme. Bulbous protrusions of stucco festooned the walls and coved ceiling, giving the place a sort of hippy-dippy atmosphere, despite the building being quite old—a section of Madrid's city wall was visible near the door.

The mushrooms were served with the stems removed and the caps filled with chorizo, oil, and herbs. Two toothpicks punctured each side of the mushroom cap, which made it easy to pick them up and eat them without spilling any of the stuffing. Zoe used the toothpicks to pick up a mushroom. "I bet that threw Gloria."

"Yeah, she was pretty shaken up," Jack said. "She didn't know what to do, but then Munez told her that he'd had Fossa under surveillance, and he knew that the two of them had met. She seemed to consider her options for a second, then started talking. She said Fossa had threatened to take her daughter unless she helped him. Fossa didn't care how Gloria ensured we brought the flash drive to him. She just had to make sure we did it."

"So she made up the story about her daughter being kidnapped, just like we thought." Zoe popped the mushroom in her mouth and savored the rich flavors.

"Gloria *did* send her daughter to stay with her grandmother. Maybe she really was afraid that Fossa would do it."

Zoe shook her head. "I don't see him snatching a kid. Too much work."

"But sometimes all it takes is the threat to motivate someone."

"I still think money was involved," Zoe said. "The kidnapping story was to convince us to give up the flash drive, and then she used it to cover herself with Munez."

"That's possible, too. Either way, Munez will sort it out. And at the very least, he now has a witness to testify in the trial against the Trullas gang. Even though Fossa isn't the head of the gang, every bit of evidence will help the case the task force has been building.

Anyway, it was right about that point, when Gloria was telling him about Fossa, that Munez got word Kaz had entered the temple."

"So how did that happen? I mean, I know Kaz knew where I was because of the tracking app on my phone, but how did he know to bring a gun—albeit a toy gun—and that Fossa would be there?"

"As soon as Gloria heard Kaz's name she went white as a sheet —I've never seen anyone's skin actually change tone like that. It was weird. I could see the color draining away. She switched over to Spanish. Munez told me later she was calling Kaz all sorts of names. After she spoke to us at the café, Kaz called her and told her he'd just arrived here. She told him about Fossa and the scheduled drop. She thought she'd warned him off, but instead of backing down, he found a play gun and crashed the drop."

"He obviously didn't understand who he was dealing with— either Fossa or Mary. I sort of admire him for rushing in there, clinging to his ideals."

"He was idealistic, but foolish, a dangerous combination," Jack said.

"Fossa would have made short work of him, if Mary hadn't stopped him. And Mary," Zoe couldn't repress a shiver, "her eyes were so cold. She only wanted that flash drive and didn't care who she hurt to get it." Zoe shook off that scary thought and reached for another mushroom.

"Any word on if Munez's task force made arrests yet?" It was a question that Zoe had meant to ask Munez, but she hadn't had the opportunity when she went over her statement. Munez had interviewed her and Jack separately so she didn't know what Munez and Jack had talked about.

"Munez was cagey when I asked. He told me two things. First, he said to check the news." Jack took out his phone. "I looked while you were in your interview. I had to search quite a bit to find an English language version of the story, but this showed up."

Zoe wiped her hands on her napkin then took the phone. She read the headline aloud, "Police Take Down International Cyber

Gang With Links to Human Trafficking and Terrorism." Zoe handed the phone back. "I'd say that's a yes."

Jack said, "The second thing he said was that he'd finally caught his big fish and most of the small ones, too."

"Which sounds like he got Mato and Fossa, too."

"Right. One thing I forgot to ask Munez about was the flash drive. We'll never know why Novall put the zero-day on a flash drive and tried to transport it in the painting. Why not send it online? It's a question that will keep me awake at night."

"I have a cure for your insomnia," Zoe said.

Jack leaned closer and lowered his voice. "I'm all ears." The gleam in his eyes was mischievous.

"Not that," Zoe said. "You'll be able to sleep because I have the answer to your question." She paused and looked at him through her lashes. "Of course, other cures for insomnia aren't off the table."

"Excellent," Jack said.

"But for now, let me tell you what Munez said about Kaz. He will recover, by the way, just like Mary said. Kaz will be back to work soon—but probably not for Thacker."

"No charges against him?" Jack asked.

"No. Apparently Kaz's knowledge of the hacker world and his testimony are more important to Munez," Zoe said.

"I imagine it would be."

A waiter stopped to check on them, and Zoe waited until he left, then said, "Okay, back to Kaz. I thought Novall sending data on a flash drive was weird, too. I mean, you and Carla set up that secure, private connection thing pretty fast, and she had access to the files on the flash drive in a few minutes. I wondered why Novall and Kaz went to all the trouble of getting it in the frame of the painting."

"Right," Jack said. "Or why didn't Novall just release it himself? Why send it to Kaz?"

"Munez wouldn't tell me much, but he did say he'd learned from Kaz that Novall was extremely cautious about moving the material out of his office. He'd done it one piece of paper at a time —printed it out, then re-typed it at home. Apparently it took him weeks to complete the process. Novall was going to release the zero-day himself, but then he got nervous. He was being watched, which Munez thinks was probably his office spying on him. Apparently, they weren't as clueless as he seemed to think. And he learned about a new hack his company was working on. Munez wouldn't tell me what it was—and I probably wouldn't have understood it if he had—but he said it scared Novall so badly that he decided he had to be absolutely sure he left no digital footprint when he sent the zero-day. Kaz offered to release it for him, but Novall wouldn't send it to Kaz digitally—he was that spooked. Kaz wanted Novall to mail it to him, but Novall didn't want to do that because it would have to pass through too many hands to get to Kaz."

"But he mailed it to Gloria. What made him change his mind?" Jack asked.

"He didn't mail it. He bribed the concierge in her building to put it in her mailbox."

"That was a risk," Jack said. "I'm surprised he did that."

"Apparently he decided it was the best he could do. He was afraid to send it digitally because of the new hack his company was working on, and he knew he couldn't move it himself."

"I wonder why not? That would have been the simplest thing. He could call in sick, then hop on a plane."

"He was afraid that whoever was watching him would keep him from leaving the country. He said the people who were following him wouldn't let him leave."

"I wonder what put him off sending it digitally?" Jack stared across the room. "Val-Tech must be working on a way to crack anonymity. If they did that..." He shook his head, "...let's just say lots of people would be extremely nervous."

"Is that something you'd hear about, if it happens?" Zoe asked.

"Oh, yeah. It'll be all over the hacker community. And speaking of that, Carla sent me a text. She said to expect an update on certain mobile devices in the next day or two."

Zoe squinted at him. "Does that mean what I think it means?"

"Yes. She finally got in touch with a friend of a friend of a friend who took the information on the zero-day. A fix is in the works."

"So no one will be able to use it to spy on anyone," Zoe said. "That's great news."

"As long as everyone updates, that vulnerability is closed to crooks and to—er—any other interested parties." Jack sipped his sangria. "And now I want to hear your news. You were on the phone with Thacker a long time."

"I'll say. That's one call that I'm glad is over. I wasn't sure how he would react because he was so angry the last time I spoke to him. But he was actually quite pleased. It was a nice change to have good news for him."

"Thacker is happy that his wife has been arrested and is involved in international cybercrime?"

"No, he didn't have much to say about Mary. I get the feeling that Thacker is one of those people that once you cross him, he cuts all ties with you." Zoe swished her hand across the table as if she were clearing the dishes off of it. "You don't exist. He barely mentioned Mary. He said he was shocked and had no idea what she was involved in. It sounded like something from a press release, honestly."

"Did you believe him?" Jack asked. "If anyone would know about zero-day hacks and how valuable they were, it would be Thacker."

"You know, I *did* believe him. It was the oddest thing. He was completely uninterested in Mary. I could hear it in his tone. He only wanted to know about the blue butterfly painting. When I mentioned that, it was like the life came back into his voice."

"So Mary won't be able to count on him for an elaborate legal defense?"

"It doesn't sound like it. I think she's on her own. He couldn't get off the topic of his wife fast enough, and then he only wanted to talk about the painting. He was thrilled to know that it was fine. He pulled some strings so that I can leave with it tomorrow. Anyway, the painting seems to matter much more to him than what happened with Mary."

"I guess collecting does become an obsession with some people," Jack said. "At least, you might have him for a future client since he wasn't wrapped up in cybercrime."

"I'm not sure I want to work with someone who sent me a piece of art from his collection to test me before he hired me."

Jack pointed his glass at Zoe. "A *copy*. I'm sure he would emphasize it was a copy."

Zoe laughed. "Yes, he would. I guess I'll worry about that, if it happens."

"He is a multi-millionaire."

"But an eccentric one," Zoe countered.

"I think that's the only kind," Jack said.

Zoe put down her glass suddenly. "Oh, and even better news. He's thrilled with the idea of owning a big blue butterfly with a mutation."

Jack paused, the glass poised at his lips. "You mean you finally got to talk to him about it?"

"Yes, finally! Kaz had only told him it was a blue morpho. Once I explained why it was unique...that was it. He just wanted it. So our family budget will stay in the black."

"That's great news. And now you have another name for your list of art dealers."

"LeBlanc may be on my list, but he won't be on the top of it. I don't trust him." Zoe sighed. "But I should never say never."

"Especially in your line of work. A dealer who drifts into the shady side of things is probably someone you need to know."

"Sad, but true."

The other tables were filling with people. A pianist sat down at a small upright and ran his fingers over the keys with a flourish. Zoe raised her voice over the music. "Thacker is planning a huge press event for the announcement of the discovery of a lost Martin Johnson Heade painting. Before we got off the phone, he was already talking about possibilities for funding a special exhibit that would display the blue morpho along with the paintings and some other specimens from his vintage butterfly collection."

Jack reached for her hand across the table. "I think you're on your way."

"On my way?"

"To being considered an art recovery specialist in your own right, not just somebody who works for Harrington."

Zoe smiled. "It's a first step. Thacker wants me to be there—at the press conference—but I think I'll follow Harrington's example of staying in the background. I only need my name out there associated with the recovery, not my picture. Was that my phone? It's so loud in here...yes, it was." Zoe dug her phone out of her messenger bag. "It's a text from Evelyn. You remember her, right? Gallery owner. I bet she heard the news about the recovery of the blue butterfly painting...No, it's something else..." Zoe read aloud, "The young Giacometti is back." She frowned. "Young Giacometti? What does she mean—oh!"

Jack said, "I'm confused."

"So was I for a second. Remember the paintings that went missing from the Westoll Museum? Evelyn at Salt Grass Gallery said a guy came in her gallery and seemed to be hinting around to see if she was open to taking shady paintings. He mentioned Canaletto. One of the pieces stolen was by Canaletto. Evelyn thought maybe the guy had something to do with the robbery. She said he looked like a young Giacometti—an artist—but there wasn't anything on the surveillance tapes. She said she would be on the lookout for him." Zoe tapped her phone. "This means she's seen him again." Zoe went back to the text and continued reading then looked up. "And she managed to get a picture. She'll send it to me as soon as she gets it from the gallery's security footage."

Jack raised his glass to her. "Sounds like another case."

"Yes, it does." Zoe clinked her glass against his. "Too bad I can't do anything about it now. I have to get the blue butterfly painting back to Thacker, but then..." Zoe sent Evelyn a quick text saying that she would be back in Dallas in a few days.

Jack looked at his watch. "I think we better move on."

"That's right. We have a Flamenco performance to see and several more *tapas* bars to check out."

"And then I thought we might visit the *Plaza de Cibeles*," Jack said. "I've heard it's spectacular at night."

"I've heard that too. We should definitely do it."

# EPILOGUE

**Six months later**

Kaz Volk twisted the key and opened his mail box. It had been a long day at the web design company where he worked. The interior decorator thought her new website design didn't have enough zazz. *Zazz* wasn't even a word. How could you design something that didn't have a definition? At least he had his part-time job at the community college teaching intro to programming.

He tossed the jumble of grocery flyers on top of the pizza box and closed the mailbox. As he climbed the steps to his apartment the sheaf of mail slid sideways, and a few pieces landed on the stairs.

A glossy postcard of a sculpture landed face-up. Kaz slowly reached for it. It captured the Christ the Redeemer sculpture, arms spread wide, poised over Rio and the blue waters below.

Kaz flipped the card over.

*Machu Picchu is next. You should come out sometime.*

Kaz shook his head. "Not on your life, buddy," he murmured as he trotted up the stairs.

# THE STORY BEHIND THE STORY

And now to sort truth from imagination...

The inspiration for the painting of the blue butterfly for this story came from a real painting. Martin Johnson Heade painted a single blue morpho butterfly sometime around 1864-1865 as part of his Gems of Brazil series. A painting of a blue butterfly with a hummingbird does not exist—at least, that we know of. As Thacker stated in the story, Heade was prolific. At the end of his career he moved to St. Augustine, Florida. Tourists bought his landscape and still life paintings and dispersed them all over the country and the world. Recently, his artwork has been rediscovered, and several of his "lost" paintings have been identified and later sold at auction for over a million dollars...so keep an eye out!

I did a deep dive into butterfly research for this book. If you're interested in more details about butterflies and the exotic animal trade, check out *Dangerous World of Butterflies: The Startling Subculture of Criminals, Collectors, and Conservationists* by Peter Laufer and *Winged Obsession: The Pursuit of the World's Most Notorious Butterfly Smuggler* by Jessica Speart.

For an inside look at art theft, I read *Hot Art: Chasing Thieves and Detectives Through the Secret World of Stolen Art* by Joshua Knelman.

Thanks to Stephen and Nicky for the tour of Grand Isle and for telling me its stories. All incidents in this book are fictional, but Grand Isle does have an interesting history.

Stories circulating on the internet report that Dalí did like to get out of paying his bills by writing checks then adding a drawing, which made the check too valuable to cash.

Madrid is a wonderful place to visit. If you're able to go, I highly recommend the *mercado* described in the book. You can see my photos of the *Mercado de San Miguel* as well as my other photos I took on my research trip to Madrid on the *Treacherous* pinboard at http://www.sararosett.com/pin/Zoe6.

For the details on cybersecurity and hacks, I combed through pages and pages of *Wikileaks'* Vault7 release of internal documents from the CIA. (I feel I need a disclaimer on my browser history: *It's research for a book, I promise!*). If you'd like to hide a flash drive in an empty lip balm tube, you can find a tutorial online. And you don't have to stop with lip balm. You can hide a flash drive in empty lipstick tubes, wine corks, or even small toys or figurines.

I'm so glad you joined me for another journey with Zoe and Jack. Sign up at SaraRosett.com/signup/3 to find out when their next adventure is out.

# ABOUT THE AUTHOR

*USA Today* bestselling author Sara Rosett writes fun mysteries. Her books are light-hearted escapes for readers who enjoy interesting settings, quirky characters, and puzzling mysteries. *Publishers Weekly* called Sara's books, "satisfying," "well-executed," and "sparkling."

Sara loves to get new stamps in her passport and considers dark chocolate a daily requirement. Find out more at SaraRosett.com.

*Connect with Sara*
www.SaraRosett.com

# ALSO BY SARA ROSETT

This is Sara's complete catalogue at the time of publication, but new books are in the works. To be the first to find out when Sara has a new book, sign up for her updates.